MAN ENOUGH

A SINGLE DAD ROMANCE

NICOLE SNOW

ICE LIPS PRESS

Content copyright © Nicole Snow. All rights reserved.
Published in the United States of America.
First published in March, 2018.

Disclaimer: The following book is a work of fiction. Any resemblance characters in this story may have to real people is only coincidental.

Please respect this author's hard work! No section of this book may be reproduced or copied without permission. Exception for brief quotations used in reviews or promotions. This book is licensed for your personal enjoyment only. Thanks!

Cover Design – CoverLuv.

Website: Nicolesnowbooks.com

DESCRIPTION

He's damaged goods. Sure chaos. Mr. Impossible.
So why am I risking it all for one more kiss?

I never knew what hit me.

Rex stormed into my little world with two adorable twin boys and no apologies.

Bearish. Short-fused. Consuming. Huge.

Torturously gorgeous.

Leave-your-heart-in-pieces wrong.

Did I mention HUGE?

He's instant trouble the second he checks into our lodge and my overprotective grandpa hires him.

Then I catch him staring with that knowing ache in his eyes.

I forget what trouble even means.

He also needs a nanny. *Sold.*

My signature cupcakes aren't the sweetest thing in this small town anymore.

Not when his cold shoulder thaws.

Not when our nights unravel me.

Not when every taste of him overrules the thousand reasons we shouldn't.

But tarnished hearts and prowling kisses have limits.

The closer we get, the harder he pulls away.

Rex won't reveal why he's really here.

I can't admit how bad I wish it didn't matter.

Of course, the chilling truth *always* strikes. Without mercy.

There's heartbreak written in our stars.

Then there's the crazy part of me that believes he's man enough to stand, to fight, to stay.

Crazy, I said. Or is it?

I: CUPCAKES FOR ROOM 205 (TABBY)

They say a woman knows it's obvious when she's found the one.

Prince Charming isn't subtle.

She remembers every first with Mr. Right. Every second, third, and fourth.

Every beat of her own enchanted heart.

His face, his smell, the mischief dancing in his eyes that makes her all tingly and weak-kneed looking back on their wedding day, and then again many years later through the fog of love.

The lyrical cadence of his voice etches on her brain forever. His first kiss – the one that *has* to happen with storybook perfection – leaves the heart drumming on infinity shuffle, an echo of sweet nostalgia in her blood.

When I first saw Rex Osborne, there was none of that.

Just the roar of his old truck pulling into our lot. Two doors slamming shut. A half-second glance at him from behind while I hoisted the snow-packed shovel over my shoulder.

Another second spent staring harder. Maybe I thought his shoulders looked a little out of place in this small town.

Too big. Too broad. Too tall. Too *heavy.*

Too much urgency in his step.

Too much man for Split Harbor, and for me.

I heard two distant little voices at his feet, murmuring the happy nothings children do. Then the three of them disappeared inside the lodge.

It lasted all of three seconds before I tucked my head down and went back to work, scraping snow off the path. I only stopped for one more thing.

A growl rumbled in the sky, almost like thunder, totally out of place in frozen dead February.

I still don't know if I imagined it.

But I didn't imagine him.

I didn't know I'd met the man who'd ruin *imagining* for good, who'd tear what I thought I knew to pieces, who'd dynamite my heart, and who'd ground himself in my life's smoking crater.

Rex taught me so many things and showed me many more. Like what's real, what's undeniable, what's worth every shred of passion in two fiery souls.

Rex taught me how to live. How to love. How to hurt.

And then Rex set me free.

* * *

I TUCK the shovel into the corner of the porch railings right next to the bucket of rock salt I'll need again first thing in the morning. So far we've only gotten a light dusting of snow, but more is predicted.

No surprises. It's winter. In Michigan.

My cheeks puff as I hold in the heavy sigh burning my lungs, wanting out. It is what it is. This is my home. My livelihood. My future.

I need to be thankful for that. All of it. And I need to be satisfied, too.

I owe Gramps big time. If not for him, Lord knows where I'd be right now. Rather than living in a lodge where people pay good money to rest, relax, and enjoy life, I might've ended up in a foster home.

Shaking off the melancholy that's been weighing heavier and heavier lately, I push open the employee entrance and remove my boots, coat, hat and mittens before sitting down on the bench to change into tennis shoes.

It'll be better when Russ returns, I tell myself. Who'd have guessed a guy could break an ankle so bad he'd need two surgeries by just stepping wrong off a ladder?

One less pair of strong hands. Which also means I'll be shoveling a whole lot more yet this winter.

"Break time's over."

I glance up and crack a smile at my grandfather's words. "Break time?"

The wrinkles around his twinkling blue eyes increase as he chuckles while walking down the narrow hallway. "I've been looking to hire someone to take over Russ' duties, but –"

I laugh, interrupting him. "Everyone knows you too well, Gramps. Most who've worked for you before aren't willing to do it again."

"Only the lazy ones."

"So, everyone in Northern Michigan?" I can't resist poking fun at my Gramps' impossible standards.

He scowls at me, which only makes me laugh harder. Pushing off the bench, I step closer to him and pat his upper arm. The softness my hand encounters reminds me he's not as big and strong as he once was.

He's run the Grand Pine Lodge for over fifty years. He'll continue until his old heart stops beating. And I'll be right beside him. Probably after, too. This lodge has been in our family since the first building sprung up over a hundred years ago.

Like it or not, I know my destiny. My place. Some days, it's just harder to accept than others.

"I don't mind shoveling the sidewalks. Never have and never will," I tell him. Truth be told, it's partly my fault that Russ broke his ankle. Fixing up the stables was *my* idea. A way to expand the services we offer, and hopefully increase occupancy and revenue. "Wes Owens will still plow. Just as long as Russ comes back by spring so we don't have to hire lawn care, we'll be fine."

Gramps wraps an arm around my shoulder, nodding his thanks. "We make a good team, Tabby-kitten."

"That we do, Pops."

He scowls again, but then we both laugh. He doesn't like being called Pops any more than I like being called Tabby-kitten. Never have liked nicknames. Tabby is close enough to a nickname all by itself, and it's all I've got. But I do love the old man, despite how ornery he can be sometimes.

"We got a late arrival," he says, kissing my temple.

"Oh? I didn't see a reservation." I saw the man with two kids from a distance while I was busy shoveling, of course, but I don't say anything. Some days, we have more quick stops here looking for directions than proper guests.

"Didn't have one. I put them in room 205. You'll need to take something up for them to eat."

I nod. None of this is unusual. Exceptional guest service in the middle of nowhere is our specialty, and being as small as we are, it's not like we're ever bursting at the seams. However, this time of year, after the holidays and before spring, we can go weeks without a single guest. "How many?"

"Three. I already told Marcy."

"All right." I plant a kiss on his soft and wrinkled cheek. "I'll see to it, no problem. You head on up to bed and I'll lock up after delivering the food." With a grin over my shoulder as I start walking towards the kitchen door, I add, "I'll see you in the morning."

"Not if I see you first."

The joke is almost as old as him, but I still laugh, mainly because he expects it. Life here would be nothing without reflexes, habits, and little rituals. I wait near the kitchen door until after he turns the corner that leads to the back stairs. Then I let out the sigh that was still inside me and push open the door.

Hustling around the large kitchen like it's on fire, Marcy takes a couple single serving milk cartons out of the double-door fridge and sets them on an already full tray. She's been with the lodge as long as I can remember, a wonderful cook. With my baking skills, we make a good team.

I lift the metal lid off the plate on the tray. "Yum, chicken salad."

"I have a sandwich in the fridge for you, too," Marcy says with a smile.

Skipping meals is my specialty. Comes with running the lodge, where there's never enough hours in the day to cover everything. "What would I do without you?"

"Me? Nonsense, Tabby. This place wouldn't run without you," she answers. "Everyone knows it. Including that grumpy old man."

Marcy loves Gramps as much as I do, and works just as hard. "I'll clean after delivering this and then lock up." Lifting the tray off the center island, I say, "Goodnight."

"Sleep tight," she says, removing the apron she wears day and night.

She has dozens of aprons, all handmade. I still don't know when she finds the time to sew them up in her room on the third floor. Both she and Gramps have rooms up there.

In that respect, I'm lucky. I live in the cabin out back – except when I have to evacuate due to a huge group of guests rolling in. Thankfully, it doesn't happen often.

I exit the kitchen and head towards the back service stairway. The large front steps, as well as the small but serviceable elevator, are reserved for guests only. I try to tread carefully. These stairs are known to creak and I don't want to disturb the few guests we have, making my way up them and down the hall to room 205.

There, I shift the tray in order to balance it against me so I can use one hand to knock. Before that happens, the door flies open. A huge hand grabs my arm, pulling me inside the room.

I manage to keep the tray from falling, but when I

meet the nasty glare of the man still clutching my arm, I dang near drop it again.

"What the hell do you want and why are you sneaking around in the hallway?"

Holy crap. Guests have rarely dumbfounded me and never scared me. Until now.

I open my mouth, but nothing comes out. Tongue-tied? Since *when?*

"Well?" he snaps before my mind has a chance to force my tongue loose.

I finally take a good look at Mr. Porcupine. My heart skips a beat. If he wasn't so scary demanding, he'd be damn near gorgeous.

"Are those cupcakes?"

"Are they for us?"

The little voices coming from across the room snap me out of my deer-in-headlights mode. My heart slides out of my throat and back down in my chest where it belongs as I turn and see two little boys. Adorable little boys dressed in red and white striped pajamas with sandy-blond hair and big blue eyes.

The same shade of blue as the man still clutching my arm. No man, at least not one with an ounce of sanity, would accost a woman in front of his kids, so I jerk my arm out of his hold and carry the tray to the table in the center of the room.

"Yes, they're cupcakes, and they're yours." My nerves are settling. Teasingly, I add, "But only if you like chocolate."

"We do!" they sing in unison.

Twins. Identical, and with those eyes, the man could

never deny parentage. Thankful my mind works again, I turn to their papa, whose scowl could rival Gramps any day of the week. Slowly exhaling my relief, because I know grumpy men far too well, I say, "I *wasn't* sneaking. I was busy bringing you something to eat. Your sons are obviously hungry."

His piercing blue eyes practically burn holes through me, but I hold my own. He's mad, that's a given, but there's something deeper in those eyes. Fear almost.

Odd.

What would scare a man like him? He's over six feet tall, buff, and certainly not a weakling. His jawline looks strong pinched tight, built like it's made for kicking butt and kissing girls stupid. And the rest of him...sweet baby Jesus. The longer I stare, the harder it is believing there's such a bastard stuffed in this Adonis. I rub my arm, hoping it won't bruise tomorrow from my grabby mystery man.

"Can we have one, Daddy?"

"Please?"

I bite my tongue to keep from answering. We've had enough kids at the lodge to teach me a thing or two. Whether I like it or not, it's never my place to get between a guest and their children.

Cagey, like a trapped beast, he walks towards the table, keeping his eyes on me. I don't move, not even a step when he stops close enough to lift the lid off the plate of sandwiches. I'm not about to let him know he's frightened me, but I do get a whiff of his cologne. That has me biting the inside of my cheek. Damn if he doesn't smell as good as he looks.

Another suspicious look from his haunting eyes breaks the spell.

Clinging to the good sense God gave me, I say, "Again, sir, I wasn't sneaking around. I'm not trying to poison you, either. Whenever guests check in after meal time, we provide them with an evening snack." He doesn't look convinced. "Try it. Simple. Delicious. Yummy."

He doesn't respond, but picks up half a sandwich and takes a bite before nodding to the boys.

You're welcome, jerk, I think to myself. *Some people.*

The boys each take a cupcake and as they peel back the paper holders, I open the two cartons of milk and insert the straws Marcy included on the tray.

Then I pour him a cup of tea, using the hot water provided. "I can make you coffee if you'd prefer. It's instant, but it's not half bad."

"No, this is fine."

He's still grumpy, but his voice has lost some of its growl.

I hand each of the boys a milk carton, who both have pink frosting mustaches by now. "My name's Tabby."

"My name's Adam."

"I'm Chase, and daddy..." The second sweet boy pauses, his eyes going big as he looks at his father.

"Rex," he growls. My sinfully handsome porcupine has a normal name. Small relief.

"Well, I'm happy to meet you, Adam and Chase." I purposefully don't extend my welcome to Grumpy. "I hope you'll have fun here at the Grand Pine Lodge."

"Do you live here?" the one I think is Adam asks.

"Yes, I do, and I work here, too. So, if there's anything you need, just ask."

"Like more cupcakes?" Chase asks hopefully.

My first instinct is to say yes, but I hold back. "That would be up to your father..."

His eyes, as cold as ever, are on me. Not my face, but my sweater. It might be because it's the same color of pink as the frosting on the cupcakes and his sons' faces, but I doubt that.

Chills criss-cross my spine. My poor battered heart beats faster. It's like he can see right through the heavy wool. My nipples tingle, harden, adding to my shame.

Why? I've been hit on by men three times my age and boys alike, but I've never had *this* reaction.

"I think one's enough," he says. "You each eat a sandwich now and drink your milk."

I grab the menu off the tray before my mind, and body, reacts to how kind and gentle he suddenly sounds. "How long will you be staying?"

He picks up the tea and drinks it down before answering. "Just a few days."

"Well, here's the menu for the next three days. You can either have your meals delivered to your room or eat in the dining room. We're small, so the meal times are also listed, however, we can provide sandwiches and other items all day."

"And cupcakes?" Adam beams like the sun.

I can't help but smile. I used to dream of having children as adorable as these two, but it'll never happen. Reality and the roots I've laid down here go deep. I'll have to just enjoy the kids who visit the lodge. There aren't many men out there willing to give up their lives in order to help manage a place in the middle of nowhere. The few who might think they're willing would soon change their minds. This is a twenty-four hour, three-hundred and sixty-five day job, that also includes one very grumpy old man. My life has no place for children.

Besides, this is a small town. Split Harbor's dating pool isn't exactly extensive or quality. One very lucky lady already landed the resident billionaire a couple years ago.

"More cupcakes?" Chase echoes.

Touching the tip of Adam's nose, I say, "Some days it's cookies."

"I love cookies!" Chase yells.

"I like cupcakes more," Adam says.

"Well, then, I guess I'll have to make both, won't I? Cookies and cupcakes. I like staying busy." I wink at them before turning back to their father and hand him the menu. As he takes it, I get another whiff of that amazing cologne mingled with his scent. It's faint, but intoxicating and very good at making heat swirl deep inside me. The sandwich must have done him some good because he's no longer scowling. He's no longer *quite* as scary. His hair is darker than the boys, but I imagine when he was young it was just as sandy blond as Adam and Chase's. He was probably as adorable as they are, too.

"Where are you from?" I'm pulling my mind back where it belongs.

He sets the menu down on the dresser. "We'll be eating in our room, but aren't fussy. Whatever gets brought up will be fine. Along with coffee and milk. The earlier, the better."

I get the hint. It's none of my business where he's from. His clothes, jeans and a flannel shirt, could be worn in the city or country, but his accent reminds me of Russ, who is very proud of being born and raised in Chicagoland.

I should leave, but for some reason, it's hard peeling my eyes off him. I'm intrigued. Curious to know where his wife is, the boys' mother, but can't simply blurt it out.

He's staring back, harder than before, which has my insides tingling again in ways it shouldn't. *Ridiculous.*

"Well, Cupcake," he says slowly. It takes me a second to realize he means *me.* "You going to stand there all night, or let us finish eating in peace?"

Fine, whatever. I deserve that. He is a guest, after all.

Still, I'm irritated. And know I need to leave before saying something that will really piss him off. "I'm going," I say, "but the name's Tabby. I'd appreciate it if you'd –"

"Short for Tabitha?"

"No. Just Tabby." I cringe a little more than I usually do, giving up my nickname masquerading as a name.

He gives me one more solid toe-to-head stare that has me holding by breath before he whips around. "Let me get the door, Cupcake."

Nicknames. They shouldn't irritate me the way they do, but I can't help it.

Not when everyone always assumes Tabby is a nickname. It's the only thing my father ever gave me – whoever he was. One among many boyfriends who came calling on mom. My throat thickens slightly as I glance towards Adam and Chase. Those two boys don't know how lucky they are. Neither does their jackass father. I give them a small wave, walking out the door that's being held open impatiently by daddy's huge hand.

"Goodnight, Rex," I say, simply because he's a guest. A jerk, but a guest nonetheless, and we can't afford to lose customers in the winter. Not even a giant asshole.

He merely shuts the door.

I huff out a breath, and though I'd like to take a moment and lean against the wall to catch my bearings, I need space pronto, so make a beeline for the stairs.

Once I'm in the hallway safely downstairs, I place a hand on the wall, taking a few deep breaths. I've never had a man affect me like Rex. For no apparent reason, too.

It's so perplexing anger mingles with the heat he's left in my blood. Okay, so most women would be intrigued by six feet of mystery and muscle, especially one *that* freakin' sexy. But it doesn't explain why I'm coming undone for a Neanderthal who just wiped his feet on my back.

Annoyed, I push myself off the wall and head for the front desk. There, I move the mouse to wake up the computer and type in the password. The main screen appears.

Rex Osborne. Blue Chevy pick-up. No license plate number listed.

No, of course not. Gramps thinks that's a silly question even though I've warned him it might be important for security. Paid cash for two nights.

I log out and walk to the front door. Tall, dark, and sometimes handsome strangers are nothing new to the lodge. Insta-fascination I really shouldn't be experiencing is.

Maybe it's because our other handsome strangers come here to unwind, relieve the stress in their lives. Not this one. The man upstairs was wound tighter than a drum, and the blue pick-up backed up so it's practically hidden beneath the trees confirms something tickling at the back of my mind since he accused me of sneaking around outside 205.

Rex Osborne is hiding *something*. Or maybe, he's hiding from someone.

Either way, I want to know more. After locking the front door and turning down all the lights, and checking the kitchen, where I also leave a note for Marcy, I put on my coat and leave through the employee entrance. Rather than taking the shoveled pathway to my cabin, I walk around the lodge, to the far end of the parking lot. I'm able to get a better look at his truck from here.

Illinois plates. I knew it.

II: SETTLING IN (REX)

I stay hidden behind the curtain so she can't see me. She's already looked up at the window twice, as if sensing she was being watched, or she might just be that nosy – something that'll get her into more trouble than she'd ever bargain for.

Cupcake. I'd called her that out of defense, needing to keep my distance. Distance from everything and everyone.

Especially soft spoken girls who look as delicious as their dessert namesake. Her with the scorned looks lodged in her honey-hazel eyes. Her with the dark chocolate hair warning me it'd feel like velvet on my fingers. Her with the hips, the legs, the ass that's divine, hopelessly hidden behind her Ms. Average outfit.

Shit. I catch myself hard and shake my head, remembering she's one more problem I don't need.

How the fuck did I end up in this predicament? By fucking, that's how. At least at the beginning.

Of all the men in the world, all the one-night stands,

I'm the one who's getting royally fucked long after the fun ended. As my anger churns harder and hotter inside my guts, guilt rises to meet it. Cupcake has already walked away from the truck, back around the lodge, so I move away from the window. Stopping near the foot of one of the double beds, I stare at my twin boys

They're sleeping soundly. So innocent, so good, they almost take the edge off old mistakes.

Yeah, they came out of that one-night stand causing the present woes, too. I don't regret that. *Never will.*

It's ever screwing the bitch who bore them I regret. Should've known six years ago when I met her she was more trouble than any man needed. She'd been hot, sexy, and all over me. I'd had a hard week laying custom shingles on the roof of a frigging Senator's mansion.

I was ready to get drunk and wet my dick. We barely made it out of the bar. I fucked her in the front seat of my work truck parked in the alley. Afterwards, we'd gone back inside and partied some more, then we both left without another word.

Typical party at a watering hole on Chicago's rust belt. I never planned on seeing her again. Nine months later, when I was served the papers about submitting a blood sample, I'd long since forgotten her name. Until reading the second page of the court document, where our history was described, vividly.

I'm no deadbeat. I gave a paternity sample, accepted the DNA results, and agreed in court we'd share visitation to Adam and Chase. Limited and supervised visitations for her. Nelia claimed she hadn't known how to get a hold of me before the boys were born. An obvious lie. The name of my construction company, T-Rex Builders, was on the side of every work truck. Any number of people from the bar that night could've told her who I was, how to contact me.

She knew what she was doing from the start. Never attempted to get a hold of me to see the twins she abandoned, just thought I'd hand over child support, and lots of it, on a monthly basis.

She'd been dead wrong.

In more ways than one. Too fucking many to count.

And now she's dead.

Only saving grace about that is Adam and Chase didn't even know who she was. When, if ever, they heard about her death, they wouldn't mourn. Mommy is something they hear in fairy tales, not a fact of life.

Call me a cold-hearted bastard, but it's a small relief. Both that my sons won't suffer her loss, and that she's permanently out of our lives. She wasn't any type of mother to the boys the past five years, nor would she have ever changed. Didn't have it in her.

Raising kids takes heart, and Cornelia Hawkins didn't have a loving bone in her body, or the slightest clue what it took to be a mom.

Hell, Cupcake's already shown more affection towards the boys than Nelia ever did. Tabby, as she prefers to be called – the very reason I'll keep calling her Cupcake – may never know how badly Adam and Chase needed those chocolate treats tonight.

Not only had they been as hungry as me, and that was a damn good sandwich, the boys needed an ounce of kindness. Two weeks of driving around, spending nights in sleazy hotels and eating greasy drive-thru burgers, was taking its toll on all of us.

If Adam hadn't had to pee, and I hadn't pulled off on a side road to give him some privacy, I'd have never seen the faded sign advertising this place.

Grand Pine Lodge: A secluded hidden gem.

That's what the sign said, and that's exactly what we need. Sanctuary. A couple days off the road to wrap my head around what's happened, and what I can do about it next.

Because I'm not spending the rest of my life in jail for murder.

Fucking bitch. I knew what she was doing, but sure as hell hadn't expected this outcome.

Worst part is, I'm not the one who killed her.

I run my hands through my hair, scratching at my scalp. It itches like hell from not being washed good and proper in a couple days. The other hotels were too run down, too caked in dirt, I'd barely had time to run my head through the sink.

This place is old, but it's actually clean. Time for a real shower. Then a good night's sleep. I'll be clearer headed in the morning, able to think things through.

I grab the duffel bag I purchased in some dinky roadside town and head for the bathroom.

The shower helps. Bed's comfortable, too. So I let my mind wander free while I'm waiting to fall asleep. Even crack a grin as the Cupcake's face forms in my mind. That pink sweater hugged her in all the right places, didn't it? And those eyes...they're not really hazel. I remember more.

A brownish-green with specks of gold that sparked hellfire at times. Especially when I'd asked if she was going to stand there invading our space all night. Her long hair was thick and dark brown, pulled back in a ponytail, making her look even younger. So did the way she hadn't worn makeup. She hadn't needed any. There was a natural beauty to her. A grace, almost. Something I haven't seen in a woman in ages.

Chicago's full of girls with hair as colorful as rainbows and decked in cosmetics. Plenty of them are pretty, some teetering towards beautiful, but there's something about Cupcake's naturalness that takes my mind off everything else. At least briefly.

Or maybe it's her attitude. I'd startled her, frightened her even, but the moment she'd seen the boys, she'd turned friendly and kind. Sweet as the name I've given her. That stirs up more than it ought to. Makes me wish things were different for Chase and Adam.

Hell, I wish that for myself. If Nelia was more like Cupcake, life would be pretty damn good right now. I wouldn't be in this mess. I'd be home, probably with something pink and delicious to come home to.

I like that thought, insane as it is. I drift off imagining the boys enjoying their colorful frosted cupcakes all over again.

* * *

MY LUNGS ARE ON FIRE, my breathing ragged, coming in gasps that hurt going out as much as the air burns going in. I grab my head as the spinning slows and the faint sunshine coming in the window confirms I'm not in a penthouse apartment, standing over Nelia's dead body.

Sweat pours down my neck and my hands shake as I tell myself it was only a dream. A fucking nightmare that

I've already lived through and will continue to. Have to for Adam and Chase.

A knock at the door makes me realize that's why it ended. In the dream, Aiden had knocked on the door. That's not what happened in real life. He'd come at me like the crazy drugged up shit-hole of a man he'd been. I'm not sorry that fucker's dead either. Never will be.

The knock sounds again. Now, wide awake, the idea Cupcake could be outside my door has me tossing aside the covers. I grab a pair of jeans out of the duffel bag. "Coming."

Without bothering to zip or snap the jeans I shove my legs through, I open the door. The gray-haired old man who checked us in last evening stands there with a grimace. I can't tell if it's a frown or a smile.

"Tabby's note said you wanted breakfast early," the man said. "If she made a mistake, I can bring it back later."

"No," I answer. "No mistake. Thanks." I open the door wide enough to take the tray. "The boys are still sleeping, so I'll grab it." They're always starving when they wake up. As he hands me the tray, I say, "Hold on, though, I'll get the one from last night."

I set the tray on the table, find the one from last night, and carry it to the door. The man was hard to read, but knowing I can't afford anymore enemies, I say, "Thanks, the boys enjoyed the cupcakes."

"Tabby will be glad to hear it. I'll give her your compliments. You need something, just push one on the phone. That rings the front desk."

I nod and close the door, then give myself permission to crack a smile. The phone system in the place is as horribly outdated as everything else here. Damned if I care, it's not a dump like some of the other roadside motels we've stayed in the past two weeks. The lodge is clean and well maintained, just old.

The building must date back to the 1950s, maybe earlier. Being the carpenter I am, I'd noticed all that when we'd checked in. The place has solid bones, and with the way it's been kept up, it could stand for another century.

By the time I turn around, still trying to gauge how ancient this place really is, Adam and Chase are up. They're sitting on their bed, scratching their mops of tousled hair. Whether the sound of voices or the smell of food roused them, I have no idea.

"Hungry?"

"Yeahhhh!"

"Shhh," I say, even though it's too late. Their shout has my ears ringing, let alone any poor souls in the rooms next door. "Other people are probably still sleeping. Don't be rude, boys."

"Sorry," they say, once again at the same time.

It's uncanny, but deep down, I love it. They do most everything at the same time. They're like any kids making innocent mistakes as they grow, but they'll never need to apologize for who they are. "It's okay," I say softly. "Come on and eat."

"Are there cupcakes?"

I smile and rub each of their heads before reaching down to remove the cloth covering the tray. "Most people don't have cupcakes for breakf..." My words fade away. Besides three plates covered with domed metal lids, there are cartons of milk, a pot of coffee with a single cup, and three pink frosted cupcakes on the tray.

I can't help but chuckle. "I guess we aren't most people, are we?"

"Nope," the boys say while climbing onto the chairs.

"Are we going home today?" Chase asks.

"No, not today." Not ever is what I really mean.

"Yippie!"

They eat the cupcakes first and I let them. It's no great sin when I feed them right most days. The scrambled eggs, bacon, toast and hash browns fill me up. Damn good. I sit back to drink my coffee while the boys devour their smaller portion of the same breakfast I just had.

It's not long before I'm pouring myself a second cup. Hot and black, just how I like it. A sinking feeling gels the food in my stomach as I watch them eat.

I have to figure out what to do. These two need me. *Will* need me for years to come.

Since freeing them from the penthouse apartment, we've bounced around Illinois, Iowa and Wisconsin, zigzagging from ATM to ATM, drawing out my daily limit. If only I'd had the foresight to up that amount. I have enough money for us to live on for years in the bank, but hadn't thought about upping the amount. Worse, knowing the transactions left a trail anyone could follow, I pitched the card out the window over the side of a bridge and headed for Canada.

What choice did I have – money or demons in hot pursuit?

We could jump in the truck right now and make it to the border in a few hours, but that's just as risky as it was yesterday. I'd have to show my ID to cross the border. I don't know who's watching or what the Chicago press is saying back home.

Hunkering down would be the best bet, let things cool off till I can contact my lawyer. Granted, Justin was a business lawyer, not a criminal one, but he'll know someone who can help.

While the boys are finishing up, I dig the tablet out of my duffel bag and turn it on. I'd bought it along with clothes, duffel bags, and a cart full of other essentials the day after leaving Chicago, using a credit card which I then flushed down the toilet in the men's room of the gas station after using it to fill the truck's tank.

My grandfather's old truck is a gas hog, but reliable. I took it out of the pole shed on his property, where it's been parked since grandpa died ten years ago, and where I left mine. My cousin lives on the farm now, and probably won't go in the shed until summer. Hopefully. If he does, I hope he sees the note I left behind. It simply says I'd borrowed it. John takes the truck out on the roads every summer, just to keep it in running order, so I knew it'd take us wherever we needed to go, about as untraceable as we could get. Which is exactly what we needed and why I threw my phone in the back of a shipping truck with Florida license plates at a gas station.

Fucking-A. What a mess.

After punching in the internet password written on a slip of paper and taped to the front of the phone book on the desk, I search hotels, resorts, and all sorts of other lodging options along the Canadian border for an hour or more. I'm not sure how long it's been, but I do know my options are crap. I only have a couple of grand, tops, in my billfold. Spending three hundred a night isn't feasible. This place, the Grand Pine Lodge, doesn't even have its own website. The price is very reasonable, too.

What I need is a job. Income. Enough money so I can pay our room and board here, saving my cash for when we have to leave. The dollar stretches a bit further over the border, but only if I've got plenty to stretch.

It's far from my biggest worry, too. The Stone Syndicate won't stop looking. They know where Nelia's money came from, and they know who killed Aiden.

They know my fucking name, who my kids are, and every sacred stretch of Chicago soil I ever frequented. We can't stop for long. We *have* to keep moving.

"Dad, there's a horse out there," Adam says, breaking my quiet panic.

"Can we go look at it?" Chase asks.

"Or ride it?" Adam pipes in.

They're getting restless. I've kept them busy getting dressed, combing their hair and brushing their teeth, all on their own, which takes ample time considering they're only five.

"Sure," I say, suppressing a sigh. "Fresh air will do us all good, I suppose." It'll give me time to look around, too, maybe see if there's a back road out of this place. Valuable info I may need if the time to leave comes sooner than I think. "Get your coats on, and don't forget your mittens."

"They're gloves, Dad," Chase corrects.

"Right, don't forget your gloves." I smile. Nelia may have given them half their genes, but they've got my looks and brains. My focus.

Small blessings. Can't fathom what the hell I'd do right now without them.

It's only a little after seven and the hotel is pin-drop quiet, so I tap my lips with a finger as we walk down the stairs. Their hushed giggles make me shake my head. This is how they've been since we left. Following my commands without questions, acting like the entire thing is one huge adventure.

Technically, it is. Just not the joyous kind they think.

I open the door and close it again behind us as quick as possible. The boys can't hold back their shouts of freedom any longer as they tear across the wide front porch and down the stairs.

Whoever does the shoveling around here must get up early. The porch, steps, and sidewalks are clear from last night's snow, as well as a wide pathway to the barn that's a good hundred yards off to the east side of the lodge. Shoveling that much wouldn't have been easy. A good two inches fell, the wet, heavy kind that makes good snow balls, snow forts, and snowmen. The boys run on toward the barn, stopping to scoop up a handful every now and again.

I scanned the area, looking for signs of trouble, or anything out of the ordinary. Whoever shovels, must not also plow because there aren't any tracks in the parking lot. It's still got my truck and the two other SUVs that were there last night.

Nearly deserted. That'll do fine.

As satisfied as I can be given the circumstances, I follow the boys, catching up with them on the backside of the barn, where they're crouched down looking between the two bottom rails of the fence at the two shaggy looking horses.

"Can we go in there, Dad?" Adam asks.

"No."

Just then a door on the barn near the fence opens and I take a double look at who comes strolling out.

Cupcake. She must love pink. I didn't know they made canvas work coats in that shade. Her hair is in another ponytail and a thick head band covers her ears. Pink again.

My morning wood is back with a vengeance, straining against my denim.

"Well, good morning!" she says to the boys, never once looking at me. "What brings you early risers out here?"

"We saw the horses," Chase says.

"Can we pet them?" Adam asks.

"And ride them?" Chase grins.

"These two are too old to ride anymore," she says softly, "but you can pet them, if it's all right with your father."

The boys look up at me, hope sparking in their eyes. So does she, which makes my heart thud oddly.

It's got to be the stress. I've had women since Nelia, yeah, but always kept them at a distance, far from me and the boys. I'm never getting burned like that again. But fuck, I'm not a monk, and a woman as attractive as Cupcake has the bewitching ability to turn me hard in a heartbeat.

"Can we, Dad?"

I turn to them and nod.

"You'll have to come through the barn." She points to the side of the building. "The door I shoveled a path to."

Testing my hearing, I ask, "You shoveled the path?"

"Yes."

"And the sidewalks?"

"Yes, why?" she cocks her head.

The boys are already running, so I simply say, "No reason."

I'm impressed, and that's got nothing to do with her dick-teasing looks. A woman who bakes and shovels is a certain rarity in this day and age. Then again this isn't the big city.

By the time I get to the door, the boys have shoved it open and darted inside.

"Be careful," she says. "Slow down."

The boys listen, slowing to a brisk walk as they make their way around piles of lumber.

"We're in the middle of a remodeling out here," she says.

I nod, taking it all in.

Big and solid, the barn is what I'd call a clean slate. This is the part of construction work I've always loved. Envisioning the potential, what the final project could look like restored. Unfortunately, I don't get to do it as often as I'd like anymore.

Most of the time, my customers have professional blueprints ready to go for my crew.

Shit, the crew. Just thinking about them twists my lips sourly.

That was one of the two phone calls I'd made before I threw my phone to the wild. To Randy, my construction manager. I told him to cut the men a month's worth of paychecks and shut everything down. It was the best I could do and it still pisses me off, but I had to make a choice. Fast.

A day or two more, and the Syndicate would be all over my company. They'd go after my men for info, hell, their families. I couldn't put more lives in danger. Protecting my boys is enough. More than enough.

The other call had been to Mrs. Potter, the nanny and

tutor I'd hired for Chase and Adam in better times. I told her I was taking them out of town on business and would call when we return. I'll cut her a severance check, eventually, but she already screwed me once. *If she'd said no to Nelia that fucked up day she came...*

No. I can't go there again.

Holding in a sigh, I follow the boys, who are following Cupcake, taking my time to examine the space. Whatever helps get my mind off poison. Like the lodge, the barn was built well and it's still solid. Even the floor. By the time I catch up to them through the back door, she's given each of the kids a bucket. A horse eats out of each one, both snorting happily to the boys' delight.

"What type of remodeling project?" I finally ask.

She eyes me critically while continuing to pet one of the big brown horses. I don't blame her, I wasn't friendly last night. After a few tense seconds, I walk over and pet the other horse, acting as if I don't care if she answers or not.

"We're turning it into more of a stable, with a large tack area room, feed storage, and office."

"For these two?" I'm not much of an animal person, but I recognize old when I see it.

"No. We'll keep them, but also bring in more, so we can offer trail rides to guests."

"What are trail rides?"

She laughs at how both boys speak simultaneously, word for word. "Horse rides."

"Yippie!" They both jump, no doubt hoping to be the first happy customers.

Picturing a layout inside the barn, I ask, "How many horses?"

"I'm thinking six," she says, "but it depends on Clayton. He's our neighbor and this will be a partnership of sorts. The man boards horses and always has more than he can exercise on his property. He doesn't have enough acreage for trails, either. I think the guests will like it, and hopefully, we'll both make some money."

It's a solid plan, though I'm not about to say it. I'm also seeing a job for myself. One that won't take long, but could pay the money I need.

"Unfortunately, the remodel is delayed right now."

"Why?" I snap, trying not to show my hand. Not easy.

"Russ broke an ankle and probably won't get back to work for a couple months. He's kinda our jack-of-all-trades around here. He was spearheading this before the accident."

Shitfire, this is too perfect. My mind goes a hundred miles per hour, estimating how long it'll take me to complete the remodel as we stand quiet for a short time.

Then Cupcake glances down at the boys and then back up at me, breaking the silence. "So, not to break up the party, but I've got other chores. Can't let you stay out here, sir. Liability reasons."

I nod. "Fine. Thanks for letting them feed the horses. Boys, what do you say?"

"Can we do it again?"

I give them a look. "Boys..."

"Thank you, Tabby!" They both lower their eyes and I give a satisfied nod.

Cupcake laughs. A soft, airy sound reminding me what kind of trouble I'm in getting too close to this woman. "Adorable. Do you two *always* talk at the same time?" she asks.

"Sometimes," the boys answer shyly.

The sound of more singsong feminine laughter makes me wonder if the boys ever heard such an angelic sound before. *Hell, have I?*

"Just you working in the barn while the help is out – Russ, right?" I ask.

Cupcake nods. "Yes. Well, I fill their water tank and feed them grain every morning and hay every evening," she says while collecting the buckets. "It's easy enough."

"How do you keep the water from freezing?" I wonder aloud.

Her eyes say she still doesn't trust me, yet she answers, "There's a pump house in the far corner of the barn that we keep heated."

Room for improvement. Another opportunity, if they'll bite.

I wave for the boys to follow. They have more questions for her as we walk through the barn. She answers each one while I scan the area again, making mental notes. The old man who checked us in last night said he owns the place, so that's who I need to talk to. Once we exit the barn, she says goodbye and walks towards the back of the lodge, a plastic salt bucket in hand. I keep the boys outside until they've worn off some energy, then lead them inside.

Off the foyer where the large front desk is located, there's a big front room with a TV and a large game of checkers set up on a coffee table. I get the boys settled in first. I haven't let them out of my sight since that night our world caved in. Don't want to now, but must, in order to talk to the old man.

I won't be far, knowing this is the safest place we've

been in two weeks, so I leave the room and cross the foyer again. There's a door behind the desk marked OFFICE. Unable to remember what the man said his name was, I scan a magazine on a side table with a subscription label. Morris Danes.

That's right. I've sold multi-million dollar construction jobs, convincing Morris Danes to pay me to remodel his barn should be like taking candy from a baby.

I knock, fully prepared to open the door upon invitation.

Instead, it opens as someone leaves.

Shit.

It's Cupcake. The old man sitting behind her bristles hostility. My shoulders want to sag. If she has anything to do with it, I won't get this job.

III: HARD BARGAINS (TABBY)

My heart thuds so hard I can't breathe. Why does he do this to me? It happened outside, too, the minute I saw him standing next to the barn. Those blue eyes are the definition of piercing. Like they can see right into my head, read my thoughts. Earlier I'd become a babbling idiot, telling him all about my plan for the stable and trail rides. Which he obviously didn't care about. The dark and brooding expression that crossed his face when he'd walked into the barn made that clear. Even though he'd tried to hide it later.

Well, I can hide a few things too. Like how easy he knots my stomach.

Lifting my chin, I ask, "Something you need, Mr. Osborne?"

"I'd like to speak to Mr. Danes." His gaze goes past me, settling on Gramps.

I'm about to say I'll help, whatever it is. Mainly because Gramps was never completely sold on the trail rides idea. It won't take much for him to re-think and shut it down. If this dark, coarse stranger blurts out anything I told him...

"Come in then," Gramps says. "Tabby, shut the door behind you."

Crap. It's too late to worry.

Rex's eyes meet mine as he brushes past. There's a hint of triumph in them, as if he's won a game I didn't know we were playing. I pinch my lips together to keep from saying something rude.

"If you'll excuse us, Ms. Danes?" Oh, suddenly, I'm Ms. Danes? Not Cupcake like he'd called me last night?

Shouldn't annoy me, but of course it does.

Keeping my composure, I leave the office and pull the door closed after he enters. Frustration pricks my blood. Gramps is dead set on nothing changing at the lodge. He won't even consider proper listings on travel sites online. It took me a year to convince him to partner with Clayton Williams for the trail ride idea. No, it's not a million-dollar game changer, but every dollar counts right now. Besides, Clayton's horse boarding has a basic website and he's promised to include our resort along with the trail rides next time he updates.

Again, not a huge money maker, but baby steps are all I dare take with Gramps. If Rex Osborne screws this up for me, he'll be sorry.

"Hi, Tabby!" Two little voices chirp.

Their father makes me steam like an engine overheating, but his children are adorable. Looking at them is sunshine. It simply fills my soul with a carefree warmth. "Well, hello again," I say, walking into the front room. "Are you two playing checkers?"

"Not really."

I'm unsure which is Adam and which is Chase, so don't know how to address the question. "Why's that? Good way to pass the time, boys."

"Because we don't know how to play," the other one says, looking down.

"You don't know how to play checkers?" I smile.

They both shake their heads. "Well, then it's high time you learned." I sit down on the floor and show them how to set up the game, and then play a couple rounds with them. They're smart and catch on quick, which is good, because I have tons of work to do. It had only snowed about two inches overnight, but Wes hasn't plowed yet, and Sarah, the weekend cleaning woman, hasn't been able to make it up the hill off the main road. I'm the lucky one filling in for her.

Gramps took the phone call while I'd been out shoveling, told Sarah she should have walked if her car couldn't hash the snow. That's what he'd have done. Gramps, who has a million stories on permanent repeat about running the lodge under waves of Michigan snow, in every recession, without anyone around to drag him down.

Ugh. This also means I need to call and smooth things over with Sarah, which will probably include begging her to keep working here. If our part-time cleaning lady goes, I'll never get a full day off.

"Great game, boys, but I have to get to work," I tell them, hearing someone's heavy footsteps on the stairs. "You two have fun."

"We will, thanks, Tabby."

"You're welcome," I say while tousling their hair. "Both of you." If they were mine, I'd have to put a dot on one of their foreheads so I could tell one from the other. I've heard of that. New mothers putting a dot on one baby's heel when she has twins, in order to keep track of who's who.

Of course, that's a silly notion to be contemplating. Rex has paid for two nights, so they'll be leaving tomorrow. Sunday. Makes sense, the boys most likely need to be back at school Monday. I'm assuming they're in school. Kindergarten, I'd bet. They look about that age.

I shuffle to the front desk, help the older couple from room 203 check out, and then collect the cleaning and supply cart.

The boys take up a portion of my mind while I'm busy, but their father takes up more. I'm working upstairs, first the third floor and then the second, so don't know if he's still talking with Gramps or not. Can't tell if he and the boys entered their room or not, either. That could have happened while I was busy cleaning Grandpa's room, or vacuuming the hallways, or resetting the room left vacant by the elderly couple who checked out this morning.

Their door has the DO NOT DISTURB tag hanging off its knob, meaning he doesn't want any cleaning. Most people staying two days don't. Just like the couple in room 202, who claim they're on their honeymoon, but arrived in separate cars, with license plates from different states.

Okay, I'm nosy, but I also mind my own business by keeping my thoughts to myself. Comes with the territory in this little town. The most excitement Split Harbor's had in years was a murder-mystery involving our resident billionaire, Ryan Caspian. Him and his wife, Kara, the high school sweetheart he settled down with after a mountain of drama, practically lived through a romance thriller. And the town lived it vicariously, too.

Newly-weds or not, the 202 guests both paid in advance and haven't left their room since arriving on Thursday. They'll be leaving tomorrow, too. There are two reservations for next weekend, but the entire week we'll be empty. Not so good when it comes to making a profit. Advertising is what we need, but other than a listing in the yellow pages, and one old worn out billboard off the old road, Gramps is against that too.

Almost as strongly as he dug his heels in against my trail rides.

I'll be thoroughly pissed off if Rex changes his mind, however carelessly. That chiseled jaw and rock hard muscle sending lightning down my spine won't be enough to save him.

The more I think about it, the madder, the more worried I become. I'm holding my breath while rolling the cleaning cart off the elevator, wondering what happened. Gramps' office door is open, the room empty.

Now, I'm spitting mad. Damn him to *hell* on a fucking white horse. This stranger knows nothing about us. He can't just waltz in here one night acting all grumpy and uppity – yes, he's uppity, too, like he's better than everyone else – and start telling us how to run this place.

My mind replays the worst scenarios as I refill the cleaning cart and then stow it and the vacuum away, and carry the used bedding to the basement, where I put it in the washer before heading back upstairs and to the kitchen.

Gramps is there eating lunch. I hold my breath for a moment, waiting for an explosion, or an 'I told you so.'

He barely looks up. Marcy, on the other hand, is as bubbly as ever.

"Sit down and eat, Tabby!" She motions to the chair. "I already carried trays up to the couple in 202 and that man and his cute little boys in 205."

"Thanks," I say. If only she knew *that man* and his cute little boys are driving me *insane*.

"It's broccoli cheese soup and turkey sandwiches on rye, just how you like them!"

Is it that obvious I'm upset? I sit down, fill a bowl from the tureen in the center of the table and place half a sandwich on a plate. "Guilty as charged," I tell her.

"I know you too well," Marcy says, placing a large glass of iced tea in front of me. "Hey, if you have time this afternoon, we *are* out of cupcakes. I gave the last few to the guests. They loved them."

"I'll whip up another batch soon."

"White with chocolate frosting?" Gramps asks.

"Sure." I wait for more, eyeing him suspiciously. Still mad enough to make sure he listens to my point of view.

He just keeps eating. Weird.

Marcy sits down and fills a bowl of soup for herself. She sees me moving like molasses, sifting my spoon through the soup. "Eat before it gets cold."

Only good advice I've heard today. I eat a few quick mouthfuls of soup, and just when I take a bite off my sandwich, have my mouth completely full, Gramps speaks up.

"Good news, Tabby-kitten. I hired someone to finish the barn stables."

I almost choke trying to get down enough of the food in my mouth so I can ask, "Who?"

"Rex Osborne."

I do choke then, and have to take a drink of tea to soothe my throat before I can speak again. "Who?"

This has to be a joke. He's pulling my leg right out of its socket.

"Rex Osborne," Marcy says. "The man with those adorable twins in room –"

"I *know* who he is," I say, cringing at how the shine in her eyes behind her wire-rimmed glasses dulls. "I mean, I'm surprised. Thought he was only staying two nights."

"He's decided to make it an extended stay, until he's done with the restoration." Gramps pours himself a cup of coffee from the insulated pot on the table, turning a sip over in his cheek as he often does. "Here's your bonus: I told him the job includes shoveling the sidewalks. You're welcome."

I'm not relieved. Not even a little.

I hold up a hand. "Wait. An extended stay?" My head spins with questions. What about his boys? School? Their mother? Where *is* she in all this?

"We need that place fixed pronto for peak season. Man's a bit down right now and needs the work. Wasn't a hard decision." He taps his chest proudly.

"Down, you said? From what?"

Gramps lets out a long sigh. "Life. The mother of his kids died recently."

I press a hand against my stomach, where a sickening sensation erupts. "When? How?" I feel my anger wilting.

"Didn't ask." Gramps shrugs. "Figured it was none of my business, but suspect it wasn't long ago. That's why he's here. Soul searching. Giving the boys some different scenery, trying to get their minds off it." He tilts his head.

"Also means a man like that'll be reliable. He'll work his keister off to forget."

I don't care. I'm just...stunned isn't even the right word.

This explains everything. His moodiness, how sweet and patient he is towards his sons. Yet, I find it hard to believe the Rex I met last night and again this morning, poured his heart out to Gramps on a whim. "He told you all that?"

"Didn't need to. Once he said their mother died recently, I put the rest together." Gramps frowns. "I thought you'd be happy? The stable will be done before spring, which is what you wanted. We need it if we're gonna give your little happy trails notion some motion."

"You didn't want to," I point out.

"I never said that," Gramps says sternly.

I can't believe this. "You fought me *every* step of the way. Now, you're on board because of him?"

"No. I fought against us paying for everything out-of-pocket. Once Clayton agreed to pay for a portion of the remodel, well, that changed things. It'll be his horses living in the barn, after all."

"We'll be profiting off his horses."

"Yes, but it'll take years to recoup the remodeling cost. Clayton's portion makes business sense. I explained all that to you."

He had, but not exactly the way he is right now.

"Rex is smarter than he looks. Man's got some ideas for a few minor fix-ups and upgrades I really liked."

A flash of anger hits me all over again. "What ideas? Clayton and I laid out the design for you months ago. One that'll work for the horses, guests, and us."

"Yes, you did, it's only a few minor changes." Gramps

pushes away from the table, a sure signal he's done with this conversation. He crosses the room, but as he pushes open the door, he says, "Rex starts tomorrow morning. Be sure to drop off breakfast early."

"Isn't that wonderful news?" Marcy asks. Her smile fell then as she says, "Oh, those poor little boys, and that man. How sad."

She's right, of course. I try to calm down, feeling guilty how I'd condemned Rex to hell before knowing his situation. So guilty I pick up my half eaten lunch and carry it across the room to the sink, dumping the remnants in the trash on the way. "I'll clean up the kitchen and bake some cupcakes if you want to go up to your room for a while."

"No, I'll help," Marcy says. "Busy hands are happy. I won't be able to sew anyway, thinking about those little boys and their loss."

I know the feeling. That's what's weighing on my mind, too.

"I wonder how long ago that was," Marcy says. "A month? Maybe weeks? More?"

"No clue."

"Well, there would have been a funeral and such." With a shoulder, she shoves me aside. "Let me get the dishes. Need something to occupy my mind or I'll go nuts with crazy thoughts."

I feel the exact same way and open the pantry door to pull out the ingredients for cupcakes.

"You know what? I have a roast in the freezer. I'm going to pull that out and put it in to bake. Nice and slow so it'll be tender and juicy. It's probably been *ages* since those little boys had a good home-cooked meal. I mean if she'd been sick for a time or something...yeah, that's exactly what I'll do. I'll make mashed potatoes and gravy and candied carrots. Everybody loves candied carrots!"

Marcy rattles on, and I hear her, but don't. My own mind's too busy. Had Rex's wife been ill?

Ill for years and then passed away? The more I think about it, the more tragic my thoughts turn. Until tears sting my eyes. Not wanting Marcy to see them, I turn off the mixer. "I have to go put the laundry in the dryer, be right back."

I keep busy all afternoon, baking and helping Marcy, between taking care of any lodge business. There's very little. A couple reservations for later in the month. I also speak to Sarah, who agrees to continue working for us, but not until next weekend. That's not an issue with just the two rooms occupied, and I call Betty, the week day housekeeper, and say she doesn't need to come in on Monday unless things change.

Both women are wonderful that way, working when we need them and taking days off when we don't. I fill in the gaps and there are a lot of them. But we're like family here.

There are so many little issues with running a lodge that Gramps doesn't seem to fully understand. Or maybe he does and I don't understand his way of relaying it to me. It seems that's how it was with the stables.

It seems that's how it was with Rex, too. I'd jumped to conclusions without knowing all the facts.

By the time supper finishes, I've worked myself into a minor frenzy, wondering how I'll face Rex again, knowing how I condemned him. Or Adam and Chase for that matter.

It's not like I have a choice, anyway. I carry the tray up

to the couple in room 202 first, just to give myself a bit more time.

My nerves literally have me shaking in my shoes. I carry the tray for his room slowly across the hallway. It's not like he completely knows all the bad things I thought about him, but I do. And that's the problem.

God, Tabby Danes. Get on with it. You're being ridiculous.

I find my nerve. Can't stall longer anyway – if I do their food will get cold – so I knock. When there's no response after what feels like an hour, I knock again. This time, louder.

Still no answer.

Surely, they haven't left. They don't seem like the type to go into town for dinner. I think I'd know that, so I hold the tray against me with one hand and slowly try the knob.

It's unlocked. Just as slowly, I push the door open a crack to poke my head in around the edge.

"Hey," I say quietly to the boys lying on the bed.

"Hi, Tabby," they say together, as if expecting me.

One of them holds up the tablet they'd both been staring at. "Dad downloaded us a checkers game!"

Glancing around the room, I ask, "Where is your dad?"

"In the shower."

I can't stop the sigh of relief that oozes out of me as I hear the water hissing. We're alone. I got lucky.

Pushing the door all the way open, I carry in the tray. "I've got your supper, boys."

"And cupcakes?!"

They're too sweet. My heart skips a beat, thinking of their loss. "Two for each of you."

"Yippie!" They launch their little bodies in the air, jumping like monkeys several times.

Closing the door, I gently warn, "But, I think your dad will want you to eat your dinner first."

"Yes, he will," one of them says, a bashful look in his eyes.

They're so well behaved.

I set the tray on the table, making sure the cloth is evenly situated, hoping it helps keep things as warm as possible until Rex is ready to eat. My smile hides how my heart bleeds sympathy every time I look at them, so I sit down on the edge of the bed. "Show me your checkers game while we wait for your daddy."

They climb across the bed and sit down, one on each side of me.

"It's fun!"

"Dad never lets us play games like this."

"Nope, never."

"Mrs. Potter doesn't either."

My neck is getting tired from twisting left and right as they each speak. "Oh, who's Mrs. Potter?"

"What the hell are you doing?"

I bolt off the bed, spin around, and find myself dumbfounded all over again. Or maybe just frozen in place.

Rex. Rex freakin' Osborne, in the flesh, and *holy hell* what kind of flesh is this sweet sorcery?

Water drips off his hair, the droplets trickling down his shoulders, his arms, his chest. He'd looked buff with clothes on, but without – Holy hell! Again.

I've never seen anything like it in my life and I can't stop my eyes from going lower. It's like God smashed an underwear model, a Spartan warrior, and a screaming rockstar together. He's big, ripped to the bone, and inked all over. Explosions of color flash on the canvas of his body when he catches the light, wild beasts and flowers with thorns.

My eyes move on their own. Straight to the towel wrapped around his waist.

I can't stop myself from thinking about his wife, how she must have enjoyed this sight on a regular basis. I can't help but feel a bit jealous, either.

What the hell is wrong with me? Jealous of a dead woman.

"I asked you a question." His growl is as fierce as his muscles.

End me.

I close my eyes because they refuse to move upwards, to his face. "I, uh...I brought your supper tray. No one answered, so—"

"The old fat woman just knocked and set it on the floor."

My eyes snap open and meet the glare he's casting my way. "Her name is Marcy and she's not fat. Or very old." She's only in her late fifties, pleasantly plump and middle-aged.

"All right, the *plump older* woman just knocked and set it on the floor." It's barely politer, but I'll let it go.

His poor wife might have loved his body, but probably despised his attitude. Or maybe not. Maybe it's just me he's this grumpy with. No longer feeling a strong desire to apologize, I say, "Did you really agree to work for my grandfather?"

"Yeah. That a problem, Cupcake?"

Hell yes. Him. That body. Inked and hard and oh my

God. Nearly naked and dripping wet, or fully clothed, it's not something I need to see every day. "He's not easy to get along with," I warn.

"Good. Neither am I."

"Really?" I don't hide my sarcasm.

The grin that lights up his face is a bit cock-eyed and it nearly knocks the air out of me. A man this good-looking should have a red danger sign taped to his chest.

"Really."

I huff out a breath. "Color me shocked."

He steps closer, and though warning bells ring loud and clear in my head, my feet are still frozen. Glued to the floor.

"You'll be glad knowing it'll only take me a couple of weeks to have that barn looking better than new. Ready for horses and guests alike. Easy work, solid pay, I would've been a fool to turn it down."

I nod, pressing my feet harder against the floor, hoping it might stop my eyes from roaming lower again, past his bulging tattooed chest, washboard abs, and that line of dark hair that disappears beneath the towel.

A bolt of heat shoots down my neck as he touches the underside of my chin with a single finger and slowly forces me to look up, into his face.

"Said you'd be glad, didn't you, Cupcake? You'll have guests for this place. Other guests a lot more pleasant than me, and probably more boring. Because they won't turn your eyes into magnets."

Damn it to hell and back in a chicken basket. Flustered, I jump back, mainly because my feet still hadn't wanted to move. "Right. Glad, Mr. Osborne. I will be."

He chuckles.

"Keep laughing. You won't find it so funny after a day or two working for Gramps," I warn. "He expects an early riser, and a full day of hard, quality work."

"That's me. Man enough for the job, darling."

Darling?! And I thought Cupcake was bad. Time to go.

I'm retreating toward the door, trying hard not to stumble, but I really don't dare take my eyes off him. I'm not sure why. Maybe because I don't want to even after his crap and the rude remarks.

Yes, I'm fully aware how messed up this is.

I step into the hallway. "We'll see if you're truly up for the task."

"Oh, I'm up for the task, Cupcake, don't worry." Again, *that* name. One brow arches as he grasps the edge of the door and eyes me up and down. "I'm up for a lot of things. Just sayin'."

Fire rushes through me just as the door closes in my face. Unable to take more than a single step sideways, I lean my head against the wall and whisper to myself, "Tabby Danes, I never knew you were such a fucking idiot."

IV: FRESH BAKED DISASTER (REX)

I've only been working for an hour, and already have a fucking blister. Who would have ever thought? Not me. The past few years is why.

I had to do more managing than real labor. Not just my company, but keeping after the money Nelia kept sucking out of me. She kept threatening to haul me to court for full custody. No judge in their right mind would have agreed to it, but that had also been the problem.

The Stone Syndicate is one of the oldest crime families in Chicago. Justice is corruptible and they've got more than one judge in their pocket, and Nelia had been fucking Aiden Stone. I'd have lost any court case she dragged me into, that much was a given.

That bitch sucked more than money out of me. She sucked out my life, maybe my soul. I can't find any remorse over the fact that she's dead. I just have to find a way out of the mess she left behind. That's what still matters. The one I'm smack dab in the middle of, in more ways than one. It's not just their deaths that set the hounds loose on my trail, it was the money laundering.

I grab the handsaw and start cutting a board in two, shaking off my dilemma. When I'd estimated the time this job would take, I mistakenly figured there'd be power tools I could use.

There are. *Hand-powered* tools. Honestly, I don't mind, delays aside.

It's a release for the anger that fills me to the point it feels as if I'm being swallowed by some hellish beast and spat back out, more pissed off than I was before. These hands are used to working miracles, and when they do, they also make me smile.

Working, building something that'll last for years, grounds me. Gives me the first sense of normalcy I've had in years. Certainly since my life went to hell in a hand basket after that one fateful fuck.

Her pussy hadn't even been good. I would have remembered if it had. I don't. I know it happened, can't deny that, and won't ever regret Adam and Chase coming out of it.

I glance towards the corner where they're sorting the bent nails from straight ones out of an old coffee can. Had to give the kids something to do to keep them busy. The sun is barely up, and it's cold, well below freezing, but they haven't mumbled a single complaint. They won't either.

Even as young as they are, they're made of tough stuff. Thank God and the blessings I'm not sure I deserve that they've got no idea killers are out there right now, somewhere, searching for us.

There are times since arriving here I've forgotten that

fact. I have to make sure I never get so focused on the here and now I forget the past. Or the present. Or the reason we're here, and how fucking evil the men looking for us are.

The click of the door latch sends a shiver up my spine, and I wheel around, ready to take out whoever walks through the door.

Then I see it. Pink. The relief rushing over me is uncanny.

So is she. Pink coat, headband, and gloves. Panties? Fuck, I wouldn't be surprised if they were pink, too. Pleased. But not surprised.

"Hi, Tabby!" the boys shout together, coming back to life.

"Good morning," she replies.

I catch the way she glances my way, her frown. She's clearly not impressed the boys are out here with me. Too bad. This is where they are and where they're staying. Within my sight at all times. Not like I've got a better choice.

"What are you doing out here?" Adam asks.

"Are you here to work, too?" Chase asks. "Like us? Helping Daddy?"

"Smart guess. That's exactly why I'm here."

A chill claws through me. Shit.

I was counting on not seeing her all day. Don't need the distraction. By the time she left the room last night after delivering our supper, I'd had a hard-on like no tomorrow. An ice-cold shower had barely helped. Neither had the second one I took after I woke up, the heat flowing through my fingers as I jerked off my frustration, my sick dreams, my unholy fixation on wanting to fuck this girl.

Now, conveniently, my boss' granddaughter. Hell, boss *and* landlord. Old Morris could snap his fingers and throw us to the wolves on a whim. I have to get my head straight. *Focus.*

"But my work is feeding the horses."

I'd forgotten that. How? I don't know. But I had.

"Can we help?"

"Only if it's all right with your father," she answers.

The boys don't ask, they just give me that look, the faces I can't say no to. Even as young as they are, they know it, the little miscreants.

I mull it over. They'll still be close, within hearing distance if not seeing, so I nod.

"Yippie!" Their little screams echo off the rafters.

She holds out both hands and they run towards her, each one grasping one of her hands. I'll never admit to being a soft-hearted man, but the sight of that does something to me. To the point my throat thickens. Irritated she can do that to me, I growl, "Boys, remember: behave."

"We will!" they say. Not just Adam and Chase.

Tabby joins them. I bite back a grin at how all three of them had spoken at the same time, and how they giggle after.

Damn it. I need to keep a clear head. She makes that near impossible.

The saw does its job, cutting through the board, and I'm surprised at how straight the cut is considering how I had my eyes on the other end of the barn, where she'd shown the boys how to pull the hose out of the small corner room and out the side door, and then how to turn on the water, the entire time I'd been working.

I take my time collecting and measuring another board, still watching her as she answers the multitude of questions the boys ask about turning the water on and off, and reeling the hose back into the small corner room. Then she helps them dump grain into two buckets and carry them out to the horses.

I have several boards ready before they're back inside. I'd been able to hear them the entire time, but even if I hadn't, I instinctively knew the boys would be fine with her.

Strange. The few times Nelia was around them, I'd been on needles. Ready to pounce. *Had* pounced more than once. She couldn't be trusted to even feed them a bottle. The one time she had, Adam almost choked because she'd shoved the nipple so far down his throat.

She'd never been able to tell them apart, either. Her own sons. That was Nelia. One hell of a mother.

Hell, where I hope she is now.

I hadn't realized the anger inside me was being taken out on the board I'd been sawing until the end split off and I looked up. Just in time to catch the way Cupcake looks at me. There are wrinkles between her brows. Something inside her eyes I can't quite describe, other than it makes me feel a touch of embarrassment.

She doesn't say anything. Neither do I.

Still holding one of Adam and Chase's hands each, she guides them to the corner and their can of nails. I can't hear what she says, but the boys both nod. Then she pats their heads and stands up. Without looking at me, she walks out the door.

Frustration bubbles inside me, but I push it down, ignore it, and pick up another board.

Hours later, the boys have long ago finished their nail job, as well as several other things I'd come up with to keep them busy. They're getting bored, and cold.

This isn't going to work. Fuck me.

I can't have them out here all day, every day. Michigan in late winter is just too damn cold, too mind-numbing. They're good kids, but five year olds have limits. I can't afford for them to get sick, either, and being out in the cold for so long...

Shit. But I *need* this job.

They need me to have this job.

There's a Podunk town not far away, Split Haven or something. The idea of finding someone to watch them crosses my mind. I instantly shove the thought aside. I can't have them that far away, nor can I trust anyone. Not when it comes to my kids.

I finish pounding two boards together, and then walk over to the duffel bag I'd brought with us. Pulling out the tablet, I ask, "How about a game of checkers? You've earned it."

The boys readily agree, perking up as I lead them to the hay bales piled along the end wall. "Climb up," I say, patting the top of the lowest stack. Mrs. Potter was dead-set against any type of electronic toys, saying the screens are bad for children's eyes and minds.

Totally overblown. It's only checkers.

The boys settle on the hay and I pull their stocking-caps down over their ears after setting the tablet between them. I'd let them pick out the hats while buying the necessities of being on the run. Adam chose a black

Batman hat and Chase a green Hulk one. Mrs. Potter was also against watching TV, but there are some shows every boy needs in his life. Every kid needs a hero or two.

I carry the ladder to that end of the barn and secure it so I can climb up to mark where I'll need to connect the wall studs.

That's what I'm doing, nailing in a stud, when the door opens again. This time I'm expecting pink.

The boys are excited to see her, but don't display the same enthusiasm as earlier. They're tired. I already knew that, but this confirms it.

She's carrying a basket and uses one foot to shut the door behind her. "Who's ready for lunch?"

My stomach does a bear impression, but I don't reply. The shouts from the boys are the answer she's looking for. Her smile says it all.

"Hope you like chili," she says. "Marcy made a big pot, and it's so delicious."

"We do!" The boys jump down and run to where she's unloading the basket on the boards I'd left stretched between two saw horses.

I climb down and follow.

She sets out three bowls with lids and several sandwiches wrapped in plastic, as well as a thermos that I hope is full of hot coffee, plus small cartons of milk.

"I also have these." She holds up two brown paper bags with Adam and Chase's names written on them, along with smiley faces. "But you have to eat your lunch first."

"That won't be a problem," I say.

She glances my way, a brief, sideways peek out of the corner of her eyes that sends a trickle of electricity zipping through me.

"I have one for you, too," she says, lifting another brown bag out of the basket with Daddy written on it.

It's crazy, but for some reason, my cheeks heat up. "Thanks."

"You're welcome." She helps Adam get situated with his lunch while I help Chase.

Even something as simple as this, her bringing us food, affects me like it shouldn't. Without attempting to in any way, she has my blood heating up and shooting to specific areas.

It's annoying how frustratingly hard she makes me in no time flat. She's the exact opposite of every woman I've ever known. Of all those I left behind. The high-maintenance broads and the sleazy ones with bad habits like Cornelia. They were fuck and dumps and I was too damn busy for anything different. Cupcake doesn't know that, of course, but I do. I know better, too. No woman will ever come between me and my sons. Cornelia had run that road right to the end, and got what she deserved.

I just wish it hadn't cost us so much.

Cupcake circles around the barn while the boys and I eat, looking at the work I've completed. I try to act like I don't care what she thinks, but I do. *Shouldn't. But do.*

"Why are you putting a wall up here?" she asks, leaning against the ladder.

"For the office."

She shakes her head and points to the area behind me. "The office goes down there."

"Makes more sense to be on that end. Near the well that you already keep heated." Meeting her gaze, I ask, "You want water in the office, right? The sink?"

"Yes."

I gesture to the ceiling. "Plumbing water the length of the barn leaves you open to frozen pipes if you have any heating issues."

"The office over here won't work. I don't want the guests to have to walk the length of the barn to check-in."

I walk over and plant a hand against the outside wall. "I'm going to put the entrance right here. You can have a nice sized parking lot outside this wall, too."

She nibbles on her bottom lip for a moment before saying, "These are the changes you talked to Gramps about?"

"Yes, and foregoing the bathroom entirely."

"We can't lose the bathroom. People will need it, especially those not renting rooms at the lodge."

"Then rent some porta-potties." I shrug. "You'll never recoup the cost of putting in a septic system, or the issues that come with it. Winter can be hard on toilets, the lines will freeze up, and that can get costly."

I've got her thinking. Seriously thinking. Both that I know what I'm talking about, and that I have her best interests in mind. I have more than that in mind, and have to shift my stance to lesson the tension in my groin.

She walks towards the front of the barn. "What will be over here then, if not the office?"

"Stables mainly," I say, and then proceed to tell her how I intend to lay out the tack area near the office, and the few other minor changes I'd suggested to Morris.

By the time I'm done, she's nodding, and the smile on her face has me putting both hands in my front pockets in order to stretch my jeans enough to relieve some of the pressure on my swelling cock. Damn it to hell, but she's getting under my skin. And I can't let her.

"A part of me doesn't want to admit it." Her smile increases as she shrugs. "But some of what you've said makes sense."

I have to look away, it's like she's sucking me into some kind of happy hole. That's when I notice the boys. Sleepy-eyed, probably from being warmed up by the big bowls of hot chili. They're leaning against each other for support like two kittens ready for a long nap.

She notices, too. "Looks like your helpers need sleep."

"Looks that way," I admit, having no idea what to do about it. They'll never be able to sleep through the sound of me pounding in nails.

"I can take them inside," she says quietly. "They'll be more comfortable and you'll probably get more work done."

I appreciate her offer, but shake my head. "No, they're a handful, can't be out of sight for even a few minutes, and you have work, too."

"Not really. You're our only guests. The other couple checked out this morning." Her smile is soft and serene as she looks at the boys. "I'll keep a close eye on them, I promise."

Damn. I want to say yes, but—

"Rex. Please." She shakes her head. "Mr. Osborne, I promise –"

"You can call me Rex," I interrupt. I like how it sounded when she said it. Soft. Gentle.

"I promise they'll be fine," she says. "And warm. They can't stay out in this cold all day."

She's right about that. Silently I battle myself as she reaches into the basket on the floor.

"Here, I brought these out for you. They're too big for me."

I take the pair of leather work gloves she's handing me and make my decision. "The boys can be a handful, and grumpy when they're tired."

Once again her smile strikes me hard and fast.

"Grumpy is something I've handled my entire life." She starts loading the basket. "Don't worry. They'll be fine."

I'll worry all right, but I'll also get more work done. The gloves will help, too. The ones I'd bought myself weren't made for winter labor. "Thanks, and thanks for the gloves." I tell the boys to behave one more time, and that I'll be in the barn if they need me, and watch them leave.

With no disruptions outside my own thoughts, which sometimes make me work harder and faster, I make progress. Not as much as I would've done with power-tools, but still a sense of satisfaction fills me as I clean up the wood scraps and get things laid out for tomorrow morning. I'm stiff, overworking muscles that I hadn't in some time, but overall feel great as I grab my thermos and shut off the lights.

It was cold in the barn, but it's freezing out here in the dark. I hurry along the shoveled walkway towards the lodge. A car in the parking lot catches my eye. A big sedan.

Fuck. I hadn't heard anyone pull in, too engrossed in my work. That shouldn't have happened.

I take the steps two at a time, barging into the lodge. The dead silence that greets me sends my intuition into overdrive. There's no one at the desk, in the office, or the front room. I race up the steps and down the hall. Our room is empty. The beds are made.

Fuck, fuck, fuck! I let my guard down for a couple of hours and this happens. Same shit that happened in Chicago.

Two empty beds. The boys gone. There's no note, not like then, stating Mommy took my boys for the night. Nelia had been no fucking mommy to them in this lifetime. They'd only seen her half a dozen times.

Mrs. Potter was out sick that day, so I'd gotten a replacement, a girl I could trust, she'd said. One who also hadn't known Nelia was to never – ever – be near the twins without my supervision.

That was the one time I'd let a stranger watch them. Until now. Whether she's hot as fuck or not, Cupcake is a stranger, too.

I slam the door shut and run down the back stairs, sliding to a stop when I hear laughter. The boys. I shove a door open as if it weighs a ton, and have the sense to catch it from hitting me as it swings backwards when my feet glue themselves to the floor.

They're both there. Jesus. And so's Cupcake. Their laughter comes to an abrupt halt when they see me. All three stop and stare like I'm some crazy lunatic intruder.

That's not far from the truth. "Whose car's parked out front?"

She frowns and wipes her hands on a towel. "A guest's. Why?"

"What's his name? Where's he from? Where's he going?" It rattles out like the automatic rifle fire I remember from my Army days.

Using the towel to wipe Adam's cheek, she says,

"Chester Hobbs from Minneapolis. Older businessman. He always spends the night here when he's on his way to and from his daughter's place in Ontario." Turning a cold glare on me, she adds, "Would you like to know how old he is, or that his wife died five years ago?"

I catch the reprimand, the way she bites her lips together before spinning around.

"Time to check on those cookies again," she says, placing a reassuring hand on each of the boys.

"We made cookies, Daddy," Adam says, looking at me over his shoulder.

"Chocolate chip," Chase adds.

The last bits of tension and fear seeps out of my body. "Smells good," I say, emulating a normal person again.

"Now, we're making cinnamon rolls," Adam tells me while crossing the room beside Tabby.

"For tomorrow morning," Chase adds from her other side. He stops what's on the tip of my tongue about them having all this sugar.

She opens a big stainless-steel oven door and peeks inside. So do the boys.

"Not quite done, yet," she says. "Let's give it a little longer."

The air is heavy, and strained. It's my fucking fault.

When she turns around and our eyes meet, hot guilt slices through me. I shrug my shoulders. "Sorry."

"Me, too," she says.

I'm not sure why she bothers. I was the lunatic, belting her with questions about some old fart who's probably stayed in this place a million times.

"We've already eaten, but saved you a plate." She opens

a door on the side-by-side fridge. "I'll warm it up. You can wash in that sink over there."

I glance to the left, and hoping to ease the tension, ask, "The one with the hand washing only sign?"

"Yes." She grins slightly. "Health code."

"Gotcha." Actually, she's the one that's got me. Right where it counts.

She's wearing an apron, pink of course, and covered in flour. There's even flour on her face, which turns my dick to diamond, picturing how I'd like to wipe it away.

Shit, let's be honest: everything about Tabby Danes turns me on.

I remove my coat and drape it over a chair before moving to the sink to scrub my hands. By the time I'm done, she's set a plate on the end of the long island that's half covered in white dust.

"Chase spilled flour!" Adam says.

"No! Didn't mean to!" Chase snaps back.

"Of course you didn't," Cupcake says, smiling sweetly at Chase, who looks like a red-faced chipmunk. "Luckily, it landed right where we'll need it. Once those cookies are out of the oven, it'll be time to kneed our dough."

"You make cinnamon rolls from scratch?" I ask. Haven't seen that since I used to spend summers with my grandma down in Kentucky.

"Of course," she says. "Is there another way?"

Clearly not for her. Should've guessed that. "Frozen," I say. "But they're never as good."

The boys pipe in then, telling me what they've done all afternoon, including baking the chocolate chip cookies she rescues from the oven. Two of the cookies end up on a plate beside me. I eat them while they're still warm and at the peak of perfection. Just like her.

I set the small plate atop the larger one that I'd practically licked clean after gobbling down the lasagna. "Where should I put these?"

"Just leave them there," she says while giving the boys each a section of white dough. "I'll get them after we get this dough kneaded."

"I could do that for you."

She eyes me skeptically. "Knead dough?"

I pick up the plates and carry them to the sink. "Yes."

"You've kneaded dough before?" She laughs. "I doubt that."

Keeping my eyes locked on hers, I walk back to the island. "These hands are good for more than just pounding nails and sawing boards."

"I'll have to take your word for that," she says.

"Why? Because I'm not covered in flour?" I swipe the tip of her nose with one finger and hold it up for her to see the flour I'd removed. "Like the rest of you?"

"Accidents happen," she says. She turns away and her cheek is sun fire.

Seeing her blush taunts every inch of my cock.

Before I can respond, she flicks her fingers my way, spewing flour dust into my face.

Tease. Her playfulness sends sparks through me, and I plant both of my hands in the flour spread across the granite counter top.

As if reading my mind, she says, "You wouldn't!"

I laugh.

"Don't you dare," she says, wagging a finger. "I already have enough to clean up."

There's a good amount of flour on the counter and floor, true. Rather than flick flour at her as intended, I elbow her instead. "Step aside. Let me show you how a man kneads dough."

"Oh, please," she laughs, elbowing me back. "This is mine, get your own dough."

I point to the empty bowl. "None left."

"Snooze and you lose," she says, laughing again.

"I never lose, Ms. Danes." I step sideways so I'm right behind her, then wrap my arms around both sides of her, just above those lush ass cheeks, burying my hands in her dough. "Never."

She wiggles, trying to shove me away. "*My* dough. You hear? I can't teach the boys how to knead with your big hands in it."

I can barely think with the way her tight butt bumps into the front of my jeans, making my cock so hard I think it'll explode. Pinpointing the ounce of attention not controlled by my hard-on, I say, "Then I'll teach them." It takes a moment to pull up memories from when I was little, but once they hit, I flip the mound of dough over.

"It's like this, boys," I growl. "You have to dig the heels of your palms into this stuff, use them to stretch the dough. Not too hard or fast, or it'll get tough."

Her ponytail tickles my nose as she turns enough to look at me over one shoulder. "Who taught you that?"

"Why? Is it wrong?"

Her eyes bounce between my eyes and my lips, which causes a ripple of chaos to jolt through me. So does the way she swallows, and the way she smells. Sweet and sexy. So fucking sexy.

"Unfortunately, no," she says.

Chase and Adam are barely paying attention. For once, I don't mind.

I fold my hands over the tops of hers, using them to gently force her hands to knead the dough beneath mine, and I step closer, damn near getting high off the way her ass feels pressed up against my dick. Hellfire churns in my balls.

I feel her tremble slightly, and for the first time since they'd been born, I wish my boys were in another room. Then I'd reach up and knead her tits the same way we're working the dough – slow, forceful, thoroughly. If these hands could wander, they'd find hard nipples and warm, wet pussy lips. If the boys weren't here, fuck. It'd be less than ten minutes before I had her bent over with my balls smacking hard on her clit, dick buried in pink, pink, so much pink perfection.

The fantasy owns my mind and it's hard to remember we're hardly by ourselves, even if they are distracted. I force her to stretch the dough across the counter top, giving me a reason to press more firmly against her ass. She melts against me, enjoying it as much as I am.

She grabs the dough and flips it over, then stretches it again, as if giving me permission to dry-fuck her. Electricity shoots through me and I give my hips a quick upwards thrust. She swallows a gasp, plants her hands on the counter, as if pulling my dick deep inside her.

It's fucking nuclear. Taking us so dangerously close to full meltdown.

Until someone clears their throat.

Someone behind us who shouldn't be there.

She freezes. So do I.

A second later, she twists slightly. "Gramps. Hey."

The old man's been behind us for God only knows how long, and must've seen the way I'm practically buttfucking his granddaughter, fully-clothed or not.

Shit!

"We can't have guests in the kitchen, Tabby."

"We won't feed these rolls to the public," she says. "It's off hours and we certainly weren't doing anything that'd get a health inspector after us."

How the hell can she sound so calm? My blood's pumping faster than a marathon runner's. I've been slowly easing away from her, not wanting the old man to see just how tightly I'd had her pressed against the countertop, but if I try to talk, I'll risk my voice cracking like a goddamn kid.

"Doesn't matter who eats them," Morris says sharply. "It matters *whose* hands have been in them."

"Everyone washed their hands," she says, gathering the dough into a ball, defiance creeping into her tone. "Thoroughly."

I drop my hands to my sides as she picks up the dough and drops it into a bowl. "Put yours in here, too," she says to the boys. Once they do, she spins around and hands me a towel.

The old man is still glaring at me. "Health codes," he says.

I nod. It's all I can think to do.

"I'll have this place inspection clean in twenty minutes, Gramps. No worries. Save the white gloves some work." She nods to the boys. "Go wash your hands, please. And don't forget the soap!"

"We won't, Tabby," they say, hurrying towards the sink.

I follow, desperate to get my mind off this fuckery. "I'll make sure."

The sink is large enough for all three of us to wash at the same time, which we do, using gobs of soap.

Morris stands at the door the whole time, watching. As soon as we dry our hands, he pushes the door open. "I'd like a word with you, Mr. Osborne."

"Of course." He wants more than a word. He'd like to knock my head off. Can't say I blame him. There must be some twisted part of me that likes this – the way I keep fucking up my life.

He leads us down the hall and into the front foyer. The boys and I follow. Morris stops near his office door, and his eyes, how they look at the boys and then the front room, tells me what he expects.

"You boys go play a game of checkers," I say. "Practice makes perfect."

They run into the front room while I follow Morris into his interrogation room, closing the door behind me. I've never been in this predicament before, and it's rather hellish, but that's nothing new. My life's been toxic for some time now.

There's a brutal pause. I'm half-expecting him to belt me on the chin, and I'm ready to stand and take it like a man. *Just as long as he doesn't fire my stupid horn dog ass.*

"I'm taking a chance on you, Mr. Osborne, and I want it to work out," Morris says at last, giving me the evil eye. "But I'll kick your ass out that door so far you'll need wings if you don't stay away from my granddaughter."

I bite my tongue as a thousand come-backs race through my mind. He's got a hold over me, one I gave him, and I can't afford to break it. Fuck.

"You understand, you say so."

"Yes, sir!" I say. Just like I'm back in boot camp.

He walks to his desk and opens a drawer. When he reaches in, I half-expect to see him pull out a gun. Instead, I hear the tinkling of metal. Wound tight, my reflexes are good, and I catch the set of keys he throws my way.

"There's a shed out back," he says. "It's full of power-tools. Get that barn done as fast as you can and then get the hell off my property."

"Thank you, sir," I say, reaching behind me for the door knob. "I will."

Hours later, long after I've read the boys a story I downloaded onto the tablet, I'm staring at the ceiling, watching how the howling wind makes the shadows cast by the moonlight flutter. I see teeth and claws and death in those dark shapes. I see my own life burned, cremated, inching up to the sky in a plume of smoke.

There *has* to be a way for me to navigate this and not fuck up again. The Stone Syndicate is out there. Aiden's bodyguard said they'd be, and I believe him. They'll find us. It's only a matter of time.

I gotta make this money. Gotta make this work. If I don't, we're dead.

Whatever Cupcake does to me, she isn't worth risking Adam and Chase. No woman could ever be.

I'll become a fucking eunuch before I put them in harm's way.

My throat burns as I glance towards the other bed, where both boys are sleeping.

Today was my last warning. If I fuck up again, we're dead.

Dead. All three of us.

V: COLD SHOULDER (TABBY)

I wrap the cinnamon rolls in tinfoil and fill one thermos with coffee and the other with hot chocolate, then place everything in the basket, including cups, plates, and silverware. The lodge has an odd vibe to it today, like it's emptier than usual.

It's not just missing people, but something more. Something that's invisible, yet warming and wholesome. It's probably just me. I had a restless night. When I did finally fall asleep, I had some pretty crazy dreams. I hate when that happens. Stress always does it. Puts nightmares in my head that wake me up early, but I can't remember them.

And the odd vibe, well, that's mostly thanks to Gramps. He wasn't happy about Rex and the boys being in the kitchen.

That, I could have dealt with, but the rest of it?

He's not happy about the position he caught me and Rex in.

I should be embarrassed. Humiliated. Ashamed.

But I'm not. I'm human. Gramps has to understand that. I'm twenty-five. Most women my age have a healthy sex life.

There's nothing wrong with it.

There's nothing wrong with *me*. Except, I'm still a virgin, and woefully aware of it.

Mainly because no one has ever lit a fire inside me like Rex did last night. I should be glad Gramps walked in when he did, but I'm not. Until last night, my sex life revolved around imagining what things would feel like.

Now I *know*.

Know and want so much more.

The heat pooling inside me while I carry the basket out of the kitchen makes me grin. Or maybe it's the thought of seeing Rex that has me smiling. I like him, for all his faults. The whys are a mystery, but I like him. There's more than the brute I met his first night here. Sometimes, when he gets that dark scowl on his face, I feel like he's scared, running from something, and my heart drums sympathy.

Breath-stealing cold, the wind, hits me the second I'm outside. Crap. How stupid am I? Heaven only knows because it takes the icy wind to wake me up enough to realize Rex *is* running from something.

The death of his wife. Pain. Memories, perhaps.

How had I forgotten?

Thinking about myself. That's how.

About how I'd like to get fucked hard and often by Rex Osborne. Soundly fucked so I know exactly what it feels like for real, not just what I've read in dirty books or seen on TV. Or made up in my own mind, like I've been doing for eons.

Great. Embarrassment hits me now. Strong but delayed. Hell, I didn't even pretend to stop him last night, right?

When did I become so...idiotic? So desperate? So sex-starved? It's never bothered me before.

Gramps has chased off plenty of men since I turned sixteen, well before anything could ever happen. It's nothing new. This is just more of the same.

But if that's true, then why am I so worried what Rex thinks of me for wanting to give it up so easy?

I'm almost to the barn door, but seriously consider turning around, until the image of Adam and Chase eating the cinnamon rolls they made last night flutters in my mind. Those two boys are adorable, and so well behaved.

Me, and my nosiness, had dropped a couple of hints yesterday while baking cookies with them about mothers, hoping they'd shed some light on what happened to theirs, but they hadn't. In fact, they'd acted like they'd never had one. The only woman they mentioned was Mrs. Potter again, who never let them play video games or watch TV while their dad worked days.

Their mother was still on my mind when Rex stormed into the kitchen demanding to know every little thing about Chester Hobbs. Of course, I dropped the convenient fact that Chester's wife died five years ago, not-so-secretly wishing it'd make him open up.

Fresh guilt stings me.

Rex was probably thinking about her. Missing her. I'd seen the sadness in his eyes. The regret. And I was the only female for miles around. Just like a siren, I'd offered pleasure, a way to forget, but had I brought him the opposite?

I open the barn door and step in. Rex is at the far end, on the ladder, and barely glances my way while pounding in a nail. The boys are happy to see me.

"I brought you some cinnamon rolls and hot chocolate," I tell them while setting the basket down.

"Cocoa? Yippie!" They do their trademark jumping thing. Makes me laugh every time.

Yesterday, I'd watched which boy took the bag with their name on it and discovered a way to tell them apart – at least somewhat. Adam is left-handed, while Chase is right. Chase also has a dimple when he grins in his right cheek. That's the closest I'll get to having an identifying dot.

"You can eat them after we water and feed the horses," I say, touching the tips of their noses, first Adam's and then Chase's.

"Okay, we will!"

Rex never stops pounding in nails, not even after we're done with the horses and back inside. The angst turning over in my belly is almost sickening.

"I brought you some coffee," I shout above the noise he's making.

He nods before pulling a nail out from between his lips and starts pounding again.

"Do you want me to take the boys inside?" I ask when the pounding stops.

"No, they're fine."

"It's colder today and –"

"They're fine," he says again, colder than the air itself.

Okay. I bite my lips. I don't need to be hammered on

the head to know I'm not wanted, so I tell the boys goodbye and head back to the lodge.

* * *

AFTER CHECKING out Chester Hobbs and cleaning his room, I dust the front room and foyer and wash a few windows, then head to the basement to transfer the sheets from the washer to the dryer.

Using the last dryer sheet, I toss the empty box into the trash and enter the storage room to get some more. I grab a new box from the shelf, but it slips out of my hand. Bending down to pick it up, I see the writing on a cardboard box on the bottom shelf.

Julia.

My mother.

I've seen the box a million times. Dug through it at least a dozen occasions, flipping through her old school albums. That's all that's really there, all that's left, along with some pictures she'd drawn when she was young and a few miscellaneous report cards. Gramps saved them all. Just like he'd saved mine.

Once upon a time, mom was his little girl. And I think he sees me as the daughter he wished he'd had.

I pick up the dryer sheets and leave the room, wondering again about Adam and Chase, and if they should be in school. Too curious not to know, I head upstairs, grab my coat, and walk to my cabin.

It's small, but cozy. Familiar. Compact, but home.

There's a tiny kitchen, living room, and two bedrooms, each with their own bathrooms from when it had been remodeled several years ago. There's also a fair-sized storage room where I keep my personal stuff, mementos, old books I like to re-read when I'm in the right mood. Whenever it needs to be rented out, all I have to do is lock my storage room and take enough clothes with me to the main lodge to bunk with Marcy until the guests leave.

I grab a water from the fridge and sit down at the table, opening my laptop. It takes a while for it to start up, being as old as it is, a hand me down Gramps never used for business. Then I Google the age requirements for Michigan schools.

Six to sixteen.

So, the boys are technically too young. They're only five. That much I'd gotten out of them yesterday. Their age.

I turn the computer off, wait for it to fully power down before closing the lid. It hits me then that I should have Googled Rex Osborne, too. *Damn.*

I consider it, but the queasy feeling in my stomach tells me not to. I'm scared I'll find more questions than answers. Worse, I'm afraid I'll just feed this obsession, this stupid crush, this thing that should *not* be happening.

Grabbing my coat, I leave the cabin and head back to the main lodge to help Marcy prep lunch. It goes smoothly.

I pack an extra basket and carry it out to the barn. Rex isn't any friendlier than he was this morning, but he does agree to let the boys return to the lodge with me. I tell him they'll be safe and warm. He grunts, the only reply I get, rude and cryptic.

I'm steaming, but it's not long before the sweet boys take the edge off. Their innocent chatter through a couple board games I have just enough time to teach them makes me forget their ass of a dad for a few blissful hours.

It's the start of a weird routine that continues for several more days. The boys spend the morning in the barn with Rex and the afternoon in the lodge with me, and the two of us, Rex and me, don't say more than three or four words to one another.

I hate his icy silence. Loathe it because I'd like to get in his face, ask him what kind of game he's playing. But I know it'd make me look like the reckless, desperate girl who's more strung up on him than she has any right to be. And Rex Osborne *won't* be seeing me like that.

Also, there are times I sense he'd like to say more, but for whatever reason, doesn't. *Torture.*

I've lived with moody men who hold their emotions like cheap whiskey since I was four years old. I've figured out Rex isn't grumpy. Whatever's bothering him, goes deeper and it doesn't fit him. This isn't the way he's meant to be. I don't know why I'm so sure, but I am. It's like we're in the middle of a poker game and he doesn't want me to see his hand. He's not ready to play them, either. Not even one card at a time. Not yet.

It's driving me nuts. *Fucking nuts*

My only saving grace is the steady flow of new guests. Not many, and none book rooms for long, but at least the constant checking in and out gives me something to do every morning while waiting to collect Adam and Chase for lunch.

Now, I can't believe I ever had a hard time telling them apart. Adam is more curious and asks far more questions than his brother. Chase is more like Rex, quiet and pondering, often figuring out the answers to Adam's questions about the same time Adam asks them. It's odd, adorable, and fascinating all at once.

This afternoon we learn a popular cartoon hero flick will be on TV tonight. The boys beg me to ask Rex if they can watch it, so I do. Surprisingly, he agrees.

The boys help me make popcorn, and here we are, watching a movie about super heroes. I'm a little lost trying to follow all the characters and the powers they have, but the boys are enjoying every second. Rex appears to be, too, when he slinks in later and sits at the far end of the sofa. So does Gramps, who gobbles more popcorn than the rest of us combined.

Then I notice headlights shining through the window, and leave the room to man the front desk, ready to check in our new arrival.

There are no reservations, so I collect his information and give him our standard spiel about amenities.

He states he'll only need a place to sleep.

I assign him a room for the night, and then swipe his credit card. While I'm waiting for the approval to go through, I ask if he's been in Split Harbor before.

"Nope, first time. Heading up to Canada to go ice fishing with my brother. Haven't seen him for five years, since he came down to Chicago."

"Well, have fun, and stay warm," I say, handing him back his card. "You're all set."

With a friendly wave, he heads for the wide staircase. "Thanks!"

I'm about to staple the credit card slip to the printout of the room assignment when the sheet of paper flies out of my hand. Flipping around, I try to re-take it from Rex, who's already scanning the printout. He holds it conveniently out of reach.

"Hey! Private information," I say, trying again to snatch the paper back, but he's too tall and his hold is too firm.

"I heard him say Chicago," Rex snaps.

"Because that's where he's from?" He's reading the slip, so it's not like I'm telling him anything he doesn't already know. I point to the top of the paper. "Sam Walton from Chicago, Illinois."

He flips the paper over, finding only a blank page of course. "Where's he going?"

"What's it matter?"

His eyes turn into narrow slits. "Where's he going?"

I finally jerk the paper away, staple the credit card slip, and file it. "Canada, to go fishing with his brother. Not that it's any business of yours."

"How long is he staying?" He's relentless. "Cupcake, how long?"

"Jesus, one night!" Flustered, I tap my cheeks and say, "What's wrong with you, Rex? Why do you interrogate me about every single male guest who checks in?"

"Just curious."

"Oh, no. You're a lot more than curious. You're like an FBI agent without a badge to flash."

He grabs my arm when I try to walk around him. "FBI, huh? Has the FBI been here?"

"No, the FBI hasn't been here! I said it because you're acting like they do on TV." Pulling my arm out of his hold, I add, "Like a total asshole."

He scowls, but then glances towards the staircase.

Wow. He hasn't actually let this go.

An eerie feeling crawls up my spine, slowly, like a spider on a mission. A creepy-ass scary spider. I can't stop myself from asking, "You aren't wanted by the FBI...are you?"

I swear my heart stops during the silence that follows.

"No," he finally says.

"You're sure?"

"Would I be here, with my sons, working on your barn if I was wanted by the goddamn FBI?"

That's his way, answering my questions with his own. Tired of playing his game, I say, "You'd better be telling the truth, Rex. Because if you aren't, I'll –"

"You'll what?" Rage flashes in his eyes. "Tell me, Cupcake. What'll you do?"

Hell if I know. Pissed, I skirt around him while hissing, "Rue the day you were born for putting my family, my business in danger."

"I –"

I stop, waiting to hear more.

"Forget it," he snarls numbly, walking past me.

He heads to the front door and I march into the front room.

"Anyone need more popcorn?"

Both boys and Gramps say yes, so I grab the bowl and leave the room. Rex is still outside, I can see his outline through the window.

Fine. I'll forget about it all right. And him. Jerk.

I stomp down the hall. *Such. An. Asshole.*

Why can't he just be honest? Tell me his wife died and he's going through a rough time right now. That's all he'd have to say, and I'd believe him.

But no. Instead, he jumps back and forth in some

stupid Jekyll and Hyde routine that's twisting my last nerve.

I make the popcorn and deliver it to the front room. Rex is back, sitting on the sofa with the boys, acting like nothing happened. I leave again. I can't do this and I've officially had my fill.

I need space. Finding myself back in the kitchen, I dig out the ingredients to make a batch of blueberry muffins, a double batch so Sam Walton can take some with on his ice fishing trip.

Screw you, Rex Osborne.

Flipping off the door while I wait for the oven makes me feel a smidge better, but I'm still fuming.

After the muffins are done, I gather the bowls and glasses from the front room, which is empty except for Gramps. The movie's over. I tell him I'll lock up after wrapping the muffins and putting the extras on a plate for the front desk in case the guests checking out want to take some.

"You doing all right, Tabby-kitten?" Gramps asks as we walk down the hallway together.

"I'm fine." I'm nowhere close and I think he knows it.

"Is it the boys? Taking care of those kids getting to be too much?"

"No way. Adam and Chase are wonderful, Gramps. Seriously."

I'm glad I don't have to lie. They're not the problem.

He casts me a thoughtful glance before saying, "Well, they won't be here much longer."

"I know." God, do I ever. I hold up the dirty dishes in my hands. "Gotta get these in the dishwasher." After kissing his cheek, I hold the kitchen door open, giving him one last glance. "Night."

Gramps is a better man than Rex. Grumpy, short-fused, but his heart is in the right place. With Mr. Osborne, I don't know what the hell I'm dealing with besides a constant guessing game.

His words ring in my memory while I finish up. *They won't be here much longer.*

Sigh. My mind goes down several melancholy paths concerning both Rex and his sons while I'm wiping the counters. I'll never hear their sweet laughter, or catch Rex's fierce blue eyes stripping me bare, or wonder for the thousandth time what makes him tick like the timebomb he is. Soon, they'll be memories. By the time I've locked the front door, I can't take any more.

None.

I'm done.

Rather than grab my coat and head for my cabin, I march up the back steps. Quietly, because I don't want to wake the boys, I knock on Rex's door.

He pulls it open and scowls. Exactly what I'm expecting.

"Why can't you just tell me the truth?" I ask.

He shakes his head, but his eyes never leave mine. Then he grabs my arm and pulls me inside.

VI: NO ESCAPE (REX)

Nothing good will come of this, but I can't take the sorrow in her eyes any longer. I can't take the shit-ton of it filling me, either, strapped around my neck like an albatross made of solid granite.

Cupcake's the reason I feel this way. At least part of it. She's done me one hell of a favor, watching the boys every afternoon, asking for nothing in return. I'd offered to pay her, but she'd refused to even consider that.

She just wanted a smile, a few kind words, a goddamned thank you or two. And I've been too screwed up to give her more than a disinterested grunt and a weight from hell she doesn't need.

Fuck. It isn't fair and I know it. I'm not oblivious.

The least I can give her is the truth – a small portion of it.

Still holding onto her arm, I close the door, and then guide her to the corner of the room furthest away from the bed the boys are sleeping in. I can't wake them up with this.

"Look, Tabby, I can't tell you everything, but what I'm about to say, is the truth."

My heart literally swells at how her face softens.

"You don't have to. I never asked for everything," she whispers.

But I want to get it out, have her understand, but there's this ugly fear in my guts she'll hate me once she knows. "You can't tell anyone a word I say."

"I won't," she says. "Promise."

I have no idea where to start, what to say specifically.

"Had she been ill long?"

I shake my head, wondering if I'd already spoken. Convinced I hadn't, I ask, "Who?"

"Your wife."

"I've never been married."

She glances towards the bed. "Grandpa said their mother died recently."

A wave of regret washes over me.

"He said you told him that."

"I did," I admit. I'd said a lot of things to get the job, most of them true, stopping at the part where I'm running for my life after an accidental murder.

"Why?" There's skepticism in her eyes again. "So he'd give you the job?"

"Bingo." I had to give Morris a normal reason why the boys and I are here. Why I needed the job so badly. He's an intuitive old goat, would've seen through any obvious lies.

"So she's not dead?"

"She's dead all right," I say.

Tabby blinks and her eyes get big. "But that's not

what's bothering you. It's not the chip on your shoulder," she says softly.

No. Fuck no. It's far more than 'a chip.' More like a thousand-pound boulder. "Some things happened a few weeks ago. Bad shit, and now I've got bad people looking for me."

The splattering of fear racing across her face has me taking hold of her hand.

"They don't know where we are. I have to believe they won't find us here." Not for a while, anyway. I'm still hoping they're following my pinged phone all the way to Florida. They'll figure it out sooner or later, and by then, I can only hope any trail I may have left is ice cold.

"Who are *they*?"

"Demons. People deep in the criminal world." I can't tell her about the deaths, but can let her know what lead up to it at the beginning. "They needed money laundered. I got blackmailed into doing it."

Her eyes pop wide again. "So, are you wanted by the FBI?"

I have no idea, but for her sake, I shake my head. "They aren't the type to go to the FBI, and no one will report the money laundering. I just refused to keep doing it. That's why I've got problems." That's what I should have done in the very beginning. Instead, fearing Nelia would find a way to take away the boys, I agreed to run a few thousand dollars worth of drug money through my construction company. Then a few thousand turned five figures, then six. I know now, as I should have then, it would never fucking stop. You give these men an inch, they'll be up your ass for miles.

"And now they're after you," she finishes.

"Yeah."

"Jesus. Can't you just...I don't know, go to the authorities?"

I shake my head. "If only it was that easy. I broke the law, Cupcake. Also not sure the police can do shit to protect us from these people. Their Syndicate has tendrils everywhere. I can't start over with the boys in witness protection, growing up with their old lives and me scorched to the ground."

Her eyes are so sweet, so innocent, nowhere cut out for contemplating something like this. Guilt blackens my heart for laying this on her, but there's also a vicious relief in giving up the truth.

She takes hold of my other hand. "There are people who can help you, Rex. I can help. You just have to let me."

I pull her towards me, close enough for me to place a tiny kiss on her forehead. "No. Nothing you can do, Cupcake. Nothing anyone can do. I'm not putting you in danger."

"Yes –"

I shake my head. "We'll be leaving soon." Nodding towards the bed, I continue, "The boys and me, we can't stay here forever once the job's done, much as I'd like it. Soon as the money comes in from remodeling the barn, we're moving on." I didn't expect this part to be the hardest confession. My heart constricts so tightly my chest burns.

Fuck.

I know this is exactly how it has to be, and if I don't get her out of this room soon, I won't want her to leave.

I lead her back to the door. "Thanks, Cupcake, you're

an amazing, compassionate, beautiful woman. I hope you never change."

I open the door then, gently nudging her over the threshold because it'd be far too easy to ask her to stay. She leaves without a fight, or maybe she just doesn't know what the hell to say. I can't blame her.

As soon as I push the door closed, I lock it, as if that'll reconstruct the barrier between us I just tore down. Why did I have to meet someone like her now? When my life's as fucked as it can possibly be?

I back away from the door, watching to make sure it doesn't magically open. When the backs of my legs bump the foot of the bed, I sit.

It's not long before I lose track of how much time passes since she left. I crawl to the head of the bed and click off the lamp. Sleep doesn't come quick or easy.

I can't stop thinking of Cupcake. Of how sad and forlorn she looked when I closed that door, wishes etched all over her face for us, for the kids, for me.

But this is how it has to be. How *I* have to be.

Distant. Detached from everyone and everything. No more midnight confessions where I might slip, say too damn much, or put too many promises in her sweet young heart.

I close my eyes, begging for sleep to come.

* * *

She's stretched out in a big tub, naked, one leg hanging over the edge.

I'm pissed.

Yell at her.

She doesn't open an eye.

Blood boils inside me as I storm into the room, calling her the fucking bitch she is.

She still doesn't move.

That's when I notice what's next to her.

Needles. Tubing. Drug shit.

"Nelia!" I shout one more time, roaring so loud my throat shifts on bone.

She still doesn't move.

I lean down to touch her.

Cold. So fucking cold.

Then, suddenly, she grabs my arm.

I jolt backwards. The air stalls in my lungs.

It's not Nelia. It's Tabby! Her sweet eyes empty, scared, lifeless.

"Cupcake!" I scream, reaching to grab her as she slips beneath the water, too deep for me to reach.

"Cupcake!"

* * *

I CAN'T BREATHE. It hurts. Agony like I've never known. I rip my eyes open, cough like mad, trying to catch my breath. It was a dream. A goddamn dream.

I press a hand to my forehead. Another nightmare. Trying to split my soul in two, or at least my head.

Nelia's dead. A fucking overdose, but Cupcake is fine.

She's *fine.*

Too afraid to close my eyes, I get off the bed. Go to the bathroom. Fill a glass with water. Drink it. Then do it again.

She's fine, you fool.

"Fine!" It comes out a harsh whisper. I barely recognize my own reflection.

For now, I'll trust she's fine without acting like a madman. And fine is how I need her to stay.

* * *

I WORK my ass off the next two days, needing to get this project done as fast as possible. The routine is the same: the boys stay with me, playing in the barn, until Tabby comes and gets them at noon. I try hard to think of her as Tabby, not Cupcake. Not the woman Nelia's dead face transformed into during that fucked up dream. And I try harder to avoid her day and night. I'm giving her the cold shoulder again and it makes me feel like shit, only a little less than pouring my heart out again, putting her in danger.

It has to be almost noon, so I climb off the ladder, tell the boys to zip up their coats and get their hats on.

"Why?" Adam asks while zipping.

Chase tugs on his Hulk hat. "Where're we going, daddy?"

"Lodge," I growl.

They race for the door, glad to have the morning over no doubt. We're inching toward spring, but more than a couple hours out here still lets Jack Frost creep into your bones.

Morris is behind the check-in desk. Good. I don't want to run into Tabby looking for him.

"I need a few things." I set the list I've written on the desk. "Mostly nails and pole-barn screws."

The old man frowns. "Can't go to town today. Several

guests are due here anytime," Morris says. "But you can go get them. I'll call Walt at the hardware store and tell him you're coming. He'll put it on my charge account."

I hadn't left the lodge since arriving over a week ago.

"The hardware store is right on main street. You can't miss it." Morris picks up the phone and nods toward the boys. "They can stay with Tabby. She's in the kitchen."

"No, she's right here."

Shit. Avoiding her hasn't changed much inside me. The sound of her voice still turns me on. Exactly why I grab the list off the desk and walk out the door.

Split Harbor's only ten miles up the road, a somewhat rough county road considering the weather keeps trying to fool us into thinking spring might be near. The last two days were in the forties, today even warmer. The ice and snow packed solid on the road for the past few months is melting fast, leaving puddles the size of craters.

By the time I pull onto the main highway and the tires start rolling along the smooth, dry pavement, my teeth feel like they're ready to rattle out of my head.

Trucks as old as this one don't have the same suspension as newer ones. Or the creature comforts.

I glance down to check my speed and notice the fuel gauge. "Asshole. Gas hog," I say aloud. Then, feeling a bit guilty putting the old truck down, I say, "Actually, you probably get better mileage than my new truck, your tank is just smaller."

Damn thing saved our life. Call me sentimental, superstitious, but I can't jinx that.

The hardware store is easy enough to find, and Walt introduces himself as soon as I walk in the door. I have a bag full of supplies in no time. I'm done in less time that it would have taken to walk to the hardware section of those big-box stores back in Chicagoland.

Seeing a gas station a block up the road, I head there next, pulling up beside the pump. After filling the tank, I head inside. No longer having a debit card, paying at the pump isn't an option. There are a couple people ahead of me, so I scan the candy bars and pick out a couple for the boys I know they'll like. One more for me.

Still standing in line, waiting for the cashier to finish showing the customer ahead of me a video of her granddaughter on her cellphone, a rumble makes the windows rattle. The hair on my arms rise as motorcycles, a good dozen of them, swarm into the gas station's lot.

Aiden always claimed to be tight with a large motorcycle gang. Said he'd been a prospect in his younger days and still wore the ink. I never cared one way or the other.

Until now.

Now, I wish I'd paid more attention to Aiden's tattoos so I could match them up against those on the men outside. Not that I can see many tattoos. These guys are all wearing black leather jackets, cuts as dark as night.

Sweat pops out on my temples as a burly guy climbs off his bike and walks around my truck, eyeing it closely. I think of the gun buried deep in the glove box, how fast I could fish it out if needed.

The man turns, and sees me through the glass. The pulse in my neck pounds spikes in my veins as he walks toward the door. Other bikers are looking at the truck, too.

Fuck.

I glance around, looking for an escape route, which there isn't.

"Oh, look," the woman in front of me says. "It's Sheriff Cahill! Now, we know it's almost spring if he's out riding."

The door opens and the biker walks in. The logos on his cut say SPLIT HARBOR PD.

I'm not very relieved and try to hide how my fingers tremble, sticking them in my coat pockets. That's when I realize I'm still holding candy bars in one of them. I drop that hand to my side, squeezing the bars so hard I feel the fucking chocolate melt.

"Hey, Sheriff," the check out gal says. "Got the day off?"

"Sure do," the biker answers. "Feels good, let me tell you. Been busting my balls since my old man turned the department over for retirement. And knowing we might not have another day like this in weeks, the boys and I are taking the bikes for a ride."

"Smart move. How's old Dixon holding up, anyway? Anything I can get for you? Just made fresh coffee in the deli."

"Nah, I'm fine, and so's dad. He's busy writing a book on that Caspian thing and the Drayton assholes, now that they're out of town. Even Ryan's taking a break from employing half the town to contribute. Says it's good for town history and all. Gonna be a bestseller," he answers, looking at me. "Enough said, though. I really just want to talk to this guy."

My heart stops. So do my lungs. With air locked in them like hot coal.

I'm fucking panicking. I never expected the Stone Syndicate to involve the law. Not on this level. A northern Michigan county sheriff? *How?*

My thoughts go to Adam and Chase at the lodge. I tell

myself they're at the safest place they can be. With Cupcake.

"That your truck, stranger?" the sheriff asks.

My lungs are searing, melting. I push out air before I can calmly say, "Yes, sir. Is there something wrong?" It dawns on me then that I've never checked the tabs. Just assumed my cousin bought them every year.

"That's a heavy-ass Chevy. Haven't seen a beast like that in years."

"Yes, sir, it is."

"Chevy only made a few, I think. Back in the seventies if I'm not mistaken. Added a few extra springs to their half-tons so they could haul more."

"That's correct," I say. "My grandpa bought it new for the same reason you said."

My head is about to explode. It's miraculous I'm smiling.

The man nods. "So, you wouldn't be interested in selling, would you?"

"No, sir. It'll stay in the family, I'm afraid."

"Can't argue with that." He turns to look out the window again. "That's a damn good-looking truck. Keep it that way."

"I do my best," I tell him, my heart finally thumping a notch slower.

He nods, gives a single finger wave to the cashier and walks back out the door.

My legs turn into rubber and I squish the melting candy bars more by slapping them on the counter to stay upright.

"Anything else I can get you?" the cashier asks. "Fresh coffee in the deli, don't forget."

"No, thanks." Not unless she's got a tranquilizer.

I drive all the way back to the lodge with the driver's window down, trying to cool my body from the amount of hot sweat coating every inch of my skin. Still hot, and sweating bullets, after arriving, I pull the ladder out of the barn and climb up on the side awning to examine a few lose shingles I'd noticed. There might not be another day this weather will let me fix them.

The fresh air helps my body and kicks my brain back to functional. "Goddamn it," I mumble. I'd never been so scared in my life as I'd been back at that gas station. Nor as jumpy. A part of me wants to run into the house to check on the boys, but there are no new cars in the lot, and deep down, I know they're safe with Tabby.

I also know I can't see her. Not right now. Not after I thought my worst nightmares were coming true.

If we're together, I'll grab on and hug her tight, just to make sure she's alive and well.

I consider that for a moment, and then make a mental note to write an informal will, stating if anything happens to me, the boys go to Tabby Danes until she can call my cousin.

It's a scenario I never want to think about, but shit, after what just happened...

No choice. I'll include Justin's name on it, he'll recognize my signature, know it's from me. He's a damn good lawyer, but I don't dare contact him. Not yet.

Lifting my head, I stare at the lodge for some time, and then let out the sigh that's grown too heavy to hold in.

There are so many if onlys running through my mind, I'm making myself dizzy. Most have to do with Nelia, her drug addiction, which is how she hooked up with Aiden and then got the idea to start blackmailing me.

I should have left the city then. Got as far away as possible. But I hadn't.

Now, I'm here. Scared shitless of a local lawman on a bike who just wanted to haggle over my ancient truck.

Fuck.

It's only a matter of time before everything catches up with me. The Danes are good people. Cupcake and her grandfather, and their cook, Marcy. They've made the boys feel at home, more at home than they've ever known. Plus they've given me this, a chance to make enough money for us to move on. Which is what I need to do so I don't have to consider Plan B and its worst case scenarios.

Tabby and Morris don't deserve to have monsters on their doorsteps. That's what's going to happen. Sooner or later, that *will* happen, the longer I stay.

I grab the hammer and start pounding, vowing to leave as soon as possible.

VII: JUST LIKE HER (TABBY)

"No, Gramps," I say, trying to keep the frustration out of my voice. Dealing with quarterly taxes does that. So does dealing with my grandfather. Every four months we go over the exact same things. "Read Richard's list again. These forms are exactly what he needs, just like how I filled them out."

"I'll call him."

I hold in a sigh. "There's no reason to call. He's been your accountant for years, and I've been sending him the *exact same* reports. For years."

"Don't get snippy with me."

I take a deep breath. "I'm not getting snippy, Gramps. Just pointing out the obvious."

His eyes squint as his bushy brows knit together. "Close the door. That damn TV's too loud."

I ball my hands into fists as I step away from the desk. His scowl hasn't scared me for years. The TV isn't too loud, either. He probably can't even hear it, but knows it's on because he saw me settle the boys in the front room before I came into his office, humoring his demands. I close the door, but not all the way.

"I warned you about spending too much time looking after those boys, Tabby."

I bite my lip for a moment, just to keep from snapping. "Yes, you did, but what did you expect when you hired Rex? That the boys would watch themselves? They're only five, way too young to stay out in the cold barn all day."

"That man's over thirty years old, no child himself. He can hire someone anytime to watch them. You're not his nanny...are you?"

I don't answer. I don't know what I am to these kids or their hot tempered daddy.

Gramps doesn't know Rex offered to pay me, or that I refused. That would piss him off. He's all about squeezing pennies. "Then I guess you'd have to pay him more."

The way his nostrils flare tells me my barb found its mark. So be it. Gramps still thinks paying someone over twelve dollars an hour is ridiculous. Rex had to hawk his experience up and down for more.

He waggles a somewhat twisted finger at me. "You're acting just like your mother."

I'm already too irritated to be offended. I was too little to remember, but sometimes I wonder if my mother left because he treated her the exact way he treats me. I have half a mind to ask, but stop myself. More arguing won't solve anything.

"Men like that are bad news." Gramps doesn't know when to stop.

Fury flares inside me. "Men like *what?*" I plant both hands on his desk and look him straight in the eye. "Men who get up at the crack of dawn and work, sweating through their clothes until sunset? Men who say, 'yes, sir, and right away, sir,' whenever you spout off about the changes you want at the last second? Because that's Rex."

He shifts the papers around in front of him. "You *know* what I mean."

I slap a hand on top of the papers. "Sure do, and you're wrong, Gramps."

Huffing out a breath, he leans back in his chair. Just as he opens his mouth, we both hear the front door open.

I spin around and walk toward the noise. It's Rex coming in. I gesture towards the front room and he nods. That's about the extent of our interactions lately. Peachy.

I'd hoped after the other night, when he'd opened up a small bit, that he'd gradually discover he can trust me, that I want to help, and he can tell me more anytime.

That hasn't happened. Nothing ever does.

"You know nothing about him, Tabby."

I close the door, turning back to face Gramps. "I know he's a good father and a hell of a hard worker." And that bad people are after him. That's hung heavy on my shoulders. My mind has spun circles trying to figure out how to help him.

"I'm sure that can be said about a lot of men."

"But you'll never say it, will you?" I challenge. "You'll never say anything positive about anyone."

"Nonsense." He stacks the papers in front of him into a pile. "I tell people what a great job you do all the time. How much I count on you."

There. Finally. The reason I've never had more than one date with the same man.

Because Gramps counts on me. I give him a look that says this won't work forever, but he's not looking my way.

He's scrolling through the list of numbers on the sheet of paper beside the phone, looking for Richard's info no doubt.

I push the burning air out of my lungs and leave the room, resisting the urge to slam the door behind me off its hinges. But I'm too reasonable a woman. Just like arguing, slamming the door won't do any good.

The fury inside me dissipates as I realize the TV's still going. I walk around the desk and across the foyer. The boys are slumped on the couch, watching cartoons. I look around the room before asking, "Where's your father?"

"Taking a shower," Adam says.

"Dad said we could finish watching our show," Chase adds.

That's unusual, but I choose to take it as a good sign. Maybe Rex realizes he can trust me, without second guesses.

I have no idea what I can do to help with whoever's looking for him, but I'll do whatever it takes. To say I was relieved to learn he'd never been married is an understatement. I was overjoyed. I know people don't have to be married to have children together, or to love each other, but my instincts tell me he was never in love with Adam and Chase's mother. And he's certainly not mourning her.

The click of the TV turning off brings my thoughts back around. Both the boys climb off the couch, and Adam sets the remote on the coffee table.

"What do you have?" I ask.

They both hold out their hands.

Candy bars? "Where'd you get those?"

"Dad gave them to us," Chase says happily, pulling at the wrapper.

From their scrunched condition, I wonder how old they are.

"He bought them in town today." Adam reads my mind.

I take one from his hand, turning it over. It's misshapen. Experience tells me the chocolate has melted and re-hardened. Knowing how stuck to the wrappers they are on the inside, I say, "Hmmm, how about I get you some new ones?"

"But, Tabby, why?"

"Because these candies are no good here. They're *perfect* for chopping up and putting on top of the cupcakes we made earlier," I say, hoping to surprise them.

They both frown.

Damn it.

"Trust me. You'll like them that way. Let me show you something better and stow these away."

I stop at the desk and take several coins from the spare change can I keep there for when the vending machines don't work like they're supposed to. We stop in the kitchen first, where I put their candy bars in the freezer. Across the hall from the kitchen, we push open the door to the exercise room. There's a treadmill and a bicycle, along with an old video game machine. Our makeshift gym doubles as the world's shoddiest arcade.

Gramps bought all three at an auction a few years ago. I'd envisioned something more when I'd suggested we spruce up the amenities, but at that point, he'd agreed the kitchen remodel was more important. There, Gramps had given Marcy free rein, and it turned out beautifully.

Someday, we'll finally fix up this area, as well as the hot tub and sauna in the adjoining room. At one point, I'd imagined an indoor pool, but knew Gramps would never fork out that kind of money. Not for the remodel or the upkeep, either.

I give the boys the money and show them how to deposit coins and make their selections.

"We can play?" Adam asks.

"Sure can."

The game has two seats and controllers. Once they're seated, I show them where to put in the money and how to work the controls. It's some kind of space alien destroyer game I've never really played, so other than reading the directions, I can't give them any pointers. The noises they make rival the space war on the screen, though, which tells me I've done something right.

While they're playing, I walk over to straighten the towels on the shelf next to the door leading into the hot tub and sauna room. The door has a small window. Movement catches my eye.

My heart skips a beat as Rex walks out of the corner sauna room. It's small, eight-person max. No one would want to sit that close together in a sauna. He looks huge and clean and magnificent coming out.

He crosses the room, to the shower area, giving me a quick flash of the wicked ink striped down his back muscles. I pinch my lips together as he turns the water on and reaches up to run his hands through his hair. I've seen plenty of men in swimming trunks, but his form is masculine perfection. Sculpted from head to toe. So wonderfully hard and rough I can't pull my eyes off him.

Water cascades down his back, igniting a coil of heat

in my core. I shift my inner thighs together, trying to stifle the incessant burn.

He shuts the water off, wiping his face with a hand, brushing his hair back into shape. Then he walks toward the hot tub.

The commotion inside me steals my breath. Hot, wild thoughts race through my mind, visions of how amazing touching him would be.

Touching, kissing, and so many other things.

He steps onto the first step leading down to the hot tub. Then the next. Hard muscle ripples, bends, taunts me with the things his body can do to mine, almost effortlessly.

My toes curl inside my shoes as I watch. Shame and desire fight to paint my cheeks red. His trunks are dark blue and hang low on his hips. *So low.*

Something tells me to look up. It takes effort, but I manage, taking my time and enjoying the view of his stomach, chest, neck, chin, nose.

My breath stalls as our gazes meet. There's a simmer in his eyes. As my eyes dart about, trying to escape, I catch the smirk on his face.

I should look away. But can't. Won't. Don't want to. Instead, I look directly into his eyes, biting my bottom lip as my own grin forms.

He lifts a brow.

So do I. Well, I can't lift just one. Never been able to.

My heart thuds as his grin increases, and I have to tighten my inner thigh muscles again at the hellfire burning hotter and hotter inside me. My ovaries could melt me through and through.

He hooks his thumbs inside the waist of his trunks.

"Jesus," I whisper. He can't be doing what I think he is. He can't...

I squeeze my thighs again, my pussy beyond soaked, and wrap my hand around the doorknob for support. If he flashes me, how could I not go in?

"Tabby? What are you looking at?"

"Can we see?"

I almost fly out of my skin.

"No," I say slowly, tearing my eyes off Rex. Turning, I glance down at the boys. "It's nothing. Nothing at all."

Make that a whole *lot* of nothing. I can't stop myself from taking a final peek through the window.

He's sat down in the water, has his arms stretched out along the edge of the tub. He's laughing. It doesn't steal anything from the massive bulge in his trunks.

I stick my tongue out at him and turn again. "Come on," I say to the twins, "let's go chop up those candy bars." I'm about as amazed I have the wherewithal to remember the candy bars as I am that I can still walk.

This man may be the death of me. A slow, painful death from sex starvation.

* * *

It doesn't take long to chop up the frozen candy bars and sprinkle the pieces on top of the chocolate frosted cupcakes. It's a new recipe and it's turned out really well. Figuring Rex has returned to his room by now, I lead the boys out into the hallway, fully prepared to walk them upstairs.

To my surprise, Rex is in the lobby, talking with Gramps.

Crap.

My concerns ease when I see he's smiling.

Smiling?

That's unusual.

So is Gramps' smile.

Jesus. They're laughing.

What. The. Hell?

I nearly knock the boys over in my rush to get to the foyer. Nothing good can come from Gramps and Rex smiling and laughing together like two old soldiers.

"Rex is eating in the dining room tonight," Gramps says.

I'm so shocked nothing comes out of my mouth when I open it. I cough and try again. "Um, why?" I ask, looking at Rex.

He shrugs. "Why not?"

"Rex met Sheriff Cahill today, the new boy," Gramps says. Boy is quite a stretch, and Cahill's been on our little town force for over a decade, but anyone under fifty seems like a child to the old man.

My heart stops. I remember Rex mentioned money laundering. Had the sheriff heard about that? "You did?"

"Yeah." He shakes his head, but his smile doesn't fade. "Thought it was a biker gang, silly as it sounds. Turns out it was your sheriff and his guys taking their bikes for a ride."

"I told him they do that at least once every winter. Like clockwork!" Gramps snaps his fingers. "That's how we're made up here. Hardy. Used to be more."

"Or crazy," I say.

Gramps shakes his head, but Rex lets out a deep chuckle. The sound is amazing. I haven't heard him laugh, and can't help but think how well it fits him. It makes him more handsome somehow – which should be impossible – and of course I still can't stop staring. Even when he lifts a brow, like he did through the window, sending heat pooling inside me all over again.

"Marcy made meatloaf for tonight," Gramps says. "But you can also order more off the menu."

Rex winks while saying, "Meatloaf sounds great."

Gramps lays a hand on my shoulder. "Seat them in the dining room, Tabby." With a nod towards Rex, Gramps starts down the hallway towards the kitchen.

"This way," I say, gesturing towards it. Our dining area is small, more of a cafeteria with big windows overlooking the land. Only eight tables, but they're rarely all full at the same time, so it works just fine.

"Thanks. Now how 'bout you join us?"

I'm going to have a heart attack with the way he keeps making my heart stop and then start up again, beating so fast it might fly right out of my chest. Reality settles in and I say, "If I were to join you, Rex, you won't have a waitress."

He smiles. "Goddamn. Anything around here you don't do, Cupcake?"

I pretend to think about my answer for a moment, only because I'm enjoying standing next to him. Lately, the tension between us has been so thick, the pressure alone forced me to keep my distance.

It's different tonight. He's not just friendlier, the air around him feels different.

Warmer. Open. Welcoming.

The other couple staying at the lodge walk into the dining room. With a shrug, I finally say, "No, there's not." I hold up a hand. "Other than using power-tools. Gramps won't let me. Thinks I'll cut off a finger or something." I roll my eyes.

He stops next to a table and gestures for Adam and Chase to sit down before he says, "You almost did, didn't you? Cut off a finger or something? He's looking out for you."

I laugh because I can't deny it. "Look, in my defense, I wasn't a lot older than these two." I nod toward the twins.

"You've lived here your entire life?"

I nod again. "Mostly. Can't really remember not living here. Even then, in Michigan. Always in-state."

"What about college?"

I bite my lip. That dream was snuffed out years ago. "Didn't go. Gramps needed me here." Story of my life, and it's a short one. I point towards the menu I'd printed this morning and put in all the table stands. "This time of year, our cuisine's pretty limited, but there are a few things on there besides the meatloaf. I'll be back to take your order."

I cross the room, make small talk with the middle-aged couple at the other table, and take their order before walking back to his table. Knowing he isn't a pop drinker, and neither are the boys, I ask, "One coffee and two milks?"

"Perfect," Rex answers. "And three meatloaf dinners."

"Coming right up."

To say I'm disappointed to not be joining them is an understatement. But it is what it is.

This is my life. Has been for almost as long as I can remember. Many times, I wished for different, but in truth, I have no better options. I wanted the college experience, if I'm honest. Never had a clue what I would've studied.

Besides, Gramps needed me then, and he needs me now. That's my life, stuck between a rock and a hard place existence I really can't do much to change, or second guess. Better to accept it and make the most of it, just like everybody else in Split Harbor. Even this town can change, without changing its soul – Punch Corp, Ryan Caspian's company, has made a lot of locals a whole lot happier and richer. That never would've happened if they hadn't stayed.

My mind hangs on muddy existential thoughts and I pause slightly as I walk to the swinging door that joins the kitchen to the dining room. *What if I'm not making the most of life here? What if I'm too stuck on what-ifs instead of changing where I'm at?*

Pondering that, I enter the kitchen and cross the room to collect a tray to deliver the drinks to Rex and the boys as well as the other couple. Gramps sits at the table, a plate of meatloaf and mashed potatoes in front of him, and Marcy is at the stove, looking at me, waiting to hear what the guests ordered.

My mind makes a decision then. "*Six* meatloaf dinners," I say.

"Coming right up," Marcy says.

"Six?" Gramps asks, taking a headcount of our five guests on his fingers. "Who else is out there?"

"No one," I say, filling two carafes with coffee. After putting four cups on the tray, I grab two cartons of milk out of the fridge. "I'm eating my meal with Rex and the boys."

He's already figured that out and he's glaring. "Tabby

Danes, we have *rules* against dining with guests. Etiquette and health –"

"Since when?" Marcy cuts in. "You eat with them all the time, bossy-pants."

I smile and walk to the door. It's not very often, but once in a while Marcy puts Gramps in his place like no other. Besides, Gramps is just being his usual curmudgeonly self. He'd been laughing with Rex just a short time ago.

After delivering the coffee to the couple, I walk over to Rex's table. As he's eyeing the second cup I set down, I say, "Good news. I'm joining you after all."

The boys let out little yips, banging their forks excitedly on the table, while Rex just grins. A grin sexy enough to knock me flat. Heat stings my cheeks, then kisses other parts of my body. "I'll be right back."

In the kitchen, where the atmosphere is most certainly charged, I mind my own business, filling a tray with warm rolls, butter, and glasses of water. I leave the kitchen, delivering half the food to the couple and the rest to Rex and the kids.

"Who needs ketchup?"

"Me!" the boys say at the same time.

"And me," Rex says.

"Good," I say. "I just didn't want to be the only one."

Rex grinned. "Just the opposite, Cupcake. We love the stuff. You fit right in."

I head back to the kitchen. Gramps is still stewing.

Marcy smiles as she picks up a tray with two plates. "I'll take this one out."

I grab a bottle of ketchup and add it to the tray with four plates before I lift it and follow her out of the room.

I'm done setting the plates down on Rex's table by the time Marcy walks past, and hand her the tray.

"Thanks," I say.

"You're welcome," she replies. "Enjoy your dinner."

My life hasn't allowed me too many dates. I get a case of nerves as I sit down.

"Looks great," Rex says, opening the ketchup bottle. "Smells divine, too."

"Marcy is an amazing cook," I say. "Don't know what we'd do without her."

"She been here long?"

"Yes. She used to live in town, but moved out here after her husband died. That must have been...ten years ago." Almost an eternity, and I hadn't realized it until now.

Rex gives both boys a generous dash of ketchup, and then holds the bottle over my plate. I've never had someone pour my ketchup for me, but nod, and tell him thank you. It's weirdly sweet, especially coming from this man.

He finishes adding some over his meatloaf, and we all start eating.

"Did you go to college?" I ask, both because it's quiet and I'm curious.

"No. Went into the army straight out of high school. Did my time in Afghanistan after 9/11, then started working construction after I got out. After a few years, I started my own company, T-Rex Builders."

The boys stop eating, making little dinosaur noises, holding their hands out clumsily in front of them like the king of reptiles. We both laugh.

"What kind of construction?"

"Started out with houses mainly, residential, but the

past few years it's been more commercial development. Good money with the economy humming along. Chicago and the outer 'burbs have grown like mad."

That explains why his changes for the stable area made so much sense, and why Gramps caved and hired him. "Where, exactly?"

"Lombard. Naperville. Villa Park. Wherever, when I'm not picking up the slack downtown. A lot of crews don't have the turn around we do. Word was getting around." There's a soft edge in his voice when he says *was*, very much past-tense.

Of course, I knew the where part from his license plates, but I'm cautious about pressing for too much detail. I don't want that door to slam shut again. "Sounds nice. I've never been there."

"Where have you been? Travel?" He quirks an eyebrow.

"Split Harbor."

He grins, thinking this little town only ten miles away can't be my whole world. Nobody could be that boring, right? "Where else?"

I shrug. "Don't know for sure. Marquette, briefly, I guess. I was in Detroit real young, but considering I was only four, can't remember much about it." I leave it there. I have secrets, too. Like the weird nightmares about a church there, and the run down house I'd been taken to before Gramps collected me.

"Otherwise you've never left here? Split Harbor?"

He sounds shocked.

"Haven't had a need to leave."

He took a drink of water. "If you could go anywhere in the world, where would it be?"

"Hawaii," I reply before he's barely stopped talking.

"Hawaii?"

"Yes, sir."

"Why? I mean, it's beautiful, but why?"

"Just 'cause." I could explain it's because that's the furthest place I can go without a passport. Gramps would have a cow if I ever applied for one of those. Honestly, Hawaii is everything I know Split Harbor and northern Michigan isn't. Bright. Warm. Tropical. It's another world, an inversion of sorts, and I've always wondered if I spend enough time in a place like that, maybe I'll come home happier.

Noticing the couple across the room was almost done with their meal, I say, "Excuse me. I'll be right back."

I visit the couple's table, asking if they need anything, and then walk to the kitchen to collect the desert included with the meal. Time for my chocolate candy cupcakes to shine.

Seated at the table with Gramps, Marcy lays down her napkin, leaning in her chair. "Ready for dessert?"

"Yep, I got it," I say.

"How long have the guests been waiting?" Gramps asks. I notice the sharpness in his voice.

"They're just finishing their meals," I answer. Opening the fridge, I take out the can of whipped cream and a jar of cherries to complete the top of the cupcakes.

"They'd better be."

"You hush, now," Marcy says to Gramps.

"No. Her catting-around has already taken up too damn much of her time. The girl's just like *her*."

His derogatory tone sticks me deep and hard. "What did you just say?"

"You heard, Tabby."

"Yes, I did." I give each cupcake a quick shot of whipped cream and drop a cherry on top, trying to quell my indignation. I don't know who that old man thinks he is sometimes.

I'm in my mid-freaking-twenties. I'm practically a nun.

Catting-around? He's always grumpy, but right now, he's being cruel.

Marcy knows it, too, and quietly reprimands him.

"What's up with you?" I ask, trying not to set him off all over again, even though he deserves it. "That's the second time today you've compared me to my mother." He's never tried to hide anything, even when I was a kid. Maybe I didn't know what catting-around was when he'd picked me up in Detroit, but he said that's what my mother was doing plenty of times. And that was always the reason I had to come live with him like I do now.

"Because you're acting like her," he says coldly. "Following in her footsteps."

"Morris!" Marcy snaps. "Enough."

"You stay out of this," he tells her. "You're just an employee here."

She slaps the table, an outburst I've never seen from the normally calm, lovely cook. "You know what? You're right. That's *all* I am. And I can quit any time."

My stomach twists. Once when I imagine how screwed up this place will be without her. Again when I see the tears nipping at her eyes.

Damn it, Gramps, what have *you done?*

Gramps scowls, unfazed. "You won't quit. You're too old for another job."

"Don't push me, old man. Final warning." She's too gracious.

I have the urge to step in. This is my fight, after all, not hers, but I don't have it in me right now. Once again, any enjoyment I've had tonight is nearly ruined.

I don't even bother looking at Gramps as I leave the kitchen.

The couple tells me they'll take their cupcakes up to their room for later. I force a smile, wrap them up for them, then carry the tray to Rex's table.

The boys are excited about their cupcakes. I smile, a real one this time, and agree they're delish when they tell Rex about the candy bars we'd chopped up and sprinkled over the frosting.

"Aren't you going to eat yours, Tabby?" Adam asks once his cupcake is devoured.

But my appetite is gone. "No. You two can share, if that's okay with your father."

Rex looks at me questioningly and I look away.

The kitchen door opens and my insides sink until I see Marcy walk out. I was certain it'd be Gramps first, being his own deflated grumpy self. I quickly look away. He's embarrassed me before, and made me mad, but I don't remember being this hurt by him before.

Marcy smiles across the room, but it's strained.

"Is everything okay?" Rex asks.

I swallow, pursing my lips together. They're probably turning white.

Damn.

Why can't I have a happy evening? Just one? Is that too much to ask? "Everything's exactly how it always is," I say. "Excuse me, Rex, I need to help Marcy for a second."

She's clearing off the other table, and when I arrive, she shakes her head. "You're sweet, doll, but I don't need your help. And neither does your grandfather. I'm going to carry these dishes to the kitchen, and watch as he washes them and cleans the kitchen. Then I'll watch him lock up, and don't you even think about helping him. It's time he *learns* just how much he takes for granted around here."

I'd never heard or seen her quite so mad. I can only imagine how angry Gramps is. "I'd better –"

"Tabby," Marcy draws in a deep breath. "Please. He's made me too mad this time. *Too. Mad.*"

I have to let her give the old man a lesson and risk God only knows.

We're screwed if she quits. Totally screwed.

She picks up the tray. "I'll see you tomorrow."

I mumble a goodnight, watch her leave, forcing myself not to follow. Normally I would, but Gramps deserves what he's getting right now. Whatever happens next is on him.

"You sure everything's okay?" Rex stands behind me, his voice close and deep.

I shake my head, then nod. "Yeah. Gramps just pissed her off royal. You should take the boys upstairs before the kitchen explodes."

"What're you going to do? You need some help?"

"I'll tell you what I'm not going to do," I say. "I'm not going in that kitchen until morning."

"Do you want me to –"

"No. No. Just take the boys upstairs." He has too much to worry about. Asking him to get in the middle of a spat at the lodge is just insufferable.

"Cupcake? You're *sure?*" He doesn't stop. Neither do his eyes, concerned and strong and so consuming.

It was kind of him to ask. Gallant even. A word I never thought I'd put next to Rex Osborne. "I'm sure. Don't worry."

"Thanks for doing dinner. It was nice."

"It *was* nice." Until Gramps rubbed his nose in it.

He ushers the boys out the doorway, and I stand where I am for a moment, until the kitchen door opens again, then I shoot around the corner. Unable not to, I peak around the frame.

Gramps. With a tray.

Afraid he'll catch me watching him clear the table I'd just sat at, I tip toe down the hall. A splatter of guilt crosses my stomach, but I tell myself to ignore it. I'm still pissed at him, after all. He's burned out any sympathy points tonight, and then some.

I rarely go to my cabin before ten, but there's nothing else for me to do. After grabbing my coat, I stand at the door, with my hand on the knob. Pushing the heavy air out of my lungs, I open the door and step outside.

The door almost closes before it opens again. Half expecting Gramps, I frown when Rex steps out.

"It's me, isn't it? That's what your grandfather's so pissed about."

"No, not really. He..." It could be any man. I know that, shaking my head. "It's me."

"You? Bullshit." I say nothing until he asks, "Cupcake, why? What's the story?"

He'd been open with me, so it's only fair I fill him in. "My grandma died when my mother was in her teens. She stayed here, took Gramps' attitude for a while, but then left. She couldn't handle him like me. Ran away. Did bad stuff, or so I hear. Gramps didn't get a word from her for five years. Then, he got a call from the Detroit police. I'd been dropped off at a church with his name and number pinned to my shirt."

"How old where you?"

"Four."

"And you've been here ever since?"

I nod.

"Where's your mother now?"

I shrug. "No idea. She's called a couple of times over the years, but I've never talked to her. Just Gramps. Each time he only said she wanted money."

"Cupcake," he growls, pulling me into his enormous arms. "I'm sorry."

Maybe it's his whisper, or his inked muscles, or the human twinkle in his eyes. Or all of the above.

Either way, tears drown my eyes as he holds me against his chest, suddenly bigger than the stars spanning the night sky.

Amazing. All of it. His arms around me. His wonderful scent, strong and piney and somehow masculine to its very soul. How solid, how strong, how *right* he feels.

I've heard hugs were good for people. They stir up some chemicals, do things to the brain, the whole system, but until this moment, I never realized just how incredible it feels to be held so close and so tight. My entire being is safe and secure in the special, secret kingdom Rex Osborne hides between his arms.

I relish in all of that for as long as I dare, and then lift my head. "You've got nothing to be sorry about, Cupcake. You hear? *Nothing*."

"No, no, I do. You have all this on your plate, so much horror, and here I am, dumping more."

He's looking at me, straight in the eyes, and it's as if I can see inside him. See the pain and anguish. God, how is he this strong?

I don't want him feeling another burden. I know what it's like.

My eyes go to his lips and I stretch onto my toes.

The moment my lips touch his, my heart opens. All the emotions I've kept bottled up inside pour out.

It's exciting. It's electric. It's hot and sweet and just a little bit wet. It's exactly what I need tonight, tomorrow, maybe forever.

And our kiss accelerates with phenomenal speed. His lips are hungry, all over mine, his tongue curling and twisting, spiraling around mine.

Heat explodes inside me, around me, as he plants his hands on my butt and presses me so hard against him. *Yes.*

I love it. And want more. So much more.

A tiny voice says I shouldn't be doing this. Gramps could walk out the door any minute. Then another voice says, *So the hell what? He's already accused you of catting-around so there's no reason not to.*

I grind my hips against his, loving the sensations, hating the material between us, and softly catch his tongue between my teeth to swirl mine around it. I think I could kiss this man forever. And then a little longer.

His hands slip inside the waistband of my jeans and the delight of his bare skin against mine makes me gasp. My knees shake, terrified he'll see how wet I am if he drifts a little lower.

"I know a place," I whisper. "My cabin."

Excitement, surprise, and animal lust sparks in his big blue eyes. He goes still and then pulls me even tighter against him. His sigh echoes in my ear.

"Tabby, fuck. You know damn well I want to, but the boys are alone, up in my room."

I slide my hands inside the back of his jeans. One handful of his amazing ass, and I'm well aware it has the power to fuck me to the earth's center. *Holy hell.*

"There are two...two bedrooms in my cabin." I'm stammering, imagining what he can do, what I want him to do to me tonight so bad.

He pulls away, but only far enough to look at me. "Cupcake, you're *sure* you want this?"

I lean up and kiss his lips gently. "More than sure. Need it."

"Okay. It'll take me a couple of minutes to get them ready. Wait for us."

Excitement laced with pure happiness sends a giggle to my throat. "Oh, I'll be waiting."

VIII: HOT COFFEE AND COCOA (REX)

I take the stairs two at time and stop myself from throwing open the door, needing a second to collect myself. I'm so fucking spun my cock throbs lightning, my mind already hooked on what it'll feel like inside Cupcake.

My vision is practically pink. I see her hair fisted in my hand, hear her soft little moans, dream how I think she'll cry out once I'm in to the hilt. A fuck like this comes around once a lifetime. It's not just my woes – it's this woman.

Christ. After bedding Tabby, I may never come down, wherever my life goes from here.

My control strains its limits. I take a deep breath, focus on breathing, and then open the door. I have to push her out of my head for the twins.

"We put on our pajamas like you said, Daddy," Adam says, pride ringing in his little voice.

"Can we play on the tablet now?" Chase asks.

"Put on your boots," I growl. "New plan."

I do a double take. Guilt stabs me at how harsh I sound as they look up, quiet and confused.

I pull up a tight smile, crouch down, and ruffle the hair on their heads. "Tabby invited us over to her cabin tonight. It'll be a sleepover."

"Sleepover? Wow, yeah, wow!" they shout.

Sweet relief. That was close. No sex will ever come between me and making these kids grin.

Not even if it's guaranteed to leave me spent, happy, and triumphant over Tabby's tight bod. *Fuck.*

"Bring the tablet, boys." It'll give them something to do while I'm otherwise occupied.

"Tabby has movies at her cabin, Daddy. Lotsa them," Chase says.

"She does?" My grin gets bigger. Even better. The boys love to play their hero flicks loud and it'll be the perfect cover.

"She let us watch some. Big boomer speakers too!" Adam beams.

"And snacks! Popcorn!" Chase is like me, a sucker for late night junk food sometimes. I rub his head again.

"Good deal," I say. "We've got business, her and I. While we're doing boring grown-up stuff, you can watch some more."

They're sold. They chatter away to each other about which movies they'll watch as I hurry them along, putting on their boots and coats. As we leave the room, I put a finger to my lips to keep them quiet. The last thing I want is for Morris to hear us sneaking out the back door.

I probably should be taking in the consequences of that, but can't right now. The old man runs a tight ship, but he's a bastard with Tabby. Working her day and night.

He's jealous. That's what he is. Wants her all to himself, shackled to this place. Doesn't let her be an adult, a free agent, a woman.

Too damn bad. Tonight, Rex is taking over, and I swear up and down I'll show her the magic of her own majestic flesh. Every sweet fucking inch of it.

I know I'm not thinking completely clearly, mainly because I'm thinking with my cock and not my head, but Cupcake deserves attention, and I want to be the one to give it to her in droves.

Long and hard and deep, all the way till dawn.

All this time we've been running, I've never felt the thrill that shoots through me as we slip out the back door. The boys giggle as we hurry along the pathway towards the little wood cabin. The lights glow jack-o-lantern orange inside, casting a warm, welcoming heat through the windows.

For just a second, I stop and stare. Jesus. I can't remember when something felt so right.

The door opens as soon as we step onto the porch and the shine in her eyes makes something remarkable happen inside my chest. My heart pounds like a hammer, more than it should with this animal lust coursing through my system. Can't say why – don't fucking dare – but I feel it, and it makes me smile.

"Hello, hello," she says softly.

"Hi, Tabby!" the boys shout. "Can we watch movies?"

She laughs. "I had a feeling that's what you'd want. I'll find you the remote."

The boys are already kicking off their boots. I tell them to put them by the door and hang up their coats on the back of a chair she has by the door.

"We know, Dad," Chase says.

"We've been here before," Adam points out.

I haven't, but am damn excited to be here now. I toss my coat over the back of the same chair, stepping out of my boots.

"Any preferences?" she asks.

My mind goes several directions, all focused on her. Preferably naked. In bed. With me. Maybe something silky and pink to start, which I'll rip off with my teeth.

Her grin is gold, and her hips sway with a sexy hitch as she steps closer.

She touches a button on my shirt with one finger. "I'm referring to the movie. More cartoons? Or maybe one you might like better?"

"I don't give a shit about movies," I whisper in her ear, nipping at her ear lobe. "The boys can have their pick, as long as it's not too violent or crude for their age."

She slips a hand in my back pocket. "It's a small cabin, Rex. We should wait until they're asleep."

Easy for her to say. My dick is about to explode through my pants. But damn it if she isn't making sense.

"I know," I growl reluctantly. "They need something boring. Or something so intense it tires them the hell out."

Her giggle makes my cock jolt as she turns and walks away.

The cabin is tiny, but quaint and homey, and I feel more at ease than I have in weeks, maybe months and years. I don't pay much attention as the boys pick out a movie and she sets it up on their system. Another superhero thing with plenty of comic villains and big explosions.

Both boys flop onto the floor, on their stomachs

with their hands under their chins. She gives them a big blanket with black and brown bears on it. Big and warm and certain to make them tired before long. Smart move.

"Care for some coffee?" she asks.

I glance towards the little alcove that's the kitchen. Shame the tiny space doesn't lend the privacy we'd need for the scorching hot kind of coffee I *really* want. "No, thanks. I'm good."

"Sit down?" She gestures to the couch.

No privacy there either. I haven't been so stirred up, so damn ready to throw her against the nearest horizontal surface since I got a girl naked on prom night the first time. This is nuts. Absolutely *loco*.

How the fuck can she make me feel almost twenty years younger? One thing's for sure: with her, I'll have the same gusto, same vigor, same need to fuck until my bones give out that I had at eighteen.

I grab Cupcake's hand and tug her towards the kitchen area, searching through the fridge for water bottles. She puts a small bag of popcorn for them in the microwave and we wait, impatient as all hell.

I can't resist once my hand finds hers. I grab her hair, bring her in for a kiss, long and hot and melting. My tongue previews every way I'll be between her legs soon. Growling, I lead her to the farthest corner of the tiny kitchen.

She leans up against the counter and toys with the buttons on my shirt with both hands. "Careful. They'll hear us."

"Not if we're quiet," I say as my lips catch hers again.

Fuck she tastes good, and the way she grinds her pussy

against my cock is enough to drive me crazy. There's no space between us, but it's still not close enough.

I want more. *Need* more. So does she.

The passion in her kisses intoxicates me, crawls down my spine and puts lava in my balls. My hands roam her back, her sides, her ass. I cup her lush cheeks and slam her harder against me.

My cock is screaming. Howling to be cut loose from the restraint of my jeans and dive inside her hot, wet pussy. Maybe it's good we'll have to wait for later, until we're out of this kitchen. Otherwise, I would throw her against the counter. Shit *would* break.

She leans her head back. Her eyes are hooded, halfway closed, but the pleasure shining on her face is the hottest thing I've ever seen. I trail more kisses down her neck and then dive lower, into the V left open by her pink top's neckline. Cupcake arches her back, thrusting her tits forward, nipples hard as sin through her shirt.

Another hour. Maybe less. That's as long as I'll last before I push my dick into this woman or die first.

Trading my hold on her ass for those palm-sized tits, I wish I could see them, taste them. Suck the pebbled ends my thumbs keep stroking through her shirt.

"Dad, did you see that?!"

We both go still at the sound of Adam's voice.

"Dad?" Chase asks.

She sucks in a breath before saying, "Who wants hot chocolate?"

"We do, we do!"

I'm amazed at her ability to speak. She serves the boys their bowl of popcorn and then comes back to me, a knowing look in her eye. My teeth clench, insanity pinching them shut, no thanks to the dynamite blazing in my jeans.

"Two hot chocolates, coming right up." She plants a tiny kiss on my lips. "Go sit down." I watch her scoop the cocoa powder into two cups, adding plenty of milk, pulling out a bag of mini-marshmallows to go on top.

"Can't, Cupcake," I admit. "Too damn wound up."

"Me, neither," she whispers. "But we don't have a choice. Soon, Rex. *Soon.*"

Fuck me, the way she says it...

She's just amazing. Body, mind, and soul. Putting my kids before her needs. I'm used to doing that, but right now, I wouldn't mind them nodding off and then hauling her to the bedroom.

"Go," she says.

Reluctantly, I walk to the couch, stiff legged, and sit down.

In no time she carries in a tray with four cups of steaming hot chocolate. Melting marshmallows float on the top. There's less milk in our cups than the two for the twins.

Here, too, I'm amazed how she doesn't warn the boys to be careful or not spill. Instead she just smiles at them like they're as precious to her as they are to me. I'm reminded then of what I thought about before, sending a note to my lawyer that says the kids go to her if something happens.

Sure, my family will get involved sooner or later, but there's no one better to keep them safe until then if the unthinkable comes down. Shit. I wonder if it's legal to include a way for her to have access to my checking accounts so she'll have money to take care of them?

Assuming the fucking Feds don't decide to come down like a ton of bricks and seize all my money thanks to Nelia and her criminal fuckboy.

"You like it? The hot chocolate?" she whispers.

I've barely touched it. Pausing, I take a big sip, then turn her way, pushing my lips to her ear. "Delicious, Cupcake. But just between you and me, I'm looking at the only hot thing I really want."

"Stop!"

The teasing in her voice says more and the sexy glimmer in her eyes betrays flattery.

Unbelievable. Hasn't anyone ever told her how sexy she is? How bad they want to spread her out and take her over?

"Patience," she whispers. "Looks like they're getting tired."

The boys are noticeably calmer. Their little heads are nodding as they sip their drinks, eyes glued to the TV, half the popcorn uneaten. The movie drones on, a damsel in distress shrieking on the screen as the bad guy laughs.

"Darling, I'm trying." Like hell I am.

She's sitting on the couch next to me and folds her legs up under her while sipping her hot chocolate. "Question, Rex? Why didn't you marry their mother?"

It's only fair that she'd be curious, and that I tell her the truth.

"Their mother was a whore."

She frowns.

"Almost literally," I say. "She was certainly reckless. Drawn to anyone strong with an edge in their eyes. I didn't know the danger at the time, but should have. We met in a bar, got all hot and bothered, had sex in the parking lot. She didn't ask for any money, no. I never imagined I'd see her again. Didn't think about her habits, her drugs, the guys she slept around with to get her next fix. Nine months later, I get a letter in the mail about a paternity test. Court ordered. The twins were born early, spent a few weeks in the hospital thanks to her stupid ass. Don't know what the fuck she put in her system while she was carrying them, but damn, it could've been worse. My kids walked away clean, reasonably healthy, and so did I. No diseases. I've been tested plenty. She didn't have any health insurance, either, so the state paid full medical and wanted to recoup that money. I paid my fair share, and hers, too."

I keep glancing towards the boys. Hard to believe that was more than five fucking years ago.

Long time, but also like it was only yesterday. No matter how they came into this world, or how I found out about their existence, it never changed how much I love them. Not since the second I laid eyes on them the first time, cradled their tiny little bodies in my big hands.

They came out beautiful from something ugly. They made me believe in miracles.

"Several guys took the DNA test, but I was the lucky one." I look her way so she knows I'm serious. "No sarcasm, Cupcake. They're mine. Always were from the instant I found out. I took charge and never looked back."

"I know, and I can see how much you love them." Her eyes soften, staring at me like I'm one of the heroes crawling up the skyscraper on the screen. I'm actually a little ashamed. I'm no damn hero, or I wouldn't have put anyone in this predicament.

"I do love them. Didn't know I had a love that strong

and deep inside me. My sons changed everything. Forever."

"What happened then?"

"My lawyer petitioned the court that if my health insurance was footing the bill, and I was picking up the extra, that I should have full custody. Had a stable job, a business, and against her it was no contest. My wish was granted, but I had to allow her visitation. I agreed, but only if the visits were supervised. Not that it really mattered. She only saw them twice when they were babies. Never tried again for *years.*"

Memories float back and I reach down for the mug of hot chocolate just to have a distraction till the worst of them fade.

"Nelia, that was her name. She was a drug addict. A royal piece of dog shit. I still count my lucky stars to this day she didn't infect them, screw up their system, or leave me with some crap I'd never get rid of. The doctors assured me that wasn't the case, thank God. Anyway, when the boys were about two, she hooked up with a drug dealer. An asshole with mob connections in an underground crime syndicate. An asshole with ties to a lot of money and power in the city. A dangerous asshole. She started threatening me. Said if I didn't help him launder some money, she'd take the boys away."

"Oh my God." Her little hands cover her mouth and then slip away slowly. *"That's* how the blackmail started?"

"Yes. And continued."

"Until recently?"

I nod. "I came home one night and the boys were gone. I found them, saved them, really, and then we left town. We didn't have a choice. Nelia died of an overdose that night." Not wanting the memories, the nightmare of that night to come between us, I change the conversation.

"Tell me about your Hawaiian dreams."

She stares at me for a long time, silent. I hold my breath, really not wanting to subject her to all that had happened that night. There's some crap I'm still not ready to tell.

She looks away, hiding a creeping smile. "Oh, Hawaii. I'll go there someday. I *know* I will. I won't even let Gramps stop me."

"Damn straight, you will, Cupcake. You've got grit." I shake my head at the irony of her dream location and say, "You can say hi to my old man. He's out there."

"In Hawaii?"

"Yeah, Oahu. With wife number three."

"Where's your mother?"

"Italy. Venice, in fact, but some seasons it's Rome. They got divorced, because of wife number two, while Dad was stationed there. Spent a long time in the Air Force and retired late. Mom remarried a rich European guy and never left."

"Has she seen the boys?"

"Absolutely. She comes back almost every year." There's no need for me to mention my father's only seen the boys once, disappointed I'd never married their mom.

Christ, if he only knew...but he doesn't know the truth. He'd curse me out like the hard paragon of perfection he pretended to be while I was growing up. We had a few good times and he's still my dad, but family love doesn't blind me to what a huge asshole he can be.

"Did you ever live there? In Italy?"

"Very briefly. Just for a few months between the army

and my business. It's not all it's cracked up to be. Loved the food, though."

She chuckles.

I can't believe I'm telling her all this. That's unusual for me, yet it feels good. Like it's been bottled up inside me forever, needing to be let go. "I was an army brat. Air Force, technically, and that's what led me to the service, too. My dad wouldn't have had it any other way. He was disappointed when I didn't re-up after my initial tour, but hell, several years in Afghanistan was enough for this life. I've spent my time watching people kill and I don't much like it."

"What did you do then?"

"Went to the only real home I'd ever known. To my grandparents' house in Illinois. I'd spent a couple of summers with them growing up and always enjoyed it."

"Are they still there?"

"No, they died a couple years before the twins were born. First my grandfather, and then a couple months later, grandma. Nothing tragic. Just old age. They lived good lives."

"But you still miss them."

She's intuitive. "Plenty. Grandpa taught me a hell of a lot about building, how things work. Got me my first construction job. Wasn't long before I learned to run a crew and sell contracts."

A thoughtful expression covers her face as she glances around the room. "Grandfather's are like that, I guess. They teach us a lot."

I smile, know exactly who she's talking about. Prickly SOB or not, Gramps means well. He loves her.

I reach over to lay a hand on her knee. The desire she

evokes is still raging, but has cooled just enough so I'm no longer ready to pounce on her in the open. Won't take much to reignite the flame, but I also want to know more about her. "What about this place, Cupcake? How long's it been in the family?"

"My great-great grandfather started this lodge, I think. It was a stopping point for traders and hunters over a century ago, and it's been passed down from generation to generation ever since." Her smile glows, thoughtful and genuine as she nibbles on her bottom lip. "I guess it was quite a madhouse during the roaring twenties. Gramps has stories."

"Bootlegging?"

She nods.

I grin. "Makes sense this close to Canada. Out in the middle of nowhere."

With a smile that could brighten even the darkest day, she whispers, "Al Capone rented a cabin here. Lived here an entire winter with one of his many girlfriends, they say. I don't know if it's really true, but Gramps swears it is. Crazy."

"Shit," I whisper softly, walking a hand up her thigh. "Wonder what they did to stay warm?"

She stifles a giggle, sliding a bit closer. "Do you *really* wonder?"

Fate is finally on my side because the cartoon ends right then. "Time for bed."

"Aw, no fair," the boys mumble with disappointment, fighting the obvious sleepiness in their voices.

"You can play a game on the tablet till you fall asleep," I tell them, glad I'd grabbed it while walking out of our room at the lodge.

"We don't want to go back to our room," Adam says.

"We're comfy. We like it here," Chase says. "At Tabby's."

"Then you'll be happy to know you're sleeping here tonight," she says, pointing to one of the bedrooms. "It's a sleepover," she reminds them.

"Sleep-over! Sleep-over!" They chant, burning a little of their sugar rush.

I nod. Then hold my breath, wondering if they'll ask where I'll sleep.

Thankfully they don't. They're too busy jumping off the floor to follow Tabby into the room.

I get off the couch and cross the room to pick up the tablet I'd set on the chair by the door. "Anyone need a drink of water first? Or the bathroom?"

Her smile shines as I follow her into the guest bedroom for the boys. "There's a bathroom in here. With glasses for water. There's even a little step stool so you guys can reach the sink."

She helps Chase under the covers while I help Adam and then pass over the tablet. It's too perfect.

"Share, boys. Play as many rounds as you want till you're asleep."

"How many games is that?" he asks.

A random number pops into my head. "Six." I have no idea. They should fall asleep before then.

I hope.

The look she gives me says she does, too. Then I'm instantly hard all over again.

Cupcake leaves the room first, and I mirror how she told the boys goodnight before following her and pulling the door shut.

Stopping near the coffee table, she sets all the empty

cups on the tray, glancing at me over one shoulder. We're alone. *Finally.*

The glimmer in her eyes and the coy smile on her lips sends a jolt of electricity through me. I follow her into the kitchen and stop directly behind her.

She leans back against me, her ass rubbing my hard-on, slow and teasing. She's too good at this, the little minx.

I slip my hands under her shirt and rub the lace covering her tits. "Anything I can do to help?"

"You can turn off the lights. The switch is right behind you."

Wondering if her bra is pink, I leave one hand where it's at and use the other to shut off the light. "Done. Now, I want you," I say, raking my stubble and my lips up the side of her neck.

She wiggles her ass against me. This time harder. "No way. I couldn't tell."

"Your loss," I growl back, kisses coming faster. My cock grinds through my jeans, into her ass, way past ready to be in her.

Laughing she spins around. I settle my hands on her sides, loving how soft her skin feels on mine. She plants both hands on my chest and pushes.

I take a step back, following her urging.

She pushes again. "Keep going."

The excitement in her eyes fuses to mine. Has my blood churning full force. I can't, not anymore, can't fucking *wait* for her pussy wrapped around every inch of me.

"Straight back," she says. "Just a little more."

Trusting her guidance, I keep walking backwards,

enjoying the sway of her hips beneath my hands as she walks with me step for step.

"Almost there," she says.

I cross the threshold, assuming the light switch is in the same place as the other bedroom. I reach over and flick it on. The room isn't large and the back of my knees bump into the bed. She's in the room, too, and uses one foot to make the door swing shut behind her. It closes with a soft click.

"Finally." My voice is so low I sound like a bear, and she laughs.

I grasp the edge of her pink shirt. It's soft and loose, like a long sleeve T-shirt. "First thing's first."

Her head tilts sideways as she asks, "What's that?"

"I've been dying to know if everything you wear is pink."

She tosses her head back and holds her arms over her head. I take the invitation and slip the shirt upwards. The bra isn't pink. It's beige, the same color as her skin, but there's a pink bow smack dab in the middle of the tits I'm itching to taste, suck, and rule.

"Sorry to disappoint. A girl needs *a little* variety in her wardrobe."

I toss aside her shirt. "Cupcake, you've got nothing to be sorry about."

No fucking way.

"I do have some pink," she says.

"You'll show me later," I say, running a finger along the lace covering one tit. My dick jerks in my pants.

"I can put one on right now."

I'm now teasing both tits in my hands. Her eyelids

flutter, pleasure overwhelming her. "I'd rather you take this one off."

She arches her back so her tits jiggle slightly. "Your hands are in the way. The clasp is in the front."

I find it, right under the pink bow. "This?" I say slowly.

I know it is, but love teasing her. Love how her eyes are smoldering and her breathing comes shallow and husky. Love how I'll feel her screaming in my hand very, *very* soon.

"Yes!"

"Do you want me to unclasp it, Cupcake? Talk to me."

She tries to cover up a little moan and a surge of adrenaline fires through me. It's amazing I can play this game at all. I haven't been this excited, this into a woman, in years. Maybe fucking *never*.

"Only if you want to see what's underneath it," she says, giving me a look that says, *you'd better*.

This beautiful woman has no clue.

"Never wanted anything more," I tell her, unclasping the hook.

The cups of her bra separate and her tits bounce free. It's almost as if they're calling my name, and that isn't something I can resist. I push the straps off her shoulders, sitting on the bed. Then, I pull her forward, draw her between my knees as I latch onto one tit with my mouth.

So soft. So sweet. So fucking mine.

Cupcake makes a sound that's all breath and no voice. It's so decadent my cock seethes, begging to come right now. But won't. That would be a damn waste I'd never get over.

I want this to go on and on. All night. Into morning.

It might be torturous, waiting for the finale, but it'll be so, so, so fucking good.

Just like these tits. Her nipples are hard nubs and I nibble on one and then the other, slowly, fighting the ache building inside me.

Her hands are in my hair, holding my head as I suck and lick, and teasingly bite her tits. We both groan at the pleasure taking over.

After another thorough suck that has my cock oozing, I lift my head and lick her skin all the way up to her neck. She lets out a hoarse little moan, and then another as I unbutton her jeans.

They fit snug, but not too tight. My hands easily slip in and snag her panties. "Fuck, yes," I say, smiling. "Pink."

"I'm glad you approve." She's too modest. They could be ugly sweater green and they'd be the sexiest stuff on any hips ever.

I give the jeans and panties a quick shove down her thighs in one rough fistful. "You'll impress me more once they're gone."

She takes a step backwards. I lean down to push everything down around her ankles. Her curly trim bush is right before my eyes and I breathe deep. It's the most wonderful scent I've ever smelled. I can't wait to taste her, grasping her hips.

She comes up easy and I hoist her into the air as I flip around. We both land on the bed. She's laughing. So am I. Damn, but this feels good.

All of it feels good. And right. So very, very right.

I inch her upwards, so her head is on the pillows, then take her hands and tuck them under her head, one at a time.

She looks at me oddly.

"Trust me," I say, giving her a quick kiss. Then, I part her legs, bending her knees so her pussy is revealed. It's like the rest of her. Pink and fucking beautiful.

I run a hand up the inside of her thigh.

Her breathing stalls and she swallows before asking, "Aren't you...going to get undressed?"

"In good time," I answer, spreading her thighs a bit more. I kiss her tits again, running a finger over the lips of her pussy. She moans again, and fuck I love that sound, and how it tells me she's entranced in everything I'm doing.

I find her clit, swirl a circle, and then press against it with the tip of my finger.

She shudders sweetly. "Oh, yes!" She whimpers, barely audible.

I press again. More firmly this time, roll it around beneath my finger. It's soft, delicate, and ready for my touch. My tongue. My everything.

"When..." She takes a deep breath. "Rex, when will you get naked?"

I give her tit another long suck before lifting my head to look at her. My hand is still teasing her pussy. "Are we in a hurry, Cupcake?"

I feel her muscles tightening beneath my hand and slip a finger inside her. I find the spot that makes her hips arch, smiling proudly when they do.

Her hips buck up, again, desperate and accepting. "No, Rex, no. But – oh, there!"

"But what?" I whisper, stroking her with my finger. She's as hot, as wet, as fucking amazing as I'd imagined.

"There's, well, there's something I need to tell you."

I thrust my finger deeper inside her, loving how she comes into it, into the friction I'm giving. "Then tell me, Cupcake," I say. I wouldn't consider myself a kinky person, but I'm more than willing to do whatever she wants.

She gasps and then lets the air out slowly. "Rex, I'm sorry. I'm a virgin."

IX: THE THINGS SHE'LL LEARN
(TABBY)

My mind screams *idiot* the second he freezes.

Fuck it all to hell. I should have lied. Or just pretended otherwise.

But he's experienced. Vastly more than me.

The way my body reacts proves that, and he'll soon discover I'm not. It's been easy so far. Just going with the flow. He's made it that way. Sooner or later, he'll expect me to do something, and I won't know what. How can I? I'm a freaking virgin. And just told him so.

I close my eyes as his fingers, the same ones giving me unimaginable pleasure only seconds ago, slip out of me. He lies down, stretching out beside me and lays a hand on my stomach.

"You're honest. Shit," he says. I wonder if he's amazed anyone would be this stupid.

It's over. Me and my big mouth have screwed me out of getting screwed. Heat burns my face as I whisper again, "Sorry. Rex, I didn't mean –"

"Wrong. There's *nothing* to be sorry for, Cupcake."

I look up, catch his sky blue eyes, and fall into his trance for the millionth time.

I'd dreamed of this. Of an amazing man coming to stay at the lodge and taking me, taking my V-card, making love like I'd only read about in dirty books. The dream was *so close*, but now...

"I had to tell you," I admit. "Just didn't want you to be disappointed. And now, I..."

He leans over and looks me in the eye, his gaze going nuclear. "You actually think I'm disappointed?"

I shrug. I don't know what he means.

He shakes his head. "Fuck that, Cupcake. I'm honored. I'm excited. I'm lucky as hell no man's ever been inside you and I don't have to fuck so hard you'll forget them."

A chill sweeps up my spine. He's serious.

I think. *Holy hell.*

I'd love to believe it, but I've been disappointed too many times in life to even hope.

"Need to know one thing before we continue," he says, lifting my chin with a finger. There's no escaping those bottomless blue eyes.

My heart skips a beat at the idea of starting up where we'd left off. "Continue?"

"Fuck yes." He strokes my stomach with his hand, then trails it to my hip. "I have to *know* this is what you want before we go any further. You have to say you want this, want me owning every inch of you."

"It is!" I blurt out. "More than you can know."

"Cupcake," he growls my name, waiting for the rest. "Word for word, Tabby."

"I want you owning me," I say, a new fiery blush mingling on my cheeks. "Every inch, Rex."

He kisses my temple. "How old are you, anyway, Cupcake?"

It's funny. I've always hated nicknames before him. Foolish, maybe, because even though I bake them regularly, I don't like eating cupcakes all that much. Chiding myself for letting my mind wander down such stupid paths, I answer, "Twenty-five." Heat rushes my cheeks again. If we weren't lying on top of them, I'd crawl under the covers to hide. I'm probably the oldest virgin in the state. And I'm naked in bed with this tiger of a man, not having sex.

"Perfect. Then you're old enough to appreciate every-fucking-thing I'll do, darling. You're beautiful, amazing, and so damn mine. Tonight. Tomorrow. Long as I'm here, this bed is ours. Shit. I find it hard to believe another man —"

"There's never been another man I've wanted," I interrupt. There's no need for me to tell him about Gramps. He's met him. But what I'd said is a hundred percent true. I've never stood up against Gramps over a man before Rex. Or had a man willing to fight for me like him.

I've never invited a man to my cabin, either. Completely, deep down, wanted to invite one. Until he stormed in and brought the stars to my world.

He leans in, brushing his lips over mine. "You still want me, Cupcake? You want me inside you?"

"Yes!" It's a whimper. Brutally honest.

"Good. Because now that I've heard the truth, I want you even more."

I want to believe it's stupid surface flattery, trying to

make me feel better, but his face says otherwise. The honesty in his voice, in his twinkling blue eyes, makes me smile. *It's true.*

"But Cupcake, I have to know it's really what you want, because we're not stopping again."

I lift his hand off my hip, pulling it toward my right breast. "This. This is what I want, and I don't want you to stop. Not even for a second, Rex. I'm just not sure what to do. Show me."

He grins. "I'll teach you everything, Ms. Danes. Proud to."

"I think I'll like that."

"Fuck yeah, you will."

His hand folds around my nipple as he kisses me, adding a delicious pressure. At first, I'm hesitant, having just admitted so much, but the anxiety doesn't last long.

I can't control myself when it comes to him. His touch, his smell, the hard inked canvass hiding his soul makes me come undone.

Rex Osborne, I surrender. His hand, his lips, his touch, his kiss, delivers a sweet amnesia, wipes away everything except the here and now. And this present with him is the best place I've ever been. It's wonder, ecstasy, and it's so damn real it hurts in all the right ways.

His mouth adds its heat to my nipple and I sigh, melting into him. Rough stubble teases my skin, a soft, scratchy sensation I never thought I'd love. But I thought a lot of things before Rex turned what I knew upside down.

More hands roam free, his fingers stroking my hips. I arc upwards, inviting him to touch me there again. To enter me.

He does just that, and in no time has me focused on nothing but how amazing it feels.

Oh. Dear. God.

I've lost my grip on earth. The bedspread bunches in my hands as he starts teasing my clit like before. That burn is relentless, intense and all consuming, and I spread my legs wider, giving him all the room in the world to continue. He sucks my other nipple, growling into my flesh, teasing fresh blazing fire through me, this time with his teeth.

Mercy. I'm throbbing in places I've never imagined.

"More, Cupcake?" he says, lifting his head, a glimmer in his eye that says, *beg.*

"Please!" It comes out shamelessly. I'm too addicted to his touch, his lips, to be dragged down by anything.

Narrowing his eyes, he kisses me harder, running his fingers tight through my hair. Then he leaves a trail of kisses down my stomach as he slips down the bed, down the sheets, down my body to – *oh, no.* "Easy, woman. You like what I just did, you'll fucking *love* this. Bite your hand if you need to scream."

Shit, he's right. We can't wake the boys.

My wrist hovers over my lips as I watch his gorgeous face sink between my legs, move to my core, and –

His tongue engulfs me. Tongue and lips and holy hell, heat!

He sucks and licks my pussy open, and I feel my clit swell like never before. It's a pulsing trigger for the fire igniting in my veins. The fire that may well kill me, but I can't bring myself to care. How can I give a crap what's right or wrong or deadly when it feels so good?

My hips rise off the bed. I spread my trembling legs

wider, giving him access to every part of me. He grabs my butt and holds me tight against him as his tongue slips in and out of me several times and then adds more teasing licks to my clit.

Circles. Swirls. Driving me half-insane.

I bite down on my hand gently. And then not so gently.

I'm making noises I never knew I could make, heart beating out of my chest, overwhelmed in the very best ways. Pleasure builds, warning and relentless. I curl my toes and clutch the bedspread tighter.

"Rex," I finally gasp. "I'm not sure – I –"

He stops long enough to quickly say, "Go, Cupcake. Come for me."

His finger slips in while he tongues my clit again. Muscles inside me clench, flutter, promise an explosion, lost in several more long, glorious licks.

"Come the fuck on," he urges, lifting his head for just a second. "There's always round two. Only gets better from here, darling."

Better? Round two?

He's sucking again, and this time, I know he won't let up until I let go. The idea of round two sends my virgin brain to the brink, the edge, the end and the beginning.

Holyyy shit. Coming!

I shove my wrist into my mouth to keep from shouting, sinking my teeth in as my back arches completely off the bed. Something explodes. Many somethings.

There's no way to describe it. It's like fireworks erupting inside me, soaring to every nerve where they kiss and spark and go nova, bathing me in sugar.

Forget the words. I can't even remember my own name. The pleasure waves intensify.

One long convulsion wracks my whole body. The O lasts forever, hurling me ever higher into bliss, and just when I think I'm about to pass out, it eases its grip, lets me fall back to the mortal realm, back to him.

I flop against the pillow as my body shudders, releasing the last bits of an O so fucking amazing I'm in shock. It doesn't even exist in the same universe as the messy, repressed quickies I've given myself over the years after long work days.

Nothing could have ever prepared me for that. Nothing describes it. And nothing compares.

I just know I already want *more*.

My lungs work overtime, desperately replenishing air and oxygen. I'm drained. Can't even lift an arm. "Holy hell," I whine.

"That good?" Amusement flicks in his blue eyes. Like he doesn't know.

It takes all my effort to lift my head enough to stare at him, still crouched between my spread, bent legs. "Do I have to answer?" I let out another sigh and drop my head back on the pillow, dragging my arms over my face.

Rex chuckles sweetly and gives my pussy a parting lick before climbing up beside me. "It'll be even better next time, Cupcake."

"Better?" I shake my head. "I don't know. That one almost killed me."

"Wrong, darling." He kisses the tip of one of my nipples. "It made you come alive."

I smile. He might be right because just that little movement, him kissing my nipple, has a ripple renewing itself inside me.

It's impossible but it's happening. I thought I was spent. That there was nothing left, but of course, there always is.

After another kiss, he climbs off the bed. I'm still fried, but excitement has me licking my lips as he unbuttons his shirt. My pussy heats, wetness oozing out as I watch him undress.

It's the same chiseled body I'd seen in the pool room, but never so close.

Hard. Bristled. Dark bursts of roses, eagles, and wild beasts inked all over him.

Blue flowers with thorns that almost match the midnight shade of his eyes.

A work of raw masculine force. A storm in a human body, trying to break free.

Rex looks me dead in the eye, hooking his hands in his waistband. When the boxers come down, I can't look away to save my life.

His cock stands tall, rigid, and of course it's fucking huge. I *expected* it to be, but seeing it in the living, pulsing flesh sends my heart into my throat.

Okay, no. Whatever I imagined, this is bigger.

Almost scary big. But I still can't wait to touch.

Disappointment washes over me when he bends over and I lose sight of it. I scramble to the edge of the bed, eyes searching.

He laughs. "Easy. I'm just getting a rubber. Guessing you don't have any?"

"No, sorry." The crinkle of the condom's wrapper reminds me *this is really happening.*

"Quit saying sorry." He tosses a small package on the bed. "Here we go."

"Only one?"

His laugh is as amazing as the rest of him. "Had like five in my emergency stash. I'll pick up more this week."

Oh, yes, he will. Because I have a feeling I've just found something I could get addicted to very quickly.

"Do the honors, Cupcake," he says, ripping the foil with his teeth, grabbing my hand and putting the small rubbery thing in my palm.

"I'll try," I answer, suddenly a little nervous. I flip my legs over the edge of the bed. He's now standing between them like I was his earlier, and an idea hits me. I set the package aside and wrap one hand around his cock.

It's hard, yet almost velvety, and the way he sucks in air when I hold it is encouraging. I lean forward, licking the tip. His taste is earthy, all man, all powerful. I lick again. And again. Then open my mouth wide, taking him inside like I've only seen in X-rated movies.

He lets out a low groan. "Cupcake, fuck!"

"Mmmm-hmmm," I purr, sucking him deeper. My tongue trails the ridge of his cock, focusing on the crown, the soft underside that makes his huge body twitch.

I feel his body vibrating as he leans closer. Hoping it feels as good for him as it does for me, as everything he just did, I suck harder.

He pumps forward again, and then draws back slightly. I love this to my soul.

Heat pools inside me, another climax creeping closer, begging to come out. I know it, I love it, and I'm hooked.

As much as I love sucking on him.

After a few more pumps, he grasps my head. "Cupcake," he breathes again.

"Hmm?"

He steps back, withdrawing his cock all the way out of my mouth. "Tonight's for you," he says. "We'll save that for another time. I need that pussy."

I'm not disappointed. How can I be? I glance up at him and smile.

I feel for the condom, get ready to roll the rubber on his cock, but plant a kiss on the end first.

He growls. "Careful. You're driving me to the edge and I still need to fuck you over it."

"Join the club," I say.

"Put that fucking thing on," he snaps.

His whisper is so gruff I laugh. "So you can fuck me?" I whisper, cheeks heating, rolling the rubber slowly over his cock.

"Yeah, darling, yeah."

He grabs me under the arms and tosses me backwards, onto the bed. It's dangerously easy for him to bend me around however he likes.

Smiling, I spread my legs, opening my arms. "Show me how it's done."

He climbs onto the bed. "I'll show you lots of things, Cupcake."

And he does.

Using one hand, he guides his cock into me. It feels so good, so sudden, so – I gasp.

A sharp sting stiffens my body. A faint sensation of something ripping.

"Darling, relax," he orders. "It'll only hurt for a minute, promise."

The virgin sting fades the more we settle in. I let the air out that was caught in my lungs. The concern on his face is so tender, so sweet. I smile and nod. "Okay. Ready."

He glides the rest of the way in, leaning down, barely kissing me, but more just sharing the air we breathe. There's something intimate about that, breathing together. The smile on my face grows as he starts moving, in and out, but not all the way. His thrusts are slow and steady and the momentum builds something inside me.

A natural instinct has me moving with him, increasing the pleasure and the indescribable, fascinating pressure inside me. It's like watching a cake rising in the oven. Or maybe it's more like inflating a balloon. Knowing if you keep going it'll explode, and that's exactly what *will* happen here, to both of us.

I wrap my arms and legs around him, match his heated kisses, twirling his tongue with my own.

We move faster, the heat between us turning hotter, the pressure becomes all consuming. I throw my hips into his, biting his bottom lip, begging him to fuck me harder, faster, however he wants.

I want this man to break down, let go, and come. I want him uninhibited.

It's all I can think about, pumping against him harder, nails digging at his back. He gives me exactly what my body asks for, his thrusts quickening.

His cock slams deeper, rattling my bones, a fierce, delicious friction every time his pubic bone mashes my clit. He grinds there a second longer than I think he should, until I moan, whimper, look him in the eye.

Then, when his hand slides into my hair, catching it in

a fist and holding me down, the pleasure doubles, and I can't see anything at all.

Ecstasy-vision is white hot. Blinding. My eyelids fly open and I pull my mouth off his as I peak, muscles I never knew I had fused to the fireball in my belly.

My body goes stiff, wracked with pleasure, convulsing, and he gives a final thrust. The imaginary balloon snaps in a thousand tiny bits, pleasure confetti sparking through both of us.

"Yes, yes, amazing!" I whimper, but it's hardly enough.

Amazing, amazing.

His body goes rock hard, swells, and his hips reach frantic, a guttural cry pouring out his throat. I hold on tighter, keep my hips pressed against his, aftershocks ripping through me.

They quicken again when his fist pulls my hair, his lips engulf mine, and his face scrunches. He doesn't have to say it to know.

I feel his cock bulging. Feel his muscles go rigid, feeding their energy into his ass, which throbs against my ankles every time his balls pulse fire.

He's coming, fucking another O into me, and our heat collides.

It's forever before it ends, soft and slow, sending us gently off our highs. I sink deep into the mattress as he softens finally. Rex lowers himself on top of me. His weight isn't heavy. More like a comforting blanket.

I kiss his shoulder and a sigh empties my lungs.

He kisses the tip of my nose. "Now, that, was fucking amazing. For real."

"Maybe you're just a good teacher."

"Nah, Cupcake, I had a damn good student."

I'm starting to think he's learned to make me smile almost as easily as he makes me come. More content than I've ever been, I wiggle slightly, still enjoying the feel of him inside me. "So, teacher, is there a third lesson tonight?"

"Third, fourth, and fifth." He brings his lips to mine for another long, slow kiss. "Only price is sleep, Cupcake."

Sounds fair. Heck, I think I'll trade the whole night if the next few times are even half as good as this.

* * *

I'M TRYING, but I can't pull my eyes open. Yet, something tells me I have to.

I finally yank them open and glance around. A smile tugs at my lips as I see Rex, his glorious body stark naked. I should be embarrassed after all the things we did last night.

But I'm not. I'm anxious to do them all again. I'm anxious for him to go buy a box of condoms. Or two. We've spent everything he had, and spent them gloriously.

There's a sound. I sit up, listening intently, trying to make it out.

Then my heart stops and leaps into my throat.

"Crap!"

I jump out of bed.

"What –" Rex stops as his eyes meets mine.

He hears it, too. The pounding on the front door. It's loud, incessant, the kind that won't go away.

"Stay here! Let me." I grab my bathrobe off the hook on the open bathroom door and run for the bedroom door.

My feet slide to a stop as I enter the living room. I'm too late.

Adam and Chase are there. The cabin door is open. Gramps is standing in the doorway.

I'm dead.

Gramps levels a glare like I've never seen before, the lines in his face sharpening like pitchforks.

"So, I was right all along," he growls.

I simply shake my head at him, not willing to argue in front of the boys. They're probably nervous enough by this screwed up, surreal scene.

Gramps turns around and walks away.

My stomach sinks clear to my toes.

"What's wrong, Tabby?"

"Didn't...didn't you want us to get the door?"

"Nothing's wrong," I say to the boys. "You didn't do anything wrong."

"I did."

I spin around and shake my head at Rex. "No way. You didn't do wrong either."

He walks out of the bedroom, shrugging into his shirt. "I'll go talk to him."

"No." I grab his arm. "No, I'll talk to him. I can handle him. Smooth this over. Make sure he doesn't –"

I don't want to even say it. There's so much at risk if Gramps decides to be a royal bastard. He could fire Rex on the spot and send him packing, ban him from the lodge. And there's nothing I could do.

"You shouldn't handle this alone," Rex says, frowning. "It's more than half my fault. Hell, almost all of it."

I wish he'd stop. I don't want our wonderful night overshadowed with this, so I kiss his cheek, trying to pretend it's no big deal. In fact, it couldn't be bigger. "I'm used to it. Really, Rex, don't worry. Please, don't talk to him. Let me. I know how to talk him down."

There's skepticism in his eyes, but he nods and kisses my forehead. Then he turns to the boys. "Get your boots and coats on."

I tighten the hold I still have on his arm. "I have to get dressed, but I'll see you later."

He nods, suddenly silent, but he stops to kiss my forehead again.

It's not until I'm in the shower, later, that I realize how different the second kiss felt. *Stop imagining things,* I tell myself.

It's nerves. Ridiculous, overtaxed nerves.

I shake the foolish worries off and step out of the shower to get dressed. I blew my hair dry enough that I won't have to worry about pneumonia outside, pulling it into a ponytail. Then I grab my coat and head for the lodge.

I take a moment to catch several deep breaths outside, collecting my thoughts before walking into the kitchen. For all I know, Gramps might be back here.

And so what? I'll stand my ground, wherever he is.

"Good morning," Marcy says as the door swings shut.

"Morning." I glance around the empty room. "Where is he?"

She continues to load the dishwasher. "Doing exactly what I told him to."

"And what is that?"

"Shopping."

"Shopping?" I repeat, confused. "He never goes shopping."

"About time he learns, isn't it?"

I shake my head. "Some things, I don't think he'll ever learn."

"Ever come to grips with the idea that you need your own life? Rather than worrying what that old man's thinking?"

"Yes." Funny timing.

Marcy doesn't have a clue what just happened. I think. But the truth in her words couldn't be clearer.

"He'll have to when there isn't another choice, but that's up to you," she says.

I sigh, absorbing her wisdom, but not knowing what to do about it. A ding – the signal from the sensor that tells us when someone walks into the dining room – tells me I don't have time to ponder logistics right now. More, the sound makes my heart skip a beat, thinking it might be Rex and the boys.

It's not. The older couple is as pleasant as they were last night, going on about how much they'd enjoyed staying here, how much they liked the food, and how they regret leaving today. I thank them sincerely and take their breakfast order.

That sets the morning's pace. They leave, another guest checks in.

This time, it's a journalist with an eight-year-old son. Late twenties or early thirties. Dark eyes and darker hair. Tall. I don't really care. He's very talkative.

The man goes on and on about how much he's heard about the lodge, and apparently, he's interested in writing a history piece on it for some newspaper near Detroit. Weird.

I try to listen to his spiel, eyeing the clock every so

often because it's already after noon. I haven't had a chance to go get the boys from Rex yet. Haven't seen them at all, actually.

Marcy said Gramps fed the horses before he left, which is probably how he knew Rex wasn't out there. Naturally, we'd overslept by a few hours. If I hadn't forgotten to set the damn wake up alarm on my phone...

Finally, the new guest, Alan something or other, stops talking, sensing my disinterest. I promise him an interview with Gramps sometime later, maybe Marcy, too. Him and his son head upstairs, and I hurry down the hall for my coat.

I hadn't realized how nice it is outside today, smiling at the sunshine, until I open the barn door. It's empty. The tools are put away like Rex hasn't been here since cleaning up last night.

I stop, frown, shake my head. Something's wrong.

So wrong.

My heart skips another beat and I run for the lodge, scanning the parking lot along the way. No old pickup, either. His truck is gone.

Now, I'm scared. What the *hell* is happening?

I'm breathing hard, dragon smoke curling from my lips in chill puffs, nerves shaking every limb by the time I barge back in, run up to the second floor, and pound at his room's door.

Nobody answers 205. It's unlocked. Throwing open the door, I practically rip the safety stopper off the wall.

Empty.

No duffel bags.

Nothing except an envelope on the table.

With my name on the front.

I don't want to read it.

But I rip it open.

Cash falls out, wrapped in a slip of paper with few words.

He's left without a goodbye.

A heavy wave washes over me.

That's why our last kiss felt different. It *was* our farewell.

X: SOME WAY OUT (REX)

"Yuck, daddy. This doesn't taste very good," Chase says.

He's right. It tastes like shit. I'm right, too. There can't be a bigger fucking fool than me in this entire universe. "I know. Eat what you can."

The diner is small, and I'd bet the health department doesn't even know it exists, but the boys were hungry. My fault. I'd dragged them out of the lodge as soon as they had their bags packed. Right after I'd written that note to Tabby.

Fucking bastard. That's what I am. Leaving her a *Dear Jenny* like that. Or whatever the fuck the male equivalent of a *Dear John* letter is. If two vile words can be called any kind of letter at all.

Just thinking of the words I'd scratched turns my stomach worse than this crappy food.

"Already ate what I can, Daddy," Adam says, pushing his plate away from him. After a long sigh, he adds, "Miss Tabby's cupcakes."

The truth hurts like a B. I wish I had Cupcake, too.

She was...I shake my head. There's no way to describe her. She's too unique. Too remarkable. Too beautiful. Too kind. Too good for the likes of me.

I'd taken everything from her last night and I hadn't left her with more than numb chicken scratch.

Fuck.

But what the hell else could I do? Stay in the lodge, screw up her life with Morris, and keep them in real danger? None of us need drama.

When there are wolves on the prowl, drama is a distraction, and distractions can be fatal.

Reaching in my back pocket, I pull out my billfold and fish out a couple worn bills to pay for the meal none of us was able to eat. "Let's go."

The boys beat me to the door. Once they're strapped into the car seats that take up most of the interior, I start the truck.

"Are we going back to Tabby's now?" Adam asks. "I'm tired."

"No. Sorry."

"I like it there," Chase says. "Why can't we, Daddy?"

I don't answer. They're making this hard. Maybe it's what I deserve.

"Me, too," Adam says. "And I like Tabby, too."

Me, three.

Swallowing a sigh, I shift into drive and pull out of the parking lot.

We could head for the border, but our identities would be recorded. I'm sure the Syndicate has money to grease anybody manning the crossings. I can't risk it.

I drive on, further down the highway, pass into Split

Harbor, no fucking clue where the hell we're actually going.

If only there was someone I could contact. Someone I could trust. Fuck, and I never *did* write that note giving Tabby the right to the boys if something wicked happens to me. She's the only person I can trust with them. Will trust with them.

And now she's gone.

"I'm still hungry, daddy." Chase rubs his stomach. "Don't feel good, maybe. Oh, daddy, I think I've gotta –"

Shit! I know my boys, and this one's about to throw up.

I hit the blinker and spin the truck around, pulling into the gas station on the edge of town where I'd seen the bikers. I scramble, getting the boys out of their seats and usher them inside, straight to the bathrooms along the back wall.

No one throws up, thank God. But Adam keeps wiping his lips with his sleeve.

"Every time I burp my mouth tastes funny. Icky."

"Me, too," Chase says.

They aren't kidding about the indigestion. I'd ordered all three of us the chili, mainly because the boys had liked the bowls we'd eaten at the lodge. It was really good. Hell, everything was decent, if not awesome. What we'd just attempted to eat, not even close.

"Come on," I say. "There's a little deli here. We'll get something else in your stomachs."

Adam covers another burp. "Not chili. Please."

"No chili," I agree.

I convince them to try the chicken noodle soup, and let them each pick out something else. Not surprisingly, they choose a twin pack of cheap mass produced cupcakes. I don't have the heart to tell them the cupcakes aren't as good as they look. Nothing like hers.

There's a man dressed in army fatigues ahead of us in the checkout line. A soldier in familiar desert camo, which I haven't worn for the better part of the last decade. His outfit kicks up memories, easier times before my life was shot to hell. Finding life easier in a war zone says a lot.

The more I stare at his boots, how his pants are tucked into them, a smile tugs at my lips. Knox, an army buddy, hated that rule. Tucking things in all clean for review. Said it made us look like mannikins, not fighters.

Knox.

Shit.

Knox! Why hadn't I thought of him till now?

"Wait here," I tell the boys before spinning around. Back by the cupcakes, I find what I'm looking for. Stationary supplies. I grab a small notebook, box of envelopes, and pack of pens.

Back at the check-out, I recognize the clerk. Damn, it feels like ages ago. The boys have already set their snacks on the counter "Is it all right if we eat this here?" I assumed it was, but the set up seems odd since you have to pay for it all first.

"Of course, that's what the booths are for." She smiles at the boys. "If they need seconds on the soup, go ahead and fill up their bowls again. These little Styrofoam things don't hold much."

"Thanks, will do."

We settle into a booth. The boys don't seem to mind the soup at all. Or the dozen tiny packages of crackers they'd scooped up. While they eat, and in between opening crackers myself, I write a letter to Knox and stuff it in an envelope. The boys had just opened their cupcakes and they're excited to see sugary white frosting stuff in the center.

"I'll be right back," I say, scooting out of the booth, keeping them in sight. "Stay here."

At the checkout counter, I ask the clerk, "Where's the post office here?"

"That'd be the corner of Eight and Crescent, but Davey's next door. Saw him pull in a minute ago."

My frown must have explained my confusion as to who Davey is.

She laughs. "Davey's our mailman. He'll be in any minute. Eats lunch here a couple times a week." She smiles and nods towards the boys. "Chicken noodle is Davey's favorite, too."

I nod. "Thanks, but I have to buy stamps."

"Hold on, I have a couple in my purse you can have. Sharing is caring. That's how we work it in Split Harbor." She plants a huge bag on the counter. "Hang on, just let me find them."

"That's okay. I've got an address to Google." Hearing how suspicious that sounds, I add, "It's an old friend. I don't have his address memorized."

"Well, we've got free Wi-Fi. Here's your stamps." She peels a couple off and hands them to me.

Feeling inclined, I take them, and dig a couple of quarters out of my pocket.

"No, I don't want any money. It's just stamps. Better get moving so you can give the letter to Davey."

I nod, but the tablet is in the truck.

"Forgot your phone? Need to use mine?"

She sure is accommodating. I try not to think of Tabby, wonder if this small town attitude is part of what made her who she is.

"Mine's in the truck," I say. It's the cheap burner I bought last week and haven't switched on since it was activated. It's good for texting, pay-per-minute calls, basic internet, and nothing else.

"Go get it. I'll keep an eye on your boys."

I glance at them and then my truck.

"Go on!" she says. "I had six kids. Got seven grandkids and three more on the way."

It's always hard to walk away. I don't want them out of my sight.

There's also no way hair that yellow is natural, and fingernails that long have to get in the way, but she seems sincere. "I'll be right back," I say, taking the opportunity to make it fast.

I'm out and back inside, with the tablet in hand, in no time. "Thanks."

"No problem," she replies.

Back at the booth, I Google Knox's full name in Phoenix, Arizona. He's been there for years, made his way up in the world, the diamond trade that made his family rich. He's running a billion dollar company these days and he owns a goddamn mansion. It takes me a few minutes to find it, and then cross check the country property records with a Facebook account.

Time running short, I scratch out a brief note and quickly address the envelope. A moment later, a mailman appears next to our table.

"Shirley says you have a letter to mail?"

I eye him up and down, looking for a way to tell if he's

legit or not. His once red hair is streaked with gray and his green eyes are lined with the kind of wrinkles that come from smiling a lot. He also has on a uniform and he's carrying a U.S. mail bag.

He opens a flap. "Right in here. That's the outgoing pocket."

There are several other letters in the pouch, so I drop in the letter to Knox. "Thanks." It's like something from the seventies, but time moves slower in this town.

"No problem." He grins at the boys. "Did you like the soup?"

They both nod.

"Me, too." He leans closer to me. "Hey, pal, quick tip: don't ever let them eat across the street at The Ladle." With a wink he adds, "Stray cats don't dig in their trash. If you know what I mean."

I nod, wishing I'd known that an hour ago. As we walk out, I thank both Davey the mailman and Shirley the clerk again, and hope like hell Knox will help me out of this mess. Army bonds run deep, but we haven't kept in touch like we should. The shit with Nelia, the boys, Knox and his little girl...

Of course, I mentioned my kids. He's just like me, a single dad up till recently. I saw on Facebook he's gotten married, same chick he used to drone on about late nights overseas many years ago, a girl he called Sunflower. She's older, but just as pretty, her smile too damn bright and beautiful and too much like Tabby's.

The boys climb into their car seats and I make sure they're buckled tight before walking around to the driver's door. With every step, I wonder where we should go now. The lodge had been perfect.

Unknown.

Hidden.

And Tabby's there.

The very reason I can't return. The Syndicate is on my trail. Looking for me. Hunting.

They don't give a rat's ass that Nelia's dead, but they *do* care that they no longer have a pigeon to launder the money they make off the heroin they line the streets with. Plus they care a whole hell of a lot that I killed their own flesh and blood.

Bastards make a lot more money than I ever laundered altogether, so I was only one among many for them to feed on, but Aiden's also dead. They blame me. They will avenge him.

They'd like nothing more than to knock me off, and don't care who they have to kill in the process.

The twins, Tabby, her friends and family at the lodge...fuck. If only I hadn't been thinking with my dick last night. If I hadn't let that old man find me and her together this morning, hadn't screwed her life almost as bad as mine...

I couldn't stay and just cause drama. Hell, it might've poisoned the atmosphere there so bad we'd all be blind to any intruders. Any danger. And even though I've never been a hunted man before, I know any mistakes in this situation are lethal.

Shitfire. I should have killed Aiden's bodyguard when I had the chance. If I hadn't let the puke live, hadn't let him see my face...shoulda, coulda, woulda is an infectious, toxic thing. Besides, I knew even then they'd be after me, whether he was dead or alive, and I'm not a cold blooded killer.

Punching back, shooting in self-defense is one thing. Obliterating an injured man is a bridge too far.

I climb in and start the engine.

"Are we going home now?" Chase asks.

I shift the truck into reverse. "No." We may never go home again. Don't really have one anymore. I'm sure the Syndicate already ransacked our old house outside the city. Probably burned it to the ground, along with my shop. I miss that shop like hell, had it attached to the garage, full of old tools from my grandfather. It'd seen better days for business use, but damn, it got my mind off bad shit. Let me tinker. Helped me escape.

"But...but I wanna see if Tabby can put that white stuff in cupcakes," Adam says.

"Me, too!" Chase says. "That was good. Tabby'd do better."

It dawns on me then that they're not talking about Chicago. Home to them *is* the lodge.

Christ. I can see why. Even though we'd only been there a few weeks, we'd all enjoyed our time. Especially last night.

My cock swells just thinking about her. Being in her bed. Taking a shower with her before we both crashed, happy and spent and grinning ear-to-ear.

"Tabby can make it like that can't she, Daddy?"

Adam's still talking about cupcakes, but my mind is on all the other things Cupcake can do. "Probably," I grunt reluctantly.

"So can we go home? Daddy please?" Chase's little eyes are pleading.

"To Tabby's cabin?" Adam adds. "We like it there."

"Me, too."

I hit the blinker switch and pull into the parking lot of a big box store. I really shouldn't.

It's not very big, more like the smallest big box store in America, but it'll work. I have to conserve money, I tell myself. Buying snacks for the boys to eat will be cheaper than eating in restaurants, at least until I can figure out what to do next. That much is true, but the bigger truth is I'm dragging my fucking feet no thanks to them, leaving this place.

The boys let out hefty sighs, but don't complain when I shut off the truck. They barely say a word as we walk into the store and I grab a cart. I head towards the grocery aisles. With the boys following, I wander up and down the lanes. After eating the wholesome, good food at the lodge for so long, nothing looks the least bit appetizing. For us, it's all instant crap, granola bars and beef jerky, stuff that'll stay good on the road while we're moving.

They spy a box of cupcakes like the ones they'd eaten at the gas station, and I agree they can each get a pack. I'm sure Tabby could make some vastly tastier than those. There isn't much she can't do.

While walking past shelves of laundry soap, I let out a heavy sigh. She'd even done that. Washed all of our clothes. Regularly. They came back clean and folded, left outside our door, part of the lodge's laundry service for guests who stayed more than a few days.

And I'd walked out on her. No explanation. Barely any words.

Maybe I deserve this hell. But Chase and Adam damn sure don't. No pride or screwed up sense of justice means they ought to pay for their father's sins.

"Are we almost done, Daddy?"

Adam clings to the side of the cart, riding it, looking bored as a kid can be. Chase is on the other side, his face the same glum mask, and not just because they're twins.

"Yeah, we're done," I say.

We have to walk past the pharmacy on the way to the checkout lanes, and that too makes me think of Cupcake and the handful of condoms we'd blown through.

It also makes me think of never seeing her again.

Shit, I *will* have to talk to her. Sooner or later. She deserves that much.

There's another reason, too, one that punches me square in the guts. If Knox gets my note and decides to help, how the fuck can he if he doesn't know where to reach me? Not knowing where we're going, I'd asked Knox to send his response to the lodge. Just wrote it down, barely even thinking, along with my new burner number. But my options are a lot more limited with any phone.

If he can't call, or I can't answer, and he sends a letter to the goddamn lodge and I'm not there – kill me.

I suppress the urge to smash my fist through the wall. I can't scare the boys.

This fucking mess I'm in just gets harder and harder. Every little move I make increases the risk of slipping up, somehow leading the Syndicate to me. To us.

Running, being on the lam, is hell.

But I keep doing it.

Running.

Now, I'm not only feeling the Syndicate, I'm running from Tabby, and she sure as hell doesn't deserve it.

Fuck this.

Grabbing a box off a shelf, I toss it into the cart, and head for checkout.

Less than five minutes later, once again buckled in their car seats, the boys look at each other and sigh.

"Where are we going now?" Chase already sounds like he doesn't want to hear my answer.

I've already put her in danger. Too much danger. But she deserves an explanation. And maybe if I get down and beg, she'll help us, help me, one last time.

I start the truck. "Home."

* * *

THE AFTERNOON SUN hides behind the gray clouds moving in and huge wet snowflakes fall as I pull the truck into the lodge's parking. Winter's back like the bitch it is.

This may be the second biggest mistake of my life, but I hope not.

Hope like hell it's not.

I need Tabby to get myself out of this mess as much as I need Knox. And I want her. Want her as bad as I did last night. More now that I've had a taste of how incredible she is. I'll just have to play it cool. Not let her know how much I need her.

In more ways than one.

The boys climb out at the same time I do. Amazing how they barely need help getting out this time. The smiles on their faces explain why. They're home. At least, that's how it feels to them. I wish it was true, for all our sakes.

I'd risked a lot in order to keep my sons, and would do

it all over again. No question. Even without knowing how it'll all turn out.

Each carries a bag containing their box of cupcakes, they run for the front door of the lodge. I catch up with them by the steps. "Slow down."

Sad grimaces flash on their faces.

"Stomp the snow off your boots," I tell them while opening the door. "Be courteous."

Morris is at the front desk, glaring while we walk through the doorway. "I thought you'd left." It's not even a question in his tone.

"We had to go shopping," Adam says, holding up his bag.

Despite his grumpiness, the boys had taken a liking to Morris and weren't affected by his glare or sharp words.

He appeared even more disgusted while saying, "Tabby told me that."

Confused, I ask, "She told you we went shopping?"

He eyes me up and down before nodding. "Right after I said you'd ran out on her. Told her you'd left her high and dry."

I have no idea why she'd have told him that, bucked the obvious truth, and though I know she'd asked me not to, I nod towards his office. "Can we talk?"

He shakes his head, but walks into his office.

"Wait right here," I tell the boys, pointing towards the bench along the wall.

They climb onto the bench, and I warn, "Don't move." Then I enter the office, closing the door.

Not giving Morris a chance to start in, I say, "Look, I'm not going to apologize for what happened between us.

We slept together. I'm not sorry. I can't even say it was a mistake. It wasn't. It was something we both wanted."

He's dead silent, but he's listening. "I *will* say I don't know where it's going, whatever it is. It's too soon for that. I'm a single dad, and though I love my sons, they could be considered as baggage to some. To me, they're baggage I'll proudly, gladly carry for the rest of my life. Think Tabby understands that, but I believe it's only fair she also understands what it means. She deserves a chance to think this over, without anybody else adding their two red cents."

Morris' expression hasn't changed in any shape or form. He's still scowling.

I ignore the desire to huff out a sigh. Tabby definitely comes by her grit naturally. "You and I have an agreement. I want to finish the stable. I still want to uphold my end of the agreement and hope you will yours."

"I *told you* in the beginning, my granddaughter wasn't part of that agreement," he barks. "Consider it void! You left your keys here. You checked out. You're done, bucko."

I grit my teeth. He hadn't exactly warned me and I hadn't really checked out with anyone at the front desk, but I can't deny what's written between the lines. "I didn't terminate the job, Morris. We signed a contract, remember? Right here in this office with the terms of my pay. As for the rest, I hope you'll let Tabby and I work it out."

He slumps back in his chair and crosses his arms, looking like the world's maddest toad. "Welp, it doesn't matter much what the hell I say, you're gonna do whatever you want, just like everyone else around here." Waving a hand, he says, "Get out. I've got work to do, and so do you."

I nod, taking what little I can get from winning this little battle. I leave the office.

"Can we go see Tabby now?" Chase asks.

"She's at her house," Adam says excitedly.

"How do you know that?"

"Marcy told us!" they say together.

My own excitement at seeing Cupcake is close to theirs. Hell, stronger, but I hide it well. "Let's go."

They run down the hall. I'm on their heels as we cross the property, open the door so they can shoot out. They fly around the back toward her place, leaving me several steps behind.

"Tabby, Tabby!" they shout.

She's shoveling the walkway in front of her cabin. It's too far to see if she's smiling, but that doesn't change my reaction. The heat of anticipation hits my blood. Hasn't even been a full day, but I've missed her in ways I've never missed anyone.

The boys run towards her. I take my sweet time. The sight of her bending down to greet them, hug them, pecking two quick kisses at their cheeks, warms me to my soul.

She stands up and a second later. Something unexpected flies my way. A snowball.

I duck, then have to swivel the other way as a second flies towards me. I'm laughing, shaking my head, until I see her face. She's pissed.

Royally, undeniably pissed.

In the time it takes me to figure that out, she hurls another snowball. This time, I don't dodge quick enough, and it pelts the side of my face.

I grab a handful of snow and pack it tight. The boys

have joined in the fun. All three of them throw snowballs my way. Theirs don't make it all the way to me, but hers zing past my head like bullets.

The fight is on. I zig-zag, avoiding snowballs while firing back. She's using a tree as a shield, blocking my ammo. Hers are well-aimed. I get hit several times in my face, working my way to the tree. Who the hell knew the woman was a sniper, too?

Once I'm close enough to grab her, I pitch my last snowball and then dive around the tree while she's not looking.

She squeals as I catch her around the hips, dragging her to the ground, flipping her onto her back. I crawl on top of her, pinning her legs down with mine, her arms with both hands.

Her cheeks are red, her eyes narrowed, and her lips pinched tight. Even spitting mad, she's adorable. Her beauty radiates straight to my blood, and fuck, I want my mouth on hers.

I lean down, fully prepared to taste the sweetness I never thought I'd have again.

But her snarl sends a shiver down my spine, as do her words.

"Get *off.* I swear to God I'll bite those lips if they touch mine."

XI: NO MORE SECRETS (TABBY)

I'm livid. Thoroughly blood-scalding mad. Not even the soft blue shimmer of his eyes can change it.

Not even the boys laughter or the passive-aggressive snowball game we'd just played.

He'd left. *Left.* And now he's back as if it was merely the shopping trip to town I'd told Gramps it had been. No, I wasn't prepared to listen to my grandfather tell me, 'I told you so.'

I had to save face. I'm also not ready to forgive Rex for what he's done, either.

He lets out a grunt as Adam, then Chase, jump on his back.

"Dog pile Daddy!" they shout, laughing.

His grin, which shouldn't affect me, but does, says he's used to this. To them jumping on him. I have to pinch my lips tighter together to keep from smiling.

Bastard or not, he's a good dad. The kind many, many kids never know. Only dream about.

Adam's face appears over one of Rex's shoulders, and Chase's the other.

"Fun snowball fight, Tabby," Adam says.

"You got him real good!" Chase laughs, nodding at his daddy.

I can no longer fight smiling. Not at those two adorable faces, which I'd missed terribly today.

But after I smile at both of them, I wrinkle my face, looking at Rex. "He deserved to be hit."

He plants a swift kiss on the end of my nose before saying, "True, I did." He sits up then, and guides the boys, one with each arm, as they slowly tumble off him and into the snow. He tickles them both. "You two throw snowballs like baseball players."

Giggling, they roll away and then jump to their feet.

He still has a hold of my arms, and pulls me to my feet while standing.

"You fire snowballs like a machine gun," he says, not letting me lose.

Inside, I'm fighting the urge to lean forward and kiss him. It's a battle. One I'm afraid I'll lose. But I can't. Won't. *"Ass-hole,"* I whisper slowly, elbowing him in the side.

"Oof. Guess I deserve that, too."

"Why'd you leave? Where'd you go?" I bite my tongue to keep a good dozen other questions from spewing out. He's so flipping gorgeous and flashes of last night crisscross my mind. One look, and I recall how amazing each and every part of him is.

"We went shopping."

I pull my arm out of his hold and head for the cabin. He's more than an asshole. Right now, he's a stupid fucking asshole. Who's now walking right beside me. Following.

Hissing, so the boys won't hear, I let it out crisp and clear, "Go to hell."

"Okay."

A lightning bolt couldn't have struck faster or been hotter than the jolt that shoots through me.

He bumps me with his shoulder.

I bump him back, hard.

He laughs.

"Stop. There's nothing funny about what you did, Rex," I say.

"Not why I'm laughing. I'm happy to be back."

I'm happy, too, but sure as hell am not going to admit it. No way.

The boys meet us on the porch, each holding a plastic shopping bag. They're too adorable to be mad at. Besides, they have no control over what their father does.

I open the door for them to walk inside. "What did you buy?"

"Cupcakes!" they both shout.

I pull off my gloves and headband. "Cupcakes?"

"Yes!"

Adam pulls a box out of his bag. "Can you make some with the white stuff in the middle like these?"

"Can you, Tabby? Stuffed-cupcakes?" Chase asks, slurring two words into one. "Don't like the brown stuff, it's not very good, but the white stuff's yum!"

Having recreated those commercial cupcakes many times, I say, "Yes, I can."

"Knew it!" they shout, bumping chests.

If only it was this easy to please everyone.

I hang up my coat before saying, "Tomorrow. But you can eat one of these right now." Normally I'd say if it was okay with their father, but right now, I don't have much respect. "There's milk in the fridge, too."

"Can we, Daddy?"

I should have known. They're simply too well-behaved.

"Sure," he answers. "And you can watch a movie, if that's okay with Tabby."

I nod at all three of them. Good. It'll give me time to bitch-out their father in private. He better *not* lie to me, either.

While he helps them get their coats and boots off, I go to the kitchen for the milk, pouring a couple glasses. By the time I return, he has them settled on the floor near the coffee table, a cartoon just starting to play on TV.

I set the milk down and open a cupcake package while he opens the other. As soon as the boys are set, I hiss, "The bedroom. Now."

"Your wish is my command, Cupcake," he says, smirking.

"It's *not* that kind of wish and you know it." It's a lie. Deep down, the part of me that isn't scorned totally owns that wish. But I can't let it rule me right now.

In the bedroom, I shut the door and grab the envelope off the dresser. "What the fuck is this?" I grab the money out and toss it at him.

"To pay for our lodging."

He's so fucking nonchalant I want to scream, but can't with the boys in the next room. "Your job remodeling the barn includes room and board. You knew it when you made the deal with Gramps. I'll ask you again: what is this?"

"I left instructions for the next person. Ideas, notes saying how to finish what I started."

I pull that sheet of paper out of the envelope. "Oh, I saw them, but that wasn't part of the deal." I throw that paper at him. "You're supposed to finish it!"

"I know."

I grab the last piece of paper out of the envelope. "And this?" I toss it at him. "Two words? Two fucking words?"

I'm sorry. That's all he'd written.

He shrugs.

"I'm not asking to become your ball and chain, but I deserve more than this! After last night..." I can't finish. I wave the envelope in his face and toss it on the floor, where everything that he's left inside spills out and scatters. "Do you have any idea how fucking freaked-out I was? I was ready to call the sheriff, see if those creeps after you finally caught up, maybe found you. I was scared, Rex. Terrified. I –" I can't do this.

I shake my head as my throat burns, plugging up and preventing me from going on. Images of him and the boys hurt, seriously hurt, haunted me all day. The hours he was gone were like an eternity in hell.

"Tabby, I'm sorry. So fucking sorry, but I'm fine. The boys are fine." He steps forward and grips my upper arms. "I don't know what else to say."

"How about the truth?" I say. "Why? Why did you leave?"

He shakes his head. "Hell, I don't know. I thought I had to. That it was the only way, but now…"

I wait. When he doesn't continue, I finally ask, "But now, what?"

"I realize how much I need you. Need your help, Cupcake."

He's serious. Deadly serious. Something inside me opens up. I can't turn him away no matter how big an asshole he's been. I step closer, folding, wrapping my arms around him. "I've said from the beginning I'll help you, Rex. You just have to *let* me."

His arms hold me, and I nearly melt inside. I now know why they call it falling in love, because that's exactly what happens.

It's like you're walking along, minding your own business, and then, *bam!* The floor drops out underneath your legs and you fall. Fall so hard and fast you don't realize what's happened until you crash to the bottom. By then it's too late. You're fucking in love.

I can't let him know that. He has enough going on, but I'm glad I realize that's what happened. And I'm glad he's back, so glad it leaves my heart in a savage knot.

Jesus. He's home. I'm thankful. Not to him, but whoever or whatever brought him back.

Gramps would've gloated for months, years, the least of my worries.

"This is the safest place for us, Cupcake. For the boys and me. It's hidden, off the beaten path. Just need a little time to get things straightened out. I've contacted someone to help me. A guy I was in the army with named Knox. I mailed him a letter today, asked him to send his response here. I mentioned your name. Did it without even thinking, fucking fool that I am, but I did."

It's hard not to smile. The idea that he's finally

including me, accepting the help I've offered all along, fills me with warmth. I nuzzle his neck with my nose, drawing in a deep breath, relishing how good he smells. "You can stay right here, in the cabin, with me. It'll make things easier."

He grasps my face with both hands and forces me to look up. "Darling, listen. Don't know how long –"

"Doesn't matter," I say. "However long it takes. I'm here."

His lips touch mine like gasoline spritzing fire. A wildfire that roars, screams, and soon consumes both of us.

Memories of the many acts we performed last night makes me all the more brazen. His hands are under my shirt, teasing my already tight nipples, and his mouth keeps mine busy.

We're still standing in the center of the room. I reach down, unbuttoning his jeans. The hardness of his cock sends a shiver of excitement through me. I push down his zipper, reach inside his underwear, and wrap my hand around his erection, excited how marvelously excited I make him.

He breaks the kiss in order to suck in a breath. I stroke his cock.

"Damn, Cupcake," he mumbles. "Shit. Missed you so much."

I love how husky he sounds and stroke harder.

"I went shopping, too," he says. "But didn't pick out cupcakes."

Using my other hand, I shove the front of his boxers down, so I can see his cock and give it and my hand more freedom. "You didn't?" I ask, licking his neck.

He groans. "I picked out a full box of condoms, darling."

Lightning hits my brain. I suck on the side of his neck. "We'll need them."

He grabs my wrist. "Stop. Need to bring them in."

There's urgency in his voice, a growl, branding a gentle madness into his blue eyes. I know why. I'm driving him to the brink like he did me last night. It's weirdly empowering. I shift my legs, already aching wet, giving his cock a long stroke before letting it go. The relief in his sigh makes me smile because he has no idea what I'm about to do.

He steps back to straighten his jeans, and I drop to my knees, grabbing his fullness and lifting it to my lips before he can stop me. I bring him in long and soft and slow, wrapping my lips around him.

"Cupcake!" he groans, but his hands are in my hair.

I'd learned a lot since last night. He likes to be the one in control, the one giving. It's his turn to take it. Hard.

I close my eyes, lost in the taste of him, the way his skin feels as it glides over my lips, in and out. *In and out.*

He shifts his hips. "Cupcake, fuck, I –"

"Need to relax," I whisper, licking the tip of his cock. "Relax, Rex." I take him completely in my mouth again, stroking the base.

He pumps forward. I suck harder and give a little moan to let him know how much I like it. How his cock feels filling my mouth full. I swirl my tongue around him, licking and sucking. Needing.

It's heavenly. I'm thoroughly turned on. Squeezing my thighs together, trying and failing to relieve the steady pulse in my core.

Then there's an abrupt knock on the door.

Nightmare flashbacks of Gramps from early this morning dart through my brain.

"Daddy?" A little voice on the other side.

Holding his cock in my mouth, I walk backwards on my knees until my heels hit the door, holding it shut tight.

He plants both hands against the door and grunts as I start sucking hard again.

"Daddy?"

"What?" he asks.

"Is Tabby in there?"

He holds his breath as I giggle slightly, still sucking his cock, a bit more leisurely now. Slowly, twirling my tongue around the tip between taking him fully in my mouth again. At last I stop, keeping him in suspense, wondering what's wrong.

"Yes," he says.

"Can we have another cupcake? Ask her?"

I nod, my eyes fixed on his angry, interrupted hard-on. He tries not to laugh.

"Yes," he growls. "One more. Don't ruin your supper."

"Hey, why do you sound funny?"

I don't know if Adam or Chase asked the question, but I'm waiting to hear his answer.

"I'm...I'm blowing my nose, son. I had to sneeze," he growls. "Go eat your cupcakes! Find a movie like Tabby showed you. We'll be done talking soon."

"Okay!"

That was definitely two voices at once, and I smile up at him.

He grabs my head and thrusts his hips forward and then back quickly. My mouth returns to his cock, hungrier than before. I'm more than happy to comply. His eyes close and I see the strain on his face, in his neck.

His breathing comes short and quick. So does mine. The pleasure I'm giving him takes me closer and closer to my own climax. I have my thighs tight together. Know I'll peak soon. I suck harder, faster, as much for my pleasure as his, and when he plunges deep into my mouth, my own dam breaks.

The boys have already found a movie, I hear it through the wall, cartoon lasers and heroes taunting villains.

Perfect timing.

I suck his dick harder, taking everything he's giving, faster. My hand reaches up, presses into his balls. Rex snarls as he leans into the wall, fisting my hair, steeling himself for –

Oh, hell.

His seed rushes into my mouth. Hot and thick and potent. I struggle to keep up with the flood. My mouth quickens, up and down, back and forth, sucking him fully off while his head snaps back, facing the ceiling, contorted.

His cock twitches, explodes, sends fiery jets in my mouth. I swallow them down and try to keep going, briefly wondering how much more there'd be if we hadn't fucked so much last night. What's here...it's plenty. Then I think how it'd feel inside me, shooting in my womb, thick and burning hot.

I close my eyes, moaning into his balls, sucking until he finally slumps slightly. Both his hands are planted against the door as I release his cock. He gently falls on his knees, wrapping both arms around me.

"Fuck, Cupcake. You're good. Damn good. Never felt anything like it before."

I smile, proud and content. "Then you'll remember what happened here today if you ever want more."

"I will," he growls, touching his forehead to mine, taking my lips.

We kiss long and slow and hard. I want to push his hands between my legs, but there'll be time for that later, and a wicked part of me likes the idea of being forced to wait. We should really get out there and spend some time with the boys, maybe *try* to salvage what's left of the evening.

One more thing nags at my soul. I open my eyes, gazing into his, pinching my fingers in his hands, I say it. "And don't you *ever* leave without telling me again. Promise."

"Never, Cupcake. That's done, God as my witness." He gives me a long and leisurely kiss, sealing our pact. "Promise. Cross my heart and hope to fucking die."

* * *

THAT DAY STARTS a brand new pattern. The boys still go to the barn with him every morning, and stay with me every evening, but the nights.

God. Our nights become my favorite time. Even the nights when I have things to do at the lodge and can't come crawling into bed until after he's asleep, passed out from a full day of work, are wonderful. I've never slept as well as I do snuggled up to his huge, warm body.

I'd never slept naked before meeting him, either. But pajamas, clothes of any kind, just get in the way. I gave him a lodge bathrobe for those times the boys need something in the middle of the night.

There's definitely a skip in my step come morning, and I can't help but smile ninety-nine percent of the time. Especially after a moment like we'd just had. And there are many.

Like this morning, after Gramps took the boys over to Clayton's to see the younger horses on his land. Left alone, Rex and I had a very mind-blowing quickie in the barn. We're both busy, so besides looks we share that promise more later, it's rare we get to go for it so early in the day.

I'm heading to the lodge now, to make Gramps his favorite coconut-coffee cupcakes as a thank you. He's come a long way lately. It's jaw dropping, really. Especially when it comes to the twins. He's acting like the grandfather I'd wished I'd had.

No regrets, though. Gramps had to be my father, and mother, and grandparent last. That didn't leave much room for him to be my grandfather full time. Rex pointed that out to me, and I'm glad he did.

The other thing that 'turned' Gramps around was Marcy. He'd pissed her off that night in the kitchen, and it wasn't until after Rex returned that I learned about something they'd kept under my nose for years, yet I'd never seen it.

Marcy and Gramps are *more* than boss and chef. Which finally explains the many times I've seen Gramps' bed already made when I go upstairs to clean.

They've made up, and everything is running as smoothly as possible. It's too perfect.

I frown as I walk up the front steps. Except, our current guest, Alan Schweikert is back.

He'd stayed several days the last time, along with his son, Brandon. He'd left after a half-hearted interview with Gramps, saying he'd be back in a few weeks. Last night, he'd returned as promised, talking up the article he's 'working like hell to finish.'

I'm not sure I like him. I've seen the looks he aims at the boys when they're all in the lobby, by the fireplace, Alan looking up from his laptop like they've interrupted God himself.

He's snappy with his son, too. To be fair, Brandon's a bit of a brat, but that's not entirely his fault. If his father would *just* pay some attention to him, he wouldn't be that way. He'd stop acting out. I'm not even a mother – not yet – but I know it.

Brandon hangs out in the front room now, watching a show on TV that isn't very appropriate for an eight-year old. At least in my opinion. Some zombie thing with blood and teeth. Extremely graphic special effects. I'm frowning, wondering if I should go over and shut it off, but knowing he'll cry bloody murder if I do. It's also not my place, I know, but this *is* our lodge.

I look around, wondering where Alan is now.

It's anybody's guess. The man seems all over the place, walking the grounds, snapping photos with his phone. On his first visit, Alan said he needed pics for his small paper. Claims that's another reason he's back now that the photos are 'touched up.'

Weirdly, though, the only people he's chatted up this time are Adam and Chase, when he isn't shooting daggers out his eyes over the top of his screen. Which I try *not* to let happen.

The mail arrived while I was in the barn, too. I pick up the stack and carry it to the office, sorting out the junk I'll file in the trash can.

There's an envelope addressed to me, with no return address. I set the rest down, open the envelope and pull out a single sheet of paper.

Dear Ms. Danes,

Please tell *R.O. to call me ASAP. Thank you.*

K

That's it. No name. Just a number scrawled under his neat writing.

R.O.?

My heart leaps into my throat. This must be the man he contacted. Knox. The old army buddy.

I stick the letter in the envelope and walk out of the office.

"Ah, there you are, Tabby!"

I turn toward a voice I'm in no mood to deal with. "Yes. Is there something you need, Mr. Schweikert?" I make a point of not calling him by his first name. I don't want to be on a first name basis with this weirdo.

"My son, Brandon, wants to see inside of your barn. Horses and kids, you know..."

His smile looks as false as the rest of him. Slimy is a better way to describe him. His hair is slicked back and even though it's neat it hides too much of his head. "I've explained before that the barn's under construction, sir. No guests are allowed out there until the project's complete and passes inspection. No horses, either. Our few retired animals have been temporarily moved while the work finishes."

Try to smile. Try to be nice. Gramps told me as much, says it's good marketing if we can get him to lend us a glowing review. He *does* work for a major newspaper in a Detroit suburb. Supposedly.

Alan's smile vanishes. "He...he won't touch anything. Honest. I'll make sure of it. He's just curious. I'd also love a chance to shoot a few more pics. The stable's one of your oldest buildings, isn't it? Mr. Danes said his father had a refinery there in the old days making moonshine."

Brandon's still on the couch, staring at the TV and hasn't looked away. I really wish Gramps hadn't told him so many intimate family details.

I shake my head, trying to soften the blow. "Sorry, sir. Rules are rules. It's a big liability if anything goes wrong."

"Well, then...perhaps we need to find other accommodations."

His threat is actually my hope. I reach under the desk for the copies I rarely need, yet keep handy. "Here's a list within a fifty-mile radius. There's a Best Western closer to Marquette, within an hour."

I regret the words as soon as they're out. Kind of.

Damn it, I want him gone, but it's losing money and I

promised Gramps. And lately, he's actually been decent. He really wants this stupid article.

"Sir, if you'll reconsider, I'll talk to my grandfather. I'll see what he can do. Maybe we can set up a quick supervised tour, or something."

Alan's face brightens. "Wonderful. Just what I was hoping to hear!"

I purse my lips, studying him. Maybe he really is just an odd bird after a story. I've heard sometimes reporters are that way.

Still, I have a gut feeling I shouldn't leave him alone in the lobby, but there isn't anything he can steal, other than the ancient ten-year-old guest computer that he'd never figure out the password for. I turn and walk out the door, anxious to get the letter to Rex.

The grin he gives me when I push open the barn door fills me with delight.

"Back for more?" he asks. "Already?"

"Not quite," I say, closing the door behind me. "Well, maybe after..."

He laughs. "Thought you were going to make cupcakes, Cupcake?"

I shake my head and plant a quick kiss on his lips before I hold up the envelope. "This just arrived." I take out the letter and hand it to him. "Is it your friend?"

I already know the answer. His expression is priceless, a hope like I haven't seen fills his eyes.

He reads it quickly, and then flips it over to see the other side.

"That's it," I say.

"Let me see the envelope."

I hand it to him. "No return. Phoenix postmark." He

huffs out a sigh and examines both the letter and envelope again. "Shit."

His tone concerns me. "Wait, it's not from your friend?"

"Must be," he growls, shaking his head. "There's...just not enough here for me to be certain. For all I know, it could be a trick."

That doesn't add up. How would they know? Then again, what do I know about the monsters he's dealing with?

I take the letter. "Here, I'll call the number."

He frowns. "Tabby..."

"And ask a question only you and him know the answer to."

His face lights up. "I like it." He kisses me. "Have I told you today how fucking glad I am we met?"

"Well, maybe not *today*," I say, laughing. My heart hums happily. "Come on, we can use my phone in the cabin."

"Isn't there, like, a business cell phone? Something without your name attached to it for the lodge?"

I roll my eyes. "You know my grandfather. We'll use my landline."

"Right. Stupid question."

As we're leaving the barn, I say, "Lock the door. I don't want anyone sneaking in here and getting hurt."

He does, and then as we're walking towards the cabin says, "If it really is Knox, the call could take a while. You should go make your cupcakes while I talk to him."

I read between the lines and shake my head. "Oh, no. You aren't getting rid of me *that* easy." Looking at him as we walk, I add, "No more secrets between us. Not in the bedroom or out of it."

XII: THE WHOLE TRUTH (REX)

She's right, and she's wrong. I don't want to admit it.

There are no secrets between us in the bedroom, but I've never told her everything outside it.

And I don't want to. Not yet.

Yet, the ring I bought yesterday says it all. I have to come clean. *Have to.*

The ring isn't much. An inexpensive placeholder until I'm able to get her something nicer.

I bought it to prove I'm serious. Once this is over and I have access to my money again, I'll buy her diamonds that'll blind people.

Trouble is, I can't wait for that. I need to claim this woman and I need to do it right the fuck *now*. She needs to know how much she means to me. How hard I'll work to get this shit all taken care of. How happy I'll make her once my woes are ancient history.

"You're right," I say, drawing strength from the simple ring in my pocket.

"Ouch."

I glance her way, wondering how she'd hurt herself.

She's smiling.

Confused, I ask, "Ouch what?"

"That had to hurt."

"What?"

"You. Admitting I'm right."

Her laughter is just like her. Delightful. And sexy as hell.

Damn if I'm not smiling too. One more sign this is the woman I want to spend my life with, and the one I'm meant to.

Screw the mind, the body. She's there, always, but they've got nothing on what really matters.

Cupcake's got herself hooked in my soul. I wake up every morning thinking about her and fall asleep with the same thoughts fogging my head. I look at this old lodge with a fondness I never thought I'd have for second rate furniture and buildings that need work. It's part of her, part of the boys, and part of me.

I'm in Cupcake's world and I want her sharing mine. I want to make it ours – even if I'm still stuck wondering how I ever managed to get so fucking lucky in the worst days of my life.

I can't deny it if I tried. Tabby puts stars back in my void, and I'd be the dumbest bastard in the world not to follow their light.

Once we're back inside the cabin, I give her a long, tongue heavy kiss as soon as the door is closed. My hand wanders to her tits, cupping a satisfying palm full. I wanted more in the barn, before she interrupted me with the note from maybe-Knox, and now I'm after what I missed.

"Rex!" She pushes me back reluctantly. "Later. You keep doing what you're doing, and we'll never make that phone call."

She's right again. But I don't say it. No need to give her a bigger head than she already has. She's everything I never knew I was looking for. Even her smart-ass sassy sense of humor.

We walk into the bedroom, she sits down on the edge of the bed, picks up the receiver and punches the numbers written in the letter.

"Ask him if he eats balls," I say, recalling an old mess hall joke.

"Eats. Balls?" She blinks, innuendo written all over her face.

"Not like that," I growl. "Just ask. He'll know."

Cupcake shrugs, then speaks into the receiver as a gruff voice answers. "Hi, this is Tabby Danes. Listen, do you, um, eat balls?"

I nod, liking how discreet she's being.

She looks at me. "Porcupine?"

I grin. The mess hall made the worst porcupine meatballs. Don't know if it was the old bread they used to bind the stuff together or what, but they were hard as fucking stones. Knox always joked that they were like trying to eat baseballs. Being the bawdy soldiers we were, it didn't take long for baseballs to become a play on all kinds of others.

"He wants to know if you have a smoke," she whispers, eyes big as she looks up.

"A Lucky Strike. Only way to go," I say, recalling a sergeant we knew who smoked Lucky Strike cigarettes one after the other. He'd get fighting mad if anybody ever insisted the old brand wasn't the best; bald eagles, mom, and apple pie to the core.

There's no question. I grab the phone she's holding out.

"Knox?"

"Osborne, shit. Good to hear your voice. Too bad this isn't a catch up call."

"No, sir," I say glumly.

"It's all right. I'll help get your tit out of the wringer."

It's been years, but he still sounds the same and it's good to hear his voice, too. "You could say that," I answer.

"You'll be pleased to know I've made some progress. I've been in touch with your lawyer, Justin. He's gotten access to your tax records, says the dirty money can be traced through them. Black Rhino's got some experience going after that sort of thing, too."

There's a dark edge in his voice when he mentions his fabulously wealthy jewelry company. I'll have to get the story someday, but now's not the time.

I sit down on the bed, relieved Justin trusted him. I should have known they'd get along. That's why I included Justin's name in my SOS letter to Knox. Justin can be as tight-lipped as us, and together, with the right info, the two of them could move mountains. Hell, I'm counting on it.

"Bad news is, we need more, Rex," Knox says softly. "In order to catch these bastards, we need the whole story. Everything. Detail, detail, however minute."

"All right," I say, hissing it slowly through my teeth. "I'll do my best."

"Good. Let's go right now then," Knox says. "There's

no time to lose. I'm recording this so Justin can hear it word-for-word, too. Think back to what happened, whatever evil fuckery put you on the run. Don't leave out *anything*."

The air I draw in burns my lungs. Tabby's sitting next to me and my chest burns at the idea of her hearing what I'm about to say.

"Rex? You hear me? Hello?" He bites off.

"I'm here," I say, heart banging bullets in my throat. "And I heard you."

"Start that morning. When was it?"

"Valentine's Day," I say. "I was just finishing up a big job. Had to be at work early, and the babysitter, Mrs. Potter, called saying she was sick but she was sending over a replacement. It was a young woman. Her niece or something. I left as soon as the woman showed up, after I fed my kids. We always do breakfast together. I worked late and my phone was dead. Couldn't find my fucking field charger to save my life." The images of that day race back into my head.

How I'd dug through the truck for my backup charger when I got in, and pulled it off when I got home. I never bothered to check the messages. *Stupid.*

I close my eyes, remembering, wishing like hell I didn't have to.

* * *

THE HOUSE IS DARK, but it's late, the kids should be in bed. Asleep. The doors locked. I unlock and open it.

"Hello?"

Dead silence.

"Adam? Chase?" I call both their names and get nothing.

My phone starts pinging voice messages left behind while the battery was drained. I check the missed calls list and see several from the house phone.

Cold sweat breaks out on my temples. *Fuck.*

I hit the voicemail icon while running for the stairs. Some woman named Anita, Ms. Potter's replacement, she'd been watching the boys, and had to leave by six. Big date for Valentine's. She leaves the same message three times, then one that says, never mind, their mother picked them up.

"No!" I want to put my fist through the wall, but there's no goddamn time.

I hurl the boys' bedroom door open as her message ends. I see my nightmare.

The room's empty.

Their beds made.

My beautiful kids are fucking gone.

Shit!

I grab the piece of paper lying on the pillow of Adam's bed. It's Nelia's Satan handwriting scrawled in pink.

"Fucking bitch!" I shout. "You're no Mommy to them. Never fucking were."

Nelia says she took them for the night. It's Valentine's Day. In her warped mind, that means they should spend it with Mommy. Never mind the four other V-Days she missed, plus all the other holidays and birthdays in between.

I pinch my teeth so hard they almost break. She won't get away with this.

My heart races as I run down the stairs and out the door. I have to keep moving. They could be in danger.

I know where she's been living. I've seen the paperwork, the places and names involved when I do the dirty laundering deeds she rams down my throat. It's Aiden's penthouse apartment downtown, not far from Lake Michigan.

My truck screams down the streets, back into the city, blowing stop signs and red lights, ignoring the horns honking at me and the screeching of brakes. I'm driving like a lunatic and I don't care. I'll pay the half a dozen tickets that show up after I run the red light cameras.

I'll pay them gladly. Just as long as I've got Adam and Chase.

My sons' lives are in danger. *Real danger.*

That bitch hasn't been sober in months. She hasn't been clean in years. She might've been strung out on something when she took the notion to pick them up, for all I know. She'd also been breathing down my neck to launder even *more* money.

Tens of thousands at a time. Every week. Unholy amounts that could bring the IRS and the Feds bearing down on us like an avalanche.

Fuck. I never should've given in that first time, but I was fucked if I did, and fucked if I didn't.

I find the building after an eternity snarling through traffic. It overlooks the lake and I park up the block, knowing I'll never be allowed in the underground lot. The Stone family all but own this complex. They've donated big to enough campaigns to make every official charged with protecting us look the other way.

That won't stop me tonight. I've remodeled buildings

just like this, and know alternate ways in. Which is what I use, climbing the fire escape stairs all the way to the top, tearing the service door open.

Fucking Aiden Stone is just as much of a druggie as Nelia, too.

I know that's why I'm the useful asshole laundering his drug money, so he can cover up the amount of heroin he's shooting in his veins, hide it from the rest of his family. They're evil, but they're professional criminals. And they *would* be pissed to know the amount of money he's skimming off the top.

Bastard. They'd broken their part of the deal. The one where Nelia told me they'd stay the fuck away from my sons. They'd both agreed to that in exchange for the money I laundered. And I'd trusted them like a fool.

I hold my breath as I slip into the hallway. It's Venetian style – what else? – frescoe floors and fancy old world chandeliers European craftsman probably installed by hand. Aiden always has bodyguards nearby, so I'm cautious, careful of every door I open next, every step I take.

My heart beats my ears nearly deaf and I have to keep wiping the sweat out of my eyes. But I press on, for them, for my own flesh and blood. Any father would.

I make it into the hallway on their floor and shimmy the lock I think leads to the kitchen. Someday, they'll make locks that can't be broken into, but not in this old renovated building. I sneak through the kitchen, crouching low, wishing I'd grabbed the gun I keep in my truck's glovebox.

There's music, and voices. I freeze.

I only breathe again when I realize it's a TV coming from the open loft above.

I press myself against the wall, knowing the layout of all these penthouses are similar. I go slowly to the end. Where the bedrooms are.

Relief washes over me when I open the first door.

The boys are there. Safe. Sleeping in one bed, snuggled together like kittens.

Needing confirmation, I walk closer, listen to their breathing. They're okay.

Jesus. Thank God. *They're okay!*

I'm the one who's not. Anger roils inside me. This has to be the last damn time.

I've fucking had it.

Leaving the boys where they are, I quietly leave the room, and then bound up the closed stairway to the second floor. The master bedroom is up there.

The noise from the TV is louder, a cooking show, I think, but I'm still quiet. My heart is still pounding.

So is my fury, a beast-like bloodlust that makes me feel like a werewolf stalking its prey.

I open the bedroom door. The room's dark, but there's light shining under the closed bathroom door.

Cornelia.

I cross the room and throw it open. "You fucking bitch!"

My mouth slams shut when I see her. She's in the tub and doesn't look my way. It's a game, or something's very wrong.

"Nelia!" I storm across the room. "Nelia!"

Goddamn, why won't she *look* at me?

She still doesn't move, and that's when I see the

needles, the tubes, half-empty bags with junkie crap.

"I hope you're fucking dead," I say. I do. But I don't.

But really, it'd be the miracle I need.

I reach down to grab her arm.

It's limp. Cold.

I suck stale air in my lungs, the full enormity of her lifeless body hitting me. "Christ. I knew this would happen one day. *Knew it.*"

It's time to go. There'll be time later to work through all the fucked up things I'm feeling right now.

Wanting nothing to do with it, for the boys to have nothing to do with it, I spin around and head for the door.

Something slams into the side of my face as soon as I step into the attached bedroom. I'm rocked back. My jaw burns and my head rings, vision going blurred.

There's barely time to jump backwards as Aiden flies at me.

I can't tell what he's yelling, something about her being dead, but his words are slurred, and he's waving a gun.

I duck out of his way. He spins, coming at me, angry and relentless. I stumble against something, a dresser. Swipe my hand over the top of it, searching for something, *anything* to defend myself.

There's something there. Solid and heavy. A lamp or vase, I don't know or care, just swing as hard as I can when Aiden lunges.

Crack! The connection vibrates up my arm, metal on bone. The next moment, Aiden falls. I jump backwards, out of the way as his body, his head, bounces against the floor like a stunt dummy.

He doesn't move. Out completely cold.

The boys. I have to get the boys and leave. Now.

"Mr. Stone?"

Fuck, it's a bodyguard. Just a few feet away. I've seen him before. He's as big as a bull and just as mean and ugly. I grab the gun lying beside Aiden's hand. All I can think about are the boys. I have to get to them. Get them out of here!

A shape appears in the doorway.

"Mr. Stone?" he calls again.

I fire.

The man goes down. I run to the door. He's in the hallway, sitting against the wall and holding his leg.

"Bastard! Fuck! Right in the fucking knee!"

I grab the gun he must have dropped. "You're lucky it's dark," I growl, knowing I might have aimed right for his chest if I'd been able.

"Kill me," the man taunts. "Go the hell ahead. You're a dead man anyway."

I think about it, very strongly, but shake my head. I can't murder in cold blood, no matter how much sense it makes. "I'm not here to kill anyone. Just to get my kids."

The man laughs. "Dumb fuck, you *better* kill me. Because as soon as I tell Uncle Leo who did this, you'll be on the shit list." He laughs harder. "You're fucking fucked."

My blood runs cold. Colder.

I raise the gun, point it at his head, but my finger won't pull the trigger. Jesus, I can't.

Can't just kill a man like this, no matter how horrible he is or how screwed he says I am.

I. Can't.

I punch him instead. Hard. My knuckles burn from the contact with his jaw. His head bounces off the wall, then hangs limply. It doesn't take much to knock him out, blood slowly draining from his knee. He'll live, I think, but it's out of my hands.

Afraid there are more, I run down the stairs, stuffing the guns in the waist band of my jeans in the center of my back. My heart thumps so hard it hurts to breath as I run to the room, grab Adam in one arm, Chase in the other and then fly down the hall.

We leave the same way I'd entered, down the fire escape. The boys keep wondering what's happening, but they're happy to see me and stay quiet when I say so. The tone in my voice makes them listen and obey.

I buckle them in their kiddie car seats and drive up the road, then take the lake road that curves around parts of town that have been neglected for ages, tossing the guns in the water as I drive over the old road bridge. It's late and the boys are tired. They fall back asleep in no time.

I'm thankful for that because I'd *never* want them to see the tears rolling down my face as I drive south out of the city, knowing we aren't safe here.

The Stone Syndicate will come after us. Sooner or later, they'll come, and they'll mean to torture, to hurt, to kill.

We're hunted. Me and my entire little family.

I drive all night, stopping only for gas, taking side roads, gravel county roads at times. It's dark again when I arrive at my grandfather's old farm near the Wisconsin border, and swap my truck for his.

The boys ask why we're leaving our truck behind. I don't know what to tell them. Don't know anything. Finally, I say it's because we're going to visit friends. Some new friends they'll surely like.

I hate like hell lying to them. But the truth is even worse.

They keep asking, day after day, night after night, when we'll get to our friend's place. I keep saying soon, passing through crappy hotels, never spending more than a day or two at a time when I'm too burned out to drive from constant insomnia.

Then we find the lodge. We park, step out, and I finally tell them, "We're here."

It was meant to be another lie. But when I see the soft, sunny face of the girl in the distance shoveling snow, and hear the distant thunder – or whatever it is – up in the sky the night we arrive, I've got a strange feeling in my gut I can't shake.

Sometimes the heavens break.
Sometimes lies transform.
Sometimes they're true.

* * *

THE FLASHBACK'S OVER. The phone burns hot in my hand, almost greasy from my palm sweating all over it.

Cupcake stares at me and tears are slowly trickling down her cheeks. I caress her face, lifting her chin gently with my fingers, "I'm sorry, darling. That's it. All of it."

She shakes her head.

"Fuck, Osborne," Knox says in my ear, bringing my attention back where it belongs. "Aiden Stone is dead."

"I know," I answer. "I heard it on the radio. Didn't take the Feds more than a day or two to get involved."

"Police don't have anything to go on, Justin says. And of course the family isn't talking, working with the authorities, but with the tape I just made of your story, and your tax records...that might be our silver bullet."

"I appreciate your help, Knox." The tears on Cupcake's face has me adding, "More than you'll ever know."

"Glad to hear it, Rex, but this isn't done. For Christ's sake, lay low. The Stones aren't talking to the police because they'll do their own breed of justice. They've got their hitmen aplenty," Knox says, as if I don't know the nightmarish truth. "We have to shut them down first. Make it too much of a liability to come after you. So, hang the fuck in there. I'll contact you again the instant I know anything. This number good?"

"Yeah, ask for Tabby."

"Will do, buddy. Don't worry. We'll get these bastards."

The line goes dead.

I replace the phone in its cradle. She's looking at me, and I don't know what to say. What to do. I've never, even after all I've been through, felt so helpless as I do right now. She's the last person I'd ever want to hurt.

She cups my face with both hands and kisses me softly. Sweetly.

I don't deserve this angel. She's so, so perfect. So wholesome. So good.

She presses her forehead against mine. "I love you, Rex Osborne. I just want you to know that. That I love you."

I can't stop myself, I grab her and hold on for dear life. I feel as if I'm drowning, and the only thing keeping me above water is her.

Our kisses are crazy at first, wild and hot, but then, they grow tender and precious, as if we both know there's no hurry. It's like the sun itself surrounds us.

And maybe it does.

Love. Our love. It's strong. Real. Lasting.

I need to be in her and I'm not going to wait.

We undress each other with care, taking our time. It's not just hot sex anymore.

It's making love. Something I always laughed at before. To the old Rex, there was fucking, and nothing else.

Nothing like this.

I didn't think sex like this existed. Sharing and loving each other in a way that's so emotional, so beautiful, I feel like I'm in a dream in the middle of my nightmare. A heavenly dream that's stronger than the blackness, and leaves me knowing this is right.

She's the one I've been seeking my entire life without even knowing it.

I throw her on the bed, rip her panties away, not even bothering with her top. I take her body in long, deep strokes, pushing inside her. It's skin-on-skin and it's fucking fantastic.

"Rex!" she moans softly, enticingly, goddamn beautifully as I push inside her sweetness.

Her hands rest on my shoulders, digging in while we fuse together, hips colliding slow and hard. She's wet and warm and perfect. Doesn't take long to see her eyes roll, and fuck, I'm a goner.

I'm groaning, feeling fierce heat billow up my spine, words ripping out of me right before I hit the point of no return. "Tabby, fuck, I love you!"

Her pussy wrings hot fire from my balls, as much as it can get. My cock pulses like mad, jerks inside her, fills her for what seems like forever. We come together like something from a movie, hearts and bodies and souls in perfect sync.

I can't let this end. Can't let her get away. Can't ever give up.

We're both spent after, like usual, but it's different this time. Rejuvenating and awe-inspiring. I'm so content. So whole.

I reach over the edge of the bed and pick up my jeans, pulling up my boxers.

"Do we have to get dressed already?" she asks. "You're really something, Rex Osborne."

I chuckle. Hard to believe she's talking about me being the one with all the surprises. She'll amaze me forever.

"Love you, Cupcake. Love you so damn much." It's now or never.

Soon as I'm dressed again, I find the ring box and pull it out. "I'm sure Morris and the boys will be home soon, but I want to ask you something."

She rolls onto her side and plants the bottom of her chin on my shoulder. Her eyes are still smoldering, her smile tender. "Yeah?"

I don't know how to start. What to say. "There's a lot going on, obviously, and though I'm not exactly sure how things will turn out, I truly believe Knox will find a way to save my ass."

"I do, too," she whispers. Hope flutters in her voice.

"Much as I hope that happens, I don't want to wait."

"Wait? For what?"

This. I open the box and hold it in her face. "To ask you to marry me, darling."

Her jaw drops and she stares at me for what feels like hours, then jumps off the bed.

"Rex, holy...are you serious?" she asks. Her hazel eyes are big and bright. Vivid. Stunning.

"Dead serious." I flinch at my choice of words and try to correct them by saying, "I love you, Tabby. Love you so hard, I'm sure you'll say yes."

"I love you, too, but..." She's pacing the floor and stops to look at me, massaging her temples. "Are you saying this because we forgot to use a condom? I've been on the pill all along, you know. I think that –"

"No," I interrupt, sitting up. She needs to know this isn't about sex. "*No.* It's because you're mine, Cupcake, and I want it to be that way forever. Look, I know I come with a lot of baggage. The kids, this whole thing with the Syndicate –"

"You did what you had to." She climbs on the bed and takes my hand, understanding glowing in her eyes. "Any loving father would have done what you did. That's *not* baggage, Rex."

"The boys can be a handful, but I think you love them as much as I do. I hope –"

Tears shine in her eyes as she nods. Vigorously. "I do, and they aren't baggage, either. Not ever." She kisses the back of my hand. "I'm the one with baggage, Rex. This place. The lodge. I can't leave Gramps, you know. I can't –"

"Who said I'm expecting you to?"

"You aren't?"

"No." The sense of security I've felt since coming here surrounds me. We'll make it work. Somehow.

"We, the boys and I, love this place. It's become home. A fresh start. Everything Chicago never was. And that's what we need. There's nothing left for us there." I hold up the ring box. "I know it's not very big, very expensive, but I swear, woman, I'll buy you a nicer one as soon as I can afford to. I'll give you a rock to make every woman in this town turn green." I mean it, too. Even if I have to compete with the town billionaire, Ryan what's-his-face.

Only thing that frustrates me about leaving Chicago is knowing everything I'd worked for may be gone. I shake my head. "This won't straighten out overnight. I know you know. I'm sure there'll be restitution that I'll have to pay, untangling my corporate accounts from the drug money shit, if the Feds are kind...but there *should* be some money left over. I'll start a new company. Here in Split Harbor. It's grown a lot the last couple years, hasn't it? I'll —"

Her kiss stops the litany of plans I'm coming up with on the fly for our future. Our life together.

She sighs as our lips part and takes the box from me. "It's not the size of the ring. I don't even care. This one is beautiful. Perfect." Her grin is adorable and honest. "I don't want anything else. I'm not a flashy kind of girl."

I know. And I love it.

"I just have to know you know what you're getting, too. Me. The lodge. Gramps. It's a package deal."

"I know, and it's what I want, as long as you want my package, too."

"Of course, Rex," she whispers. "I do."

Fuck if those two soft words don't send a shiver up my spine. I hope she'll say them the same way in a few months, whenever our big day comes.

Daring to hope, I ask, "So, Cupcake...that a yes?"

She bites her bottom lip, then says, "Yes! But I just need you to do something first. One little thing for me."

A wave of doubt washes over my gut, but I can't blame her. My life is so fucked up right now. It's only fair she'll want a prenup to protect her, the family business. Or maybe she just wants to take this slow, hold off a year or more. Waiting till everything gets resolved with the Syndicate should come first. I'd jumped the gun. I just wanted this to be the new normal. Wanted her in whatever normal means for the rest of my life. I may not deserve it, but hell, I want it *bad*.

I'm too lost in my thoughts, not expecting what comes next.

"Gramps is old-fashioned, you know that." Cupcake looks at me. I cock my head in confusion, waiting for the rest. "Rex, will you please ask him for his blessing?"

XIII: SMALL BLESSINGS (TABBY)

I hold my breath, waiting for his reaction, hoping I haven't just screwed my one and only chance at true happiness. I love him beyond anything I'd ever imagined, but until this moment, never realized how much having Gramps' approval means to me.

He's a curmudgeon, a jerk, but he's family. The closest living thing I have to a father. I'll marry Rex either way. But it'd mean *so much* if Gramps approves.

Rex is quiet. I start to panic inwardly.

Silly thinking. Nothing in my life's been easy, why should I expect this to be?

Rex closes the lid on the box and I bite my lips together, wishing I could take it back.

But then he smiles, pulls me into his arms, and puts his forehead against mine.

"Cupcake, of course," he says, a weight in his voice. "Sorry. I expected something else. Hadn't thought of the old man."

Happiness surges inside me. I wrap my arms around his neck. "Thank you! Just so you know, it's a yes, no matter what. I'll marry you whatever he says."

Rex hugs me harder. Kisses me. "He'll say yes. I'll sell him. Just like I did on hiring me. Won't stop trying till he does."

Sincerity sings in his voice like a song. "I love you," I whisper.

"And I love you."

I'll never get tired of saying it. Hearing it. Living it.

Our kisses turn heated, my body responding to every touch. If he hadn't just taken me over the edge, before he proposed, I know we'd be naked again. The emotions overwhelming me while we'd made love a few minutes ago were deeper and stronger than before.

He'd taken my V-card, showed me sex. But today, he's opened my life to love. His love. Our love.

He pulls out of a long kiss where our tongues play hide and seek, and the smile on his face sends my heart reeling.

The teasing glint in his eye as he leans down and kisses above my nipple ignites a fire inside me. I arch into him, giving him full access, letting him know I'm game for round two.

More than game. Hot and oh-so-ready.

He laughs, gently slapping my thigh. "Tonight, darling. I have work to do, and you have cupcakes to bake." He isn't wrong. Grabbing my hand, he climbs off the bed, pulling me with him.

I refuse to move. "We can be quick."

"It's *never* that quick with you." He kisses my nose. "And I don't want it to be."

He lets go of my hand and stands, straightening his clothes. I can't believe what I'm seeing. "Really? You're going to get me all hot and bothered and then leave?"

"I've lost count of the number of cold showers I've taken since meeting you." He lifts his head, a seductive glint in his eye. "Tonight, Cupcake, we'll pick this up. I'll fuck you through the wall."

I sigh, ready to countdown the hours.

I watch him run a comb through his hair, back to his perfect pre-sex state again. Foolishly, because it doesn't help the burn between my legs. When he sits on the edge of the bed to pull on his socks, I sit up and wrap my arms around him from behind, rubbing my tits against his bare back. "Do cold showers even help?"

"Temporarily," he says.

I nip at one of his earlobes. "I don't want temporary."

He flips around and knocks me onto my back. I'm thrilled and hold up my arms to welcome him. Gripping both of my wrists with one hand, he plants my arms over my head and holds them there.

"You don't want temporary?"

I shake my head. "Nope."

He trails a finger down my side, making my breath catch when he doesn't quite touch the areas that make me throb. "You want more, baby girl?"

"Yes." Goosebumps kiss my skin, wanting his touch so bad. "More."

He leans down, but rather than kiss me, he whispers in my ear, "Patience, darling. Wait. Think about it all day. Make your pussy hurt. Make it fucking beg."

Oh, hell.

"Rex," I whimper, terribly frustrated.

He gives me a quick kiss, then jumps off the bed. Grabbing his shirt off the floor, he winks at me. "Love you, Cupcake. Can't wait. *Tonight.*" He growls the last word, shooting one last wicked look over his shoulder.

I toss a pillow after him and miss. His laughter lingers after the door closes. I laugh, too. I may be aching inside, but I'm also happy, eager for tonight.

He's gone by the time I'm dressed. As I'm walking out the door, I turn around and run back into the bedroom. There, I pick up the box, take out the ring, and put it in my pocket. I want to see it on my hand, but it's another sweet agony. I'll wait. Wait for Rex to slide it on my finger for the first time after he gets Gramps' approval.

The sun seems brighter, the air sweeter, the entire universe more perfect as I walk to the lodge to make cupcakes.

The evening drifts by in a happy blur. My baking is complete and the evening meal ready to serve when Gramps and the boys arrive home. Adam and Chase are full of stories about riding horses, playing with puppies, watching a cat catch a mouse. The final story was quite animated, and we're all laughing when Rex walks into the kitchen.

All it takes is one look and I'm right back where he'd left me in the cabin.

Hot and bothered.

He and the boys eat in the kitchen with Gramps, and every time I walk in, his secretive glances nearly send me over the edge. Which makes waiting on the other customers more of a chore than usual.

Especially Alan Schweikert. The way his beady eyes catch me when he thinks I'm not looking.

When will he finish his piece and leave?

Thankfully, I carry the last of the dirty dishes into the kitchen.

"You sit down and eat," Marcy says, taking the tray.

"Where's everyone else?" I ask.

"Went to the cabin."

"Where's Gramps?"

"He went with them." Marcy pointed towards the table. "And you need to give them some time, so sit down and eat."

I hadn't expected Rex to act so quickly. A part of me is nervous about the conversation he and Gramps are having. I'm also nervous about the twinkle in Marcy's eyes. "Time for what?"

"To talk."

I nod and sit down at the table.

She laughs. "There's no use pretending. Not after the way you two were almost melting every time you looked at each other."

She's right, there's no use denying it. "I thought I'd kept it hidden," I admit.

"So did he."

I sigh and set down my fork. Not hungry. At least not for food. "So you figured it out?"

She laughs again. "I saw it coming."

"How? When?"

"When you stood up to your grandfather over Rex. You've never done that before."

"No, I hadn't, had I?" Recalling that one significant

evening, I say, "You stood up to him, too. More than usual."

"I had to," she says. "He'd gone too far that night. Besides telling him he was being a jackass, I told him it was time he let you get out from under his thumb. He was going to lose you, Tabby. Lose you forever, and then this lodge."

"I couldn't really leave Gramps." It's a hard confession, but it's true. I owe him.

"I'm not so sure. If that's what you really want to be free, to have your own life, you'd have to." She waves a hand. "This place might be your birthright, but it doesn't have to be your life. You have that choice, and don't for a moment let anyone convince you that you don't." She smiles. "Choice is yours. Always. But if you've found someone who's willing to share it with you, the good and the bad, then that's your choice, too."

I ponder that while I help her do the dishes and get the kitchen in order for morning. Gramps had returned to the lodge, but he'd gone straight upstairs.

I heard him. I'm not sure if that's a good sign or a bad one. With him, it's hard to say.

"I'll lock up," Marcy says. "You go, now."

"Night," I say, walking out the door.

The air is cold and crisp, winter's last gasp. There's even a few buds beginning on the trees out front. Before I get to the cabin, I hear a snap, like a twig snapping underfoot. Not mine.

I whirl around, looking in the direction the sound came from. It's too dark to see anything, but that doesn't convince me there's nothing there.

I squint harder, peering into darkness.

I turn back towards the cabin. Rex hadn't been standing on the porch a moment ago, but he is now. I'm relieved. I jog toward him. "You're home early. What's going on?"

"Waiting for my cupcake."

I laugh. "You already *had* a cupcake for dessert. So did the boys."

"Two dessert night, darling. I'm hungry."

I couldn't be happier, or more excited, and literally glide into his arms.

He answers me with a kiss that makes me hope the boys go to bed extra early tonight.

His lips leave mine with a promise that leaves my insides smoldering like a bed of coals that won't need much coaxing to ignite.

"I spoke to Morris."

I hold my breath. "And?"

"He says he'll think about it."

"Damn." I let out a growl, eyebrows digging into my face. "That doubtful old fart!"

Rex takes my hand and leads me to the door. "But he also said he's gotten used to me and the boys being around and he'd hate to see us leave. Told me he knows I make you happy."

"Well, that's something." It's a start, I concede.

"*You're* something," he says, slapping my butt as I walk in the cabin. Echoing my words from this morning makes me smile.

Dressed in their pajamas, the boys are lying on the floor, watching a movie I know they've seen ten times.

"They've already had their baths. They'll be out in no

time," Rex whispers in my ear. "I'm going to take a quick shower while we're winding down."

I kick off my shoes, hang up my coat, and then sit down on the sofa. I'm antsy, and can't sit, so get back up. I chatter with the kids a few minutes, but they're hooked on the show. Needing something to do, I go into the kitchen and get the coffee pot ready for morning. Lately, I've been keeping more food in the cabin. The four of us have breakfast here sometimes before heading to the lodge.

It's a nice worry to have. One more change I'm really enjoying.

The stars must have aligned in some celestial way, because when I walk back into the living room, the boys are both, head down, sound asleep. I'll have to thank Gramps for wearing them out so thoroughly today.

I go to the bedroom to tell Rex that Adam and Chase are ready to be carried into bed, but he isn't out yet.

More happiness ripples through me.

The shower is still running. We've shared more than one, and each time has been amazing.

I take the ring box out of my pocket and set it on the table beside the bed before stripping down to nothing and quietly open the bathroom door.

Steam fills the room. I slip in and two steps later, peak around the edge, where the shower curtain closes to the wall.

Rex's back is to me as he massages shampoo in his hair. I step into the tub real stealthy.

He sticks his head under the water, humming gently to himself, rinsing away the bubbles. I step forward, grabbing his ass with both hands.

"What the fuck!" he shouts, spinning around.

I laugh. "Yes, please."

There's something sexy about the alarm on his face, the urgency. He'd fight to protect himself or any of us without hesitation. His fierce lion face adds to the heat between my legs.

"Cupcake. You scared the shit out of me." He grabs my waist and pulls me closer. "Please, what?"

"Didn't you ask if I want to fuck?" I run both hands over his slick, wet, chest. Another growl leaves his throat. "Because I do. I've been thinking about it all day. Just like you said. Send me through the wall."

"Fuck," he whispers, cupping my boobs. "Are the boys –"

"Sleeping on the floor. We'll have to carry them to bed later."

"Sounds like a plan." He pulls me closer, his cock pressing into my stomach. "A very good plan."

I grab the bar of soap. "Let me clean you up. Worship this body like it deserves."

We lather each other up and down with soap, teasing and playing until suddenly the water runs cold. I gasp softly because I'm the one directly under it. *Damn, these old pipes...or the tank.*

Rex quickly turns the water off and shoves back the curtain. Grabbing a towel, he flips it open and wraps it around me. It's sweet little things like this, simple acts of kindness that makes me love him all the more.

"Better?" he asks, warming me with a kiss.

I nod. *Far better.*

Using one corner of the towel, he pats my nipples dry. "Will you look at that?"

"What?" I ask, looking down.

He takes one nipple in his mouth without warning, teasing it with the tip of his tongue My knees buckle, threatening to give out from the pleasure spiraling through me. When he lifts his head, he says, "It was still wet."

"Was it?" I ask.

"This one, too."

As he gives the other ample attention, a hand saunters between my legs. Wet doesn't begin to describe the slick heat leaking from my pussy. Rex looks down, growling, noticing what I'm doing.

"No. My job," he growls, swatting my hand away. "Know how to handle this kind of wet."

Of course he does. He picks me up, carries me into the bedroom.

He lays me on the bed, whispering, "Don't go away."

That's the last thing I'd ever do. While he walks over and shuts the door, I scoot up and lean against the headboard. My legs are splayed by the time he returns. He climbs over the foot of the bed and all the way up to me, like a tiger stalking its prey.

I curl one finger, encourage him to keep crawling.

We're nose to nose when he says, "I can't get any closer."

"Yes, you can." I wrap a hand around his cock. "There are parts of you I need to lick dry, too."

He plants his knees on both sides of me, straightening upright so his dick stands directly in front of my face. "Cupcake..."

"I'm always right," I say, kissing the head of his dick. Then I lick the length of it, loving how his coarse hair tickles my chin when I get to the base of his shaft. "Oh, yes, it's definitely wet."

I wrap one hand around his length, giving it a squeeze. Pre-come spills from his tip, sticky and hot.

"Bullshit. You just love sucking me off."

Guilty. I give it another long lick. "Maybe I do." I then kiss it. "And I like making you come, too." I sink my teeth softly into the tip. "And teasing before you do."

"Cupcake." His thunder deepens, sticking in his throat, but I know what he's saying. His fingers slide through my wet hair. Doesn't stop him from fisting my hair just as well as always. I love the tingle on my scalp when he pulls.

"You like it, too. I *know* you do."

"Fuck yes." It's not even a question.

I pump his cock with my hand several times, getting him good and hard, sucking just the tip. When I release it from my mouth, I finger the end, until his huge body twitches. "And I love this. Love watching how hard you get for me."

"Fuck your torture," he snarls again, a strained smile on his face.

"You made me wait this morning. Fair is fair."

He moves so fast, I can't stop him. He grabs me, pulls me down flat on the bed, a devilish spark in his blue eyes.

"Know what's fair, Cupcake?" he asks, stuffing a pillow under my butt, then pulling my legs apart. "Fair is eating this pussy till you scream. Fucking it with my tongue till you come so hard on my mouth we both see stars." His tongue brushes through my folds, adding to the burn lit by his words. "Fair is making you fuck these fingers while I taste your sweet cunt as long as I want. Fair is you, undone, begging for every inch of me."

Holy hell. I don't know what fair even means.

I arch upwards, into his hand, gasping as his fingers slip inside me.

"And fair is how much harder I'll own this clit when I call you my wife."

I'm twisting, writhing, losing my mind. There's nothing fair about it, but he's made me love it.

And I really do love the last thing he said – *when I call you my wife.*

Rex licks again, thrusts his fingers in, finds the spot that make me seize. I'll have a lot of catching up to do if I ever want to tease him like this.

I'm fighting my O, holding it in so this delightful torment continues as long as possible.

But he says, "You're lucky I'm addicted to your tits, your ass."

He leans forward, sucking my nipple. "And I'm a lucky man."

Oh, God. He's doing everything he describes and it's so hot it hurts. My pussy aches, begging to be brought off, bringing a whimper to my lips.

He fingers me harder, his other hand plumping my other breast.

"I'd tell you to beg, but there's no hiding how wet you get, Cupcake," he says. "You're ready for this dick? Ready for release? Ready for *me?*"

"Yes!" It's a whine and I'm barely able to speak. "Please."

"Another minute," he says, pressing hard on my clit.

Even through the friction, the sweet agony, two can play at this game. I twist, leaning far enough to one side so I can grab his cock. He's oozing, too, and I use my thumb to spread it over his pulsing tip. "Maybe you're right," I manage to say. "Maybe it's not time. Why don't you sit up again, so I can make sure?"

He rises to his knees again, and in the process the tip of his dick brushes against my nipple. I gasp at the pleasure.

"There. Something we both like a whole hell of a lot," he says, rubbing his cock over my breast.

Briefly, I push my breasts around his cock, moaning while he thrusts between them. I love how he shakes my entire body, makes me think how hard he'll feel later, deep inside me. Just when I think he'll go over, let go, he pulls away with a reluctant rumble.

"No. There's something else you'll like," he whispers.

"Show me," I say, even though I'm already so enveloped in pleasure, I can't imagine more.

He flips onto his back beside me. "Come the fuck here. Sit on my face. Backwards, so I can suck your pussy the same time you do my cock."

How could I ever say no? A husky moan escapes my lips as I position myself over his face. He's impatient, grabs my hips, pushing his tongue against my clit as I lean forward and draw him deep in my mouth.

Adrenaline fills me as we suck and lick. Faster. Harder.

It's all so freaking good. Before long, I can't take any more. His cock slips out of my mouth as the pressure inside me peaks. "Rex. *Rex. Rex!*"

He jerks my hips down, sucking with no mercy as my climax hits. The release is nuclear, a full body shock, wave after wave of pleasure. I'm coming on his face, coming for him, coming forever.

Aftershocks ripple through me minutes later, leaving me feeling nothing shy of euphoric.

I flip off him, laying on my back, trying to get my breathing under control. "I don't know how you last so long."

He runs a hand over my stomach. "Because watching you come is some kind of black fucking magic."

I smile. The sound of him opening the drawer of the bedside table gives me my second wind. I sit up. "Give me that," I say, grabbing the condom he's taken out of the drawer.

I throw it to the other side of the bed, giving him a knowing glance. "Why go back? I told you, I'm on the pill. And I really loved the feel of your cock inside me before, without anything in the way."

"Cupcake, fuck," he whispers, running his hands on my hips.

Then, in one swift movement, I straddle him. Taking him deep inside me.

"Tabby, damn!" His next whisper melts into a growl, and then he's thrusting hard and deep.

The time for thoughts is over. Same for words. We're lost in the language of our flesh, our hearts, our very souls in blissful harmony.

It's glorious. Despite thinking I was spent, a sweet spiral of heat loosens inside me, full and enveloping. I ride him long and hard, slow and fast, and everything in between.

His breathing changes, his rhythm, telling me he's close. He pins me to him, flinging my body around, using it for his pleasure.

I can't take much more.

And when his hands latch onto my hips and holds me still, growling, his cock going off inside me, I marvel how his body shudders, how his climax makes me peak all over again. I can't resist the heat of his seed, how it hurls so, so *deep*.

We're in rapture.

Panting. Convulsing. Lost.

The heavenly tension that's driven us here melts away. I fall forward, landing on his chest completely spent.

His chuckle is as sexy as the tiny kisses he places on the top of my head.

"Love you, Cupcake. More with every fuck. More every day."

I kiss him again, too exhausted to put into words how right he is.

He hugs me tight. We lie there for some time, until I roll off and flop onto the bed, utterly and blissfully happy.

Climbing off the bed, he gives me a quick kiss. When he returns, he sits on the edge of the bed. "Let me put something on you."

I sit up, expecting him to hand me my bathrobe so we can put the boys to bed. Instead, he takes my left hand, holding it in his iron grip.

"This ring's a symbol of us, Cupcake. It's also a promise: I'll keep loving you forever, just like I do now. I'll keep you this happy with my whole heart and soul."

Happy tears blur my vision as he slips the ring on my finger. "I love you, Rex. I promise, too. All I can and then some to make you and Adam and Chase smile for the rest of our lives."

* * *

The days that follow are as close to perfect as they can be. Gramps hasn't yet given his approval, stubborn as ever. But he did ask me if I thought I was ready for marriage. I said yes, without hesitation.. He nodded and walked away.

I hope it means he'll crack soon and finally give Rex his blessing.

"Tabby!"

I go to the kitchen door and shove it open. "I'm here. What do you need?"

Gramps barrels down the hallway. "Where's AC?"

I smile at the nickname he's given the boys. He can't quite tell them apart, so figures AC covers both of them. I frown then, replaying his words.

"I thought...aren't they with you?"

"They were, but I had to clean up a mess that other kid made. He's a real tyrant. Knocked over the shelf with all those movies in the front room. On purpose, I believe."

Alan is still at the lodge, with Brandon, whose behavior has just gotten worse. It's reached the point where I don't like Adam and Chase playing with him. Too bad it's hard to keep them away from the only other boy here right now. Spinning around, I ask Marcy, "Have you seen the boys?"

"No."

"They're with that kid," Gramps says. "And he's up to no good."

Urgency flares inside me. "We have to find them."

Marcy tosses aside her dish towel. "I'll check upstairs."

"I'll look outside," I say. "Gramps, you search this floor, and the basement, please."

We all scatter, going our separate ways. Running out the back door, I suddenly wish Rex hadn't gone to town for supplies. I check the cabin first. Finding it empty, I recall how Alan insisted Brandon wanted to see the barn, and run that way.

The side door is unlocked, which pisses me off. Rex would have locked it before he left. I know that for certain.

I step inside. The smell of new material hits me. I love it. The remodel is almost complete and looks amazing, but the row of newly-built stables also gives plenty of hiding places.

I'm almost around the edge of the row when the door slams shut. For a second I wonder if Rex returned and didn't stop in the kitchen to let me know. That would be weird, but –

My thoughts go blank as I see the man standing beside the closed door.

Alan.

This doesn't make sense.

Unnerved, I say, "Mr. Schweikert, I'm afraid guests aren't –"

"I know, Cupcake," he cuts in. "Know all about your little rules, where guests are and aren't allowed." He steps closer, waving one of my pink T-shits. "*Some* guests, but not all, it seems. Especially not Rex Osborne, who gets to trod around wherever he damn well pleases."

He's given me the creeps before, but right now, holding a shirt I know should be in my bedroom, he scares the shit out of me.

"The same Rex Osborne who has a price on his head." His nasty laugh echoes off the walls. "My friends can't wait to get your boy-toy in their hands. Gotta give him a hand, he's got a long way from Chicago. But they're paying mighty well to bring him home."

My stomach sinks. Bile churns. I'm going to be sick.

I'm paralyzed. Afraid to say anything. Certainly nothing that confirms Rex is the man he's looking for. Even though we both know he is.

Jesus.

"You're a nice, pink ticket to my paycheck," he says, circling like a shark.

My blood turns to ice as panic tightens, noose-like on my throat. I have to get past him, get the hell away.

"What's the matter? Tongue-tied, Cupcake?"

"Screw you," I snap. "Rex will –"

He laughs. "Do *what*, exactly? Lover-boy's in town, and dear old grandpa will be too busy fighting a terrible fire to bother looking for you." He strikes a match on a board and tosses it towards a stack of hay and scrap lumber that hadn't been there when I'd fed the horses this morning.

I scream, rushing forward, trying in vain to stomp it out. "You fucking idiot!"

It's insane, what I'm doing, but I can't control the reaction. It's visceral, watching the place I've devoted my life to go up in flames.

He grabs my arm.

I kick and squirm and lash out at him, shrieking to be let go.

He swings at me, hitting my face so hard my jaw pops and I taste blood. I hit back, using my nails to claw any skin I come in contact with. It hurts him, but not enough.

"Bitch!" He shoves me backwards, hits me again, knocking me to the floor.

I scramble to get away, but he jumps on me then,

sitting on my stomach. I kick and scream, try to get him off, but then he grabs my neck.

I can't breathe.

Can't scream.

My eyes blur, struggling to stay conscious, and I can see the fire growing.

I scream for Rex inside my head as everything goes black.

XIV: SOMETHING IN THE AIR (REX)

The sun is shining, spring is in the air, and I've never been happier, so why do I have this sickening lump in my stomach? It's April. Winter's giving up its Viking grip on the town. I should be beaming like the warm sun, bringing us our first day close to seventy degrees.

Probably because I haven't heard from Knox, yet. It's only been a few weeks, but damn, I'm hoping he's found something by now, knows *something*.

I consider having Tabby give him a call today. As soon as I get home.

A smile tugs at my lips. She'll say no news is good news.

No one has a more positive attitude than her. It's rubbing off, too. I don't think I've ever been so happy, so optimistic in my entire life.

I just can't figure out why it's deserted me as I hit the highway.

Then I'm startled by the flash of metal in front of me,

the one that makes me curse and slam my foot on the brakes. I hit them so fucking hard I swerve onto the shoulder of the road, narrowly escaping a head-on impact from a car shooting the opposite direction, into my lane, in order to make the corner off the gravel road. "Fucking ass-hole!" I shout, even though the speeding bullet is already a tiny dot in my mirror.

A blue Chevy. Those small SUV's all look the same, but...

It was that fucking Alan Schweirsnopopolis or whatever the fuck his last name is.

Cupcake doesn't like him and neither do I. Can't wait for his sneaky, tight-lipped ass to leave the lodge. Him and his bratty son.

That kid should be in school. He's older than the twins. Tabby and I talked about that. Later, she'd flat out asked Alan. He said Brandon is being home-schooled and this trip counts toward a special project.

I call bullshit.

If Alan is the kid's 'teacher' and his dad, the poor boy doesn't stand a chance.

I pull off the shoulder and make the corner onto the mile-long gravel road leading to the lodge. The back of the truck is full of lumber, the final pieces I'll need to cut in the new doorway and board up the old one. The remodel turned out better than I imagined, and several people have already stopped by to see it, mainly because Morris called them, telling them they had to come check it out.

The old man still hasn't given his approval for me to marry Tabby, but I believe it's coming. Or he'll just keep it in forever and watch us get hitched anyway.

Doesn't matter to me.

Long as we live happily-ever-after. I didn't believe in happy endings before her. Now, I'm sold. Lock, stock and barrel, because I'm *already* living it.

Crawling into bed with her every night isn't just amazing, it's an adventure.

She's an adventure.

She's irrevocably mine.

I park in front of the lodge so I can tell her I'm back before driving over to the barn to unload the lumber. I've kept my promise. Never leave or return without telling her. It's worth it. Her goodbye and hello kisses keep me smiling day and night.

Something interferes with my thoughts. I pause. *Odd.*

All my months here, I've never smelled wood smoke before. I grin then, remembering how Tabby promised the boys we'd build a campfire one night soon and roast marshmallows. Make s'mores. Maybe she decided this is the night and decided to give it a trial run.

That's exactly what she'd do. As soon as she gets a thought in her head, she acts on it. I don't mind that in the least. Especially at night, after the boys are asleep...

I jog up the steps and throw the door open.

The boys are there, sitting on a bench outside Morris' office. They bow their heads when they see me. Their eyes are red. Brandon is there, too.

He hasn't been crying. Not like Adam and Chase.

What the fuck?

Hitching up his pants at the waist, Morris walks out of the office. "They're in a time-out. All three of them."

I give the boys a look of disappointment before asking the inevitable. "Why?"

"Dumping dish soap in the hot tub. The whole damn pool room's full of bubbles." Morris points at Brandon. "It's *that* young hooligan's fault. AC were accomplices, I'm afraid."

Shit. "Is that why I saw his father racing out of here?" Alan's left Brandon alone plenty of times so it's not a huge surprise. That's always pissed Tabby off and she's confronted him about it more than once. Yet, with her heart of gold, she keeps an eye on the boy when he's alone.

"Probably," Morris says, then mutters, "Jackass." He nods to Brandon. "Kid says that's where he got the dish soap. That Alan bought it for him, and told him he could put it in the hot tub. I don't buy it one bit."

"Where's Tabby?" I ask. "Cleaning up the mess?"

Morris frowns. "No. Marcy's on it. Haven't seen Tabby since...since we all went looking for these three."

"Looking for them?"

"Couldn't find them. She went outside to search, but I found them right away. It wasn't exactly difficult." Shooting a glare at Brandon, Morris adds, "Dumping dish soap in *my* hot tub."

Imagining how frantic Tabby must be, looking for Adam and Chase, I say, "I'll go find her." Pointing a finger at the boys, I add, "Stay right there. Later, we'll talk."

They nod, heads down again, and I walk back out the front door. I try not to grin, but can almost see bubbles rising out of the hot tub all the way to the ceiling. Rude or not, it's easy to imagine how exciting that would've been for the boys.

They'll still be punished for it, of course. I'll make

them help clean up the mess, teach them they can't destroy other people's property.

My mind switches gears. The smell of smoke is getting stronger.

Too damn strong.

I rush down the steps and around the lodge. It hits me all at once.

"No." Black smoke bellows out of the barn, curdling the sky. "Fuck!"

I run faster as fear strikes lightning in my veins. Trying to fight a fire in there is exactly what Tabby would do. "Tabby! Tabby!"

I'm motherfucking losing it.

There's something pink lying on the ground near the door, confirming my worst fears. I kick the door, hands cupped around my mouth, shouting, "Tabby!"

The door flings open, flames dancing wildly, spilling out the opening. I jump back, but then leap forward trying to see through the flames. "Tabby, Jesus Christ!"

The flames are too strong. I can't see through them. I grab her pink shirt off the ground, using it to fight the blaze. It's tiny. Definitely Tabby's. My heart's racing, my mind has gone lunatic, but something about the T-shirt draws my attention away from the hell that's everywhere.

Writing. Not T-shirt print. Marker.

I stretch the T-shirt between my hands, and my heart stops. It's a message.

Armitage Lighthouse. Come alone or Cupcake dies.

My heart stops. Fear pours ice in my stomach.

Fear, then scalding rage. The Syndicate has her. "Fuck." The images that flash in my mind scare the hell out of me.

Scare me because I see myself taking men by the throat, flaying the skin from their bones.

"Cupcake!"

I turn and run, nearly knocking Morris flat as I round the corner of the lodge. I grab his arms to keep him stable at the last second.

My mind is fucking spinning. Twisting. I can't think.

I can't wait. Not while she's in danger.

"Is that smell...smoke?" he says, catching his footing, blinking in disbelief.

Everything comes back. I let go of him. "The barn's on fire!"

"No shit?"

"No, shit!" I see Marcy on the steps, her shouting, "Call the fire department!"

I don't even stop for a second. Just start racing for my truck again. Morris grabs my arm. My first instinct is to shake him off, but his words ground me.

"Where's Tabby? She's not in there, is she?"

My eyes burn and I know it's not because of the smoke. It's because I'm scared. So fucking scared, and I hate myself. Scared that something will happen to Tabby, and hate the fact it's *all because of me.*

"No, Morris." My throat is on fire. "She's gone. Taken."

"Taken?" Fury and suspicion clouds his eyes. They're hazel just like hers and it rips my heart in two.

There's no time for this.

Pushing away from his hold, I head for my truck. No more distractions.

My hands are trembling so hard I can't get one in my pocket to get the keys. I finally do and drop them. Fuck. Bend down and snatch them up with one hand.

Morris is there, caught up, grabbing my arm again. "What the devil are you talking about – taken? Where's my granddaughter?!" He's unhinged, screaming in my face, and I can't fucking blame him.

I can't think clearly. Too many things smashing through my mind, the guilt another hungry demon. "The Stone Syndicate," I say. "They're after me, and now they've got her."

"Stone Syndi-what? The *mob?*"

What can I say? The uppercut he plants against my jaw is almost expected. Again, I don't blame him. I'd punch anybody responsible for something like this, too. Any stupid, reckless son-of-a-bitch who hurt my granddaughter.

Me.

Tabby.

Tabby! My eyes blur and burn.

"Mob! I *knew* you were trouble!" he shouts, throwing another punch.

That one stings, but I'm too numb to feel more than that. There's already too much pain erupting inside me. "I'll bring her back," I say, opening the truck door. "I promise, Morris. Home and unharmed."

He's still shouting, hitting the side of the truck as I start it.

One word catches my attention. "No cops!" I shout out the window. "I'll bring her back, I promise!"

I mean it, too. If I can't, I'll lose my soul.

The tires squeal as I back up and spin the truck around. Flames eat away at the barn, black smoke spiraling in all directions, filling the air. It'll be a total loss.

I slam my foot on the gas.

I'm coming, Cupcake! *I'm coming.*

Lighthouse.

Armitage Lighthouse. There's one near the lake. I've seen it while in town.

That has to be it. Has to be.

The truck bounces as it leaves the paved parking lot and hits the gravel road, and I hope like hell that's the only lighthouse around here. The only fucking one. The one where she's at.

My mind is still spinning a hundred miles an hour, but I can't figure out who took her. Someone from the Syndicate, but *who?*

There haven't been any strangers around. Then again, anyone working with the Stones would have made sure I hadn't seen them. That's part of their job. Sneaky fucking vermin.

Why had I let my guard down so far? It's all my fault. If anything happens to her – No, I won't even think it, and keep my foot firmly on the gas as I swerve onto the highway.

Firetrucks race towards me, lights flashing and sirens blowing. Unlike the other vehicles, I don't pull onto the shoulder. It's a risk if they have a police escort, but it's one I'll take.

Can't slow down. Not for anything. There isn't time.

I slap the dash, swearing out loud, asking why the lodge has to be ten fucking miles from town. Honking, I swerve around more cars, never taking my foot off the gas.

I finally hit the city limits and weave my way through Split Harbor, running stop signs and stop lights. I've been here before, racing like mad to save the ones I love.

This wasn't supposed to happen *again.*

The anguish from the night with Nelia, Aiden, and the boys is back. It's all consuming. The fear is stronger, darker, worse than I've ever known.

I'd gotten lucky then, even if it cost us our freedom. If fate doesn't smile on me again...

I shake my head. Needing to snap out of it, to focus, I tell myself, "The lighthouse. I have to find the lighthouse."

Right. Go right. Past the gas station.

I swerve right, jumping the curb to keep from hitting the car ahead of me. I slam the gas pedal to the floor again and white-knuckle the wheel as the road curves along the lake shore.

There it is! Ahead on the left. I race forward until I see the entrance, then hit the brake and turn the wheel. The truck slides sideways around the corner, but straightens, just in time for me to slam on the brakes in front of the lighthouse. There's another car.

A blue Chevy SUV.

Alan.

Asshole Alan.

She was in his car when he ran me off the road. She must have been.

I dig my gun out of the glovebox. The metal feels cold against my back as I shove it in my waistband. I take a few seconds to survey the area.

There's Lake Superior. The wind blowing chill, angry waves against the huge boulders, slapping the shores. The sunlight from earlier is gone, devoured by a cold front and grey anvil clouds.

I look toward a few low, barren bushes. He has to have her inside. I run for the lighthouse.

I'll kill the bastard. I swear I'll kill him.

The door opens, hinges creaking. It's dim inside. Hard to see. A staircase and a second door.

Locked.

A thud sounds above.

I grab the handrail and run up the stairs, taking them in twos. The steps spiral around and around, up to the old section where there used to be a beacon going out to sea.

I want to shout, tell Tabby I'm on my way, but know it could do more harm than good. It's miserable, having to decide between assuring her and keeping her safe.

She'll understand. Later.

She'll know I'm coming for her.

That I'll *always* come.

My lungs are on fire by the time I reach the top. It's taller, higher than it looked. I slow, inching my way along the small platform leading to the open door. The wind whistles an eerie tune as it blows in through the opening, icy gusts singeing my face.

I ease into the opening, glancing one way and then the next. There's movement.

Cupcake!

I leap forward. She sees me and shakes her head. Fear fills her eyes as she glances to where the platform curls around the building. Her hands are above her head, tied to the metal rail. Her chestnut ponytail is cockeyed. Tears are falling from her eyes and her face is red. Swollen. Her pink sweater is torn, hanging open, exposing her bra.

Rage shoots through me like lightning. If he fucking violated her –

"Ah, I see you found us." Alan walks around the curved edge of the building, right on cue.

I reach for my gun.

"Pull that gun, and Cupcake dies, T-Rex." Alan has a gun, too. Pointed at Tabby. He laughs. "You thought you were so smart. Getting rid of anything that could track your movements, but you didn't plan on me, did you? I'm like a hound dog. A bloodhound. Sure, it took a while, pinging your phone took me damn near to Tallahassee before I realized it was a decoy. But I always get my man in the end. That's what good bounty hunters do."

Bastard. My hands ball into fists. "She has nothing to do with this. It's me you want. Let her fucking go."

"That's right, but she brought you to me, didn't she? Just like I planned."

"You planned, plenty, didn't you? Dish soap in the hot tub? Quite the father, you fuck. Dragging your son along on a bounty mission..." It's a desperate attempt to appeal to the one thing we have in common, our kids, but I try.

Alan wrinkles his nose. "Oh, that little bastard? He's not my son. He's my cousin's kid. She let me...borrow him, let's say. I figured I'd use him to get to your kids, snatch one so you had to come rescue them, just like you are now. But you barely let those creepy twin guppies out of your sight. And Cupcake here, well, she wouldn't even let old Brandon play with your precious gems. They're too good for him, see."

My rage spikes like a dagger slamming into my brain, turning my insides black with hatred. No one, and I mean fucking no one, ever calls her *Cupcake* except for me.

That's another lesson he'll have to pay for with his life. As soon as I get my hands on him. I just have to be patient. Figure out a plan. Watch for an opening. One that won't cause more harm to Tabby. The stakes were never higher.

I need a distraction, need to throw him off kilter. "So you kidnapped him? Your own cousin's son? You sure are a fucking loser, aren't you?"

He levels the gun on Tabby again. "I'd watch what I say if I were you, Osborne."

Steam hisses inside me, screaming for me to pounce, but it's too dangerous. I can't let him know how much she means to me. How much he's holding over my head.

Trying to get the focus off her, I ask, "So what happens to the kid now?"

Alan paces between the rail and the side of the lighthouse. "That's my problem, Osborne. Not yours." He slaps the wall of the lighthouse before pacing back towards the railing.

Then he runs a hand through his hair, a good sign I've hit a nerve. "I tried to take him home, but the little SOB pitched a fit. Said he'd tell his ma, my idiot cousin, that I'm working for the mob. So we turned around and came back. The shit served his purpose. Cupcake's better bait, anyway." His ugly laugh echoes against the building. "And it worked. You're fucked."

I glance at Tabby. Wanting like hell to assure her she'll be fine.

There's more than panic in her hazel eyes. She's trying to tell me something. A subtle twitch in her pupils. The way she barely moves her head. It takes a moment to realize her hands aren't as far over her head. They've slid down the rail. She twists slightly, just enough for me to know she's working the ropes loose.

Goddamn, I love this woman. She never gives up.

"I'm a lucky man, all things considered," Alan says, still pacing, wheeling his gun back around on Tabby. "After the damn cellphone goose chase you led me on, I picked up your trail. Figured you'd head straight for the border, so that's where I went." He laughs again. "Heard a fisherman say he'd stayed the night at the lodge, met a set of twins. Frankly, Osborne, you made me work my goddamn ass off. But the hunt's paid off. And once I get the bounty on your head, I'll be set for years. Trips to Vegas, condo on the coast, whichever beach front I damn well please. It's foolproof. Won't matter what that little bastard Brandon tells his parents. My cuz will shut her yap real quick after I drop him off and flip her a few thousand. And if she doesn't..."

He laughs again, slapping his gun against his thigh, making it very clear what he's willing to do to his own flesh and blood if they don't play along. I suppress a shudder.

Fuck this freak.

Nothing about *him* is foolproof. He's talking more than he should. I just need to keep that going, bait him into one fatal misstep and use it. Use it against him. His back and forth pacing brings him closer to Tabby every ten seconds or so.

He'll soon be next to her again. He'll have to step over her legs.

I meet her eyes, see her tiny nod. It's like something clicks. Hell's bells do I *love* this woman.

She has to be scared out of her wits, hurting beyond words, and she's still got the wherewithal to read my mind.

I start counting seconds with my breath.

Take a step.

Alan trains his gun on me. "Enough chit-chat. Why the hell am I telling you all this? It's past time for you and me to leave, Osborne. I just wanted you to have one final look at your Cupcake." He grins and turns to Tabby. "Don't worry, Cupcake, someone will find you." He waves his gun as he laughs again. "Eventually. But you won't be so sweet anymore."

I'm fighting the urge to dive at him. *One more step, bastard.*

That's all I need. One last fucking step and he'll be close enough.

"I thought about bringing her to Chicago with us, you know, but she's a royal bitch," he says. "Scratched the shit out of me." He winces, like he can still feel the pain, whatever she did.

Good.

He lifts a foot as if to kick her. Alan moves quick, but not as fast as her.

Tabby strikes first, kicking his other foot.

Now!

I leap forward, kicking the gun out of his hand while he's trying to catch his footing, then I spin around and kick the side of his face with my other foot. He flies backwards, stunned, into the railing. I pause long enough to watch his head bounce off the metal and bang the floor.

He's out cold. As limp as I saw Aiden crash down in the penthouse.

"Tabby! You all right?" I ask, rushing to her.

"Yes, untie me, hurry!"

I work at the knot, loosening it, but have to kiss her.

Her forehead, the top of her head. "Did he hurt you? Where?"

"Rex! Behind you!"

Fuck. So much for out cold.

Twisting around at the sound of her scream, I push away from her as Alan tackles me. We roll across the platform, twice before I end up on top, pinning him down.

I go berserk, punching his face with both fists.

Right. Then left. Then right again.

Asshole punches back, catches my jaw a couple of times. A few teeth rattle in my jaw, the impact making my ears ring. The distraction is enough that he manages to buck me off and kicks me in the gut.

Air locks in my lungs as my back slams into the railing.

I can't breathe, but have to. *Have to.*

He kicks me again. And again.

Stop him. I have to stop this fuck from kicking me. I feel cracking and popping inside me with each kick, my ribcage on fire, and the pain tells me to give in, but I can't.

I have to save Cupcake. No choice. He'll *kill* her if I don't.

Adrenaline surges through me. I push off the railing and charge at him with all my might, driving him hard into the lighthouse's hundred year old brick wall.

He shouts. There's a groan. I can't even tell who, him or me.

I grab his hair and ram his head against the wall. The second he rocks back, I do it again.

And again.

He slumps, finally, then slithers down the wall like the snake he is.

Stepping back, I grab the gun laying by my feet. I don't know if it's his or mine, but shit, I don't care. I level it on him.

"No!" Tabby grabs my arm at the last second. "No, Rex. You're not a killer. We both know that."

I hear her, but I'm cold inside. "He deserves to die. He tried to kill you!"

"Justice, yes, but not by your hand," she says. "Not by the hand I love. This isn't you. You're *done* with all that."

Warmth spreads through me, slowly at first, then faster, filling me. It's incredible how my killing rage thaws by her voice. I drop the gun and grab her, throwing both arms around her.

"I love you," she says. "Love you so much. I knew you'd come. Knew you'd save me, and you did."

I can't speak. My throat is raw, even though holding her fills my heart. I kiss her. Hug her.

I don't want to let her go. Ever again.

My senses are coming back. I grab her arms and hold her just far enough away to look her over. "Where did he hurt you, Tabby? How? Tell me?"

If he fucking violated her, her pleas won't stop me. I'll destroy him and I'll do it with my bare hands.

"I'm okay. Just a little bruised. Nothing else." I search her eyes.

They're beautiful, honest, and so full of love.

"Rex, I'm all right."

Fuck.

She tries to smile but the side of her upper lip is too swollen to curl right. Fresh rage courses through my system all over again.

"Now that you're here, I'm all right," she repeats, stepping forward and laying her head against my chest. "I'll heal. He didn't hurt me in any way that won't."

I'm at a loss for words, except for what's in my heart. "I love you, Cupcake. Christ, I thought I'd lost you."

"I –" She pushes off my chest, terror in her eyes. "Oh my God, the boys! The barn. He lit a fire!"

"Fire department's at the lodge and the boys are fine," I say. "Can you walk? We have to get back there."

"Of course I can." Even cockeyed, her smile is as sexy as ever. "I'll show you the other things I can still do, too, as soon as we get home."

She's joking, of course. We're way too busted for anything more than resting our battered bodies after this, but damn if I don't love the soft humor dancing in her eyes. I caress her cheek, walking, moving her gently.

Home. That sounds more amazing than I'll ever admit.

A few more steps make me start feeling things again, not just the chemical reaction in my brain from Cupcake, but the blows I've taken. My ribs ache like they've had a truck roll over them. Every breath hurts and I'm starting to wheeze.

She reaches up and touches my lip, fear returning to her precious eyes. "You're bleeding."

Though her gaze is soft, there's an angry snap in her eyes. I don't want that. Don't want her to be angry or sad. "It's over," I say. "Get the rope he used on you."

"Rex, no. We need to get you to a hospital." Sighing, she mulls it for a second, then looks at me again. "We need the police. What, are you going to tie him to the rail?"

"No." I'm not exactly *sure* what I'll do with Alan yet, but don't want to tell her. "I'll tie his hands. Just in case he wakes up again before I get him down on the ground."

"I'd leave him here," she says, "but if you say we need to haul him down from here, then we will, even though I'd rather leave him to the seagulls."

Despite all we've just gone through, I smile. I'm lucky to have this woman.

Alan comes to while I'm tying his hands, but he can't do much. Besides some moaning and groaning, when I make him get on his feet, he doesn't say anything. His legs twitch once, too confused, too drained to kick.

"Back, Cupcake!" I roar. "Stay. Several steps behind me just in case he's faking," I tell her, dragging this human trash towards the door and down the spiral staircase. I'm not gentle.

His feet drop from step to step, but for the most part, Alan is dead weight. Holding him up makes my right side, where he got a couple good kicks in against my ribs earlier, ache like hell. I have half a mind to just let him go and pick up whatever's left at the bottom.

But I won't. Tabby is right. I'm not a killer.

I don't need his blood on my hands and the cops won't be far behind.

She knows what happened back in Chicago, understands it was an accident. Knows how much it's poisoned my soul.

Tabby's right. She's too good. Too amazing to ever be married to a murderer, however justified I'd be snuffing him out.

"Are you okay?"

Her question echoes off the lighthouse walls.

"Yes," I answer.

No. My lungs, my bones are in agony.

"It's not much further," she whispers.

I have to grin. I may want to believe I'd just rescued her, but in truth, she's rescued me. Not just today, but weeks ago.

The door hangs open and without gravity fighting to pull at his feet, Alan leans against me, his feet dragging.

I get him to the doorway, gasping for air because my breathing turns so shallow. This isn't me. I've forced loads for construction twice what he weighs.

But it hurts. Hurts so fucking bad to breathe. I take a moment, resting against the door frame. Just a minute to catch my breath.

I should've known there's no such thing as rest for the wicked, or anyone who's touched the truly evil.

"Hold it right there!"

"Hands in the air!"

I look up.

Fuck.

It's the biker sheriff and his friends.

XV: ALL THE PROOF (TABBY)

I run down the last three steps when I see Rex grab the door frame and hang his head. He's hurt. I know he is. Far more than I am.

It's scaring me how bad, how much he's trying to hide it. I rush forward, not sure what to do. I wrap an arm around his back. Alan is slumped against the doorway and I have the urge to shove him aside, out the door, but Rex has a solid grasp on the rope tying Alan's hands together. He's afraid to let go.

Then, over Rex's shoulders, I see men standing outside. Dark blue uniforms. Guns drawn.

It's a moment before recognition hits me.

"Sheriff Cahill!" I shout, jumping so he can see me over Rex and Alan's shoulders. "Help us! Don't just stand there, damn it! Help!"

"Miss Danes? What's happened here?"

"We need an ambulance, Sheriff, right the hell now!"

The men rush forward. Two cops bolt back toward their car and I hear radio static.

"That one needs to go to jail, and this one to the hospital." I tell him, my voice shaking, pointing first to Alan and then Rex.

"No hospital," Rex says. "Clinic, maybe."

"Hospital. Please," Alan moans.

The deputies take Alan, but Rex shoves their hands aside. "Tabby needs an ambulance, not me."

This beautiful, hard-headed idiot. He's trying so hard to seem strong when he's in real danger. I squeeze his arm.

"EMTs on the way," Sheriff Cahill says. "Should be any minute."

The sound of more distant sirens assures me he's telling the truth.

Though Rex doesn't want help, I refuse to take my hands off him and gently guide him to a bench just outside the door. "Sit down," I say.

"No."

"Please? I need to sit down." My legs are shaking, but it's nerves, not pain.

But I know Rex. The only way this stubborn man sits is because I say I need to.

He eases into a spot next to me after I sit.

"So, who wants to do the explaining?" the sheriff asks. "This won't be easy, but I need to know what's happened here."

"I will," I say quickly, before Rex can even start.

He tenses beside me. I take a hold of his hand, the one he doesn't have pressed against his ribs.

"That man, Alan Schweikert, kidnapped me. He started our barn on fire at the lodge, choked me until I blacked out, and then hauled me here..." I leave out anything to do with the Stone Syndicate, even though the sheriff presses for more and Alan keeps insisting that I'm lying. I'm crazy.

I'm not, and lay out exactly what had happened from the time I walked into the barn until Rex arrived.

The truth will eventually come out, but not from me. I'll never testify against the man I love no matter what. I'll vouch for him. I'll be a witness for him, but I'll never say a bad word against him.

Not to anyone but myself, and then only when he's being too stubborn for his own good. Like right now, him refusing aid from the paramedics.

"Will you help me to the ambulance?" I feign a cramped stomach, doubling over, softly whispering in his ear. "Rex, *please*. I might need stitches."

He jumps to his feet, and the way he hisses at the pain in his body hurts me.

"Stitches? Where?" he asks.

"Rex," I say, hooking my arm through his elbow so he thinks he's helping me. I don't need stitches, but know saying I might gets his attention.

He insists they check me out first, and because he's sitting in the ambulance next to me and has no hope of escaping medical attention, I agree.

It takes longer than I want it to, but it's soon declared I'm fine. A short time later, they think Rex has a cracked rib, possibly two broken. He claims he doesn't, that it's just bruised and refuses any additional care.

I beg him to listen. Beg.

At last, it softens his pride.

They tape up his chest as a precaution. Then at my insistence, we climb out of the ambulance.

Alan sits on the bench near the lighthouse with a bandage on his head, several on his neck – where I scratched him – and also on his hands. As if I need more to piss me off, his hands are no longer tied behind his back.

Jesus. At least they've kept him under guard, an officer standing next to him constantly.

All the anger that's been boiling inside me since walking into the barn bursts. Hissing like a car overheating, I march over to Sheriff Cahill, who's standing next to Alan a few seconds later. "You *untied* him, Sheriff?"

"Miss Danes, I'm afraid there's nothing showing this man ought to be charged with a –"

Nope. I stomp my foot. "Hey, did you not hear what I told you?! This man's a criminal, he tried to kill me!"

"He's going to the station. We'll question him in full and –"

"Tabby!" Rex calls out the same time the sheriff starts talking.

Furious, I ball my hands into fists. Unable to think of anything else to do, I step forward and plant my right fist directly in Alan's nose. There's a crunch, startlingly fast.

"That," I shout, "Is for ripping my favorite sweater!"

He bellows, then sobs, "Fuck, my nose! She broke my goddamn nose."

I spin around and grab Rex's arm. "Let's go home."

We eventually get to leave, but not before the sheriff grabs me, explaining that punch wasn't necessary. He tells me Alan is under arrest after all since searching his truck, and I could be charged with assaulting a prisoner. The Sheriff tries not to smile while saying that, knowing I have enough of Gramps in me that I don't give a shit about an assault charge.

I don't.

But I *do* care about protecting Rex, and keep a close eye on him as he drives the truck home. The sheriff lets us go, says he'll be in touch very soon.

I'll insist on Rex getting x-rays later, but I'm relieved he's breathing better. His color is no longer ashen. Still, I'm vigilant, eager to get us home.

"You're something, Tabby Danes," he growls, once we're on the highway and he no longer has to turn the steering wheel so much.

"So are you, Rex Osborne." I kiss his cheek and run a hand over his thigh, even though the movement makes my hand hurt worse. It's swelling. I can feel it. Barely able to separate my fingers. I didn't know punching someone hurt so bad.

I'd do it again, though. Punch that psycho, Alan. Seizing the only chance we'll get before he's locked up for a long time was totally worth it.

Not wanting to bring up the subject, but no longer able to hold it back, I ask, "What now?"

"I'll call Knox as soon as we get home, see if he's made any headway in my case, and..." He huffs out a sigh and shakes his head. "Shit. We have to make sure Alan's the last who comes our way for a while. I need Morris to vet every new person who checks into the lodge like our lives depend on it. Because, honestly, darling, they might."

Knowing fretting won't do any good, I change the subject. "You said the boys are okay?"

"They were in a time-out when I arrived."

"Time-out? That's Gramps' favorite punishment. His only punishment when I was little. What'd they do?"

"Poured dish soap in the hot tub."

"Holy crap, no!" I can't believe it. Those sweet boys?

Amusement flicks in his eyes as he nods. "Several bottles from my understanding."

I cover my mouth with one hand to hide my smile. It's not funny, but to two little boys, all those bubbles would've been delightful. Clearing my throat to wash away any giggle, I say, "That had to have made a mess. Bet Marcy's fit to be tied, too, if they used up her dish soap."

"Morris said Brandon told him Alan gave him the dish soap. Told him to pour it in the hot tub. Didn't believe it at the time, but now it makes sense."

Yikes. The perfect diversion. "That *asshole!* I hope he gets life. Ruined two good shirts, too."

"I know. That's how I knew where to find you."

"How?"

"He left a ransom note on it."

"On my shirt?"

"Yes."

Although I'm pissed, I say, "Good. More proof for us. There's no way the sheriff won't have plenty."

Damn. I'm supposed to be avoiding the subject. "So, did you see the bubbles?"

"No. Morris is the one who found them."

We chat about a few other things, but don't say a lot. We are both too deep in thought, which only increases as we pull into the lodge's parking. It's almost dark, but I can see the charred shell of the barn on the horizon. It stabs my heart in ways I hadn't expected.

"I'll rebuild it, Cupcake. Bigger and better than ever,"

Rex says, seeing my glum face. "Don't even care about the money."

I shake my head, trying to make the tears burning my eyes dry up before they can escape. "The whole horse riding thing was a silly idea any way."

"Hell no, it wasn't. You still have two horses that need shelter and plenty more to come."

I draw a deep breath and let it out. "You're right. We'll take some time. Think about this."

"Ouch," he says. "That had to hurt."

I smile and then shake my head before kissing him. My familiar joke sounds even better coming from him. We both flinch at the end of the kiss.

"You have a fat lip," he says.

"You, too."

He shuts off the truck and I notice the number of vehicles in the parking lot. "Shit. Is the whole town here?"

Rex goes still. Stiff. I turn and freeze at the look in his eyes.

Dread. Pure dread.

Shouts filter into the truck. A mob walks out the front door of the lodge. I smile as the boys run down the steps, closely followed by Gramps and Marcy, but quiver at the number of men wearing three-piece suits who then walk down the steps and towards the truck.

"Who are they?" I ask, forcing the words out.

"I'd guess the FBI." There's an eerie stillness in his voice. Like it's not our world ending *again*.

XVI: FOR US (REX)

"I can't believe it," I say, squeezing Tabby's hand. We're sitting on the couch in the front room of the lodge.

Right where Morris insisted we park to get settled before answering the many dicey questions about to rain down on our heads. Marcy has the boys with her in the kitchen. I'm grateful for that.

They were crazy excited to see us when we came in, which makes me happy. Almost as happy as the news we've just got.

"Believe, buddy," Knox says, slapping my shoulder. "Can't promise it'll hit the news tonight, but the Stone Syndicate will all be behind bars by this time tomorrow."

He's finally here in the flesh. The tall man with dark hair and steely blue eyes I remember, just a few years older than me. He was already on his way here when we called. It's easy to get around when you've got private jets at your beck and call.

Knox had come through for me. In ways I hadn't even

expected. The FBI agents sitting across from us are here for our protection. Not our ruin, after all.

Same with the ones who'd left a short time ago to see Sheriff Cahill about Alan.

"The Chicago Syndicate's been on our radar for years," Agent Sutton says. He's tall, dark, and could easily have a man squirming in his boots. "We were convinced Aiden was blackmailing you, plus several other business owners in the area, but couldn't get the evidence we needed for a warrant. You were too good at covering your own tracks."

"Yeah. My sons' lives depended on that," I reply. I still can't believe all this evil fuckery might finally be ending.

"Certainly, Mr. Osborne." Agent Sutton nods at Tabby. "And let me assure you both that we're on your side. We'll make this right in the end."

"She's not part of this," I say.

"She is now, after being abducted. And that's why we'll be here, with you, Miss Danes, and your sons under our protection until we're one-hundred percent certain there are no other hit men looking for you." Sutton then looks at Morris. "Mr. Danes has given us a government discount on our rooms here at the lodge."

The brief wide grin on Morris' face has me believing that his government discount is more than twice the amount other guests usually pay.

I look at Knox. "I don't even know what to say, except thanks."

He shakes his head. "No thanks needed. You'd have done the same for me, and believe it when I say, I came damn close to cashing in some favors last year. Hurt like hell prying Black Rhino away from my fuck of a business partner." I see his jaw clench. The partner he's talking about was also the low life granddad of his kid from the baby mama who disappeared. We've got so much in common it hurts sometimes. "Don't say you wouldn't have helped because I know better, Rex."

"Damn straight," I agree, wondering how the hell I'll ever repay him for this.

Tabby squeezes my hand. I look her way, see the shine in her eyes and the happiness on her face, and it feels like the entire world just lifted off my shoulders. Not caring who's in the room, who might hear me, I say, "It's over, Cupcake."

"Finally," she breathes out.

"I love you."

"I know you do," she says. "Almost as much as I love you."

Knox is watching, grinning like a fool. "Sorry to cut this short, Osborne, but I've got a plane to catch. Gotta get back to Phoenix. Sunflower's showing off some new shoes in LA this weekend. A man *never* ought to get between a woman's work and her ice cream when she's expecting."

"Congrats again. Give my best to your wife. Bet your little girl's gonna love having a sibling, too." I give his hand another squeeze as he nods. I see the knowing look in his eye.

Shit. In a few more years, maybe less, I'll be in his place. My eyes shift to Cupcake again, her soft, perfect belly. My dick twitches for under a second, drunk on the thought of knocking her up.

Knox stands, getting the stuff he's had laid out for the FBI back in its briefcase.

I want to kiss Tabby, but don't want to hurt her. That only lasts a moment. The pain will be worth it. She'll agree. The kiss we share is soft and gentle, but so heartfelt I swear my chest swells, and not from the ribs that ache like no tomorrow.

"Excuse me."

Our lips part as we both glance towards the doorway.

"Evening meal's all ready," Marcy says. "And your servers will be three very well behaved young gentlemen. With my help, of course."

Tabby looks at me. We both slump slightly, then smile.

She grimaces, taking in the Federal Agents and my buff friend filling the room. I imagine her thoughts are the same as mine.

With the kids serving dinner, we'll soon have a room full of FBI men with food spilled all over their crisp suits.

"You two stay," Marcy says, eyeballing me. "You'll eat your meal here. No need to move around more than necessary. I've also prepped a room upstairs for you so you don't have to walk all the way to the cabin."

"That's not necessary," I say. "I'm not hurt that –"

"Humor her," Morris snaps. "And them." He nods towards Knox and the FBI agents walking out of the room.

We're the only three left in the room when he adds, "And me. I uh, well, damn, I guess I..." He swipes his fingers across his mouth, inhaling a long breath. "I owe you both an apology."

Now I know Cupcake and I are thinking the same thing.

Ouch, that had to hurt.

She squeezes my hand again.

"Listen, I'd be a real jackass if I can't admit when an old man's wrong. About more than one thing. I've been hard on you Tabby-kitten. I'm sorry about that, but you were all I had. I was afraid to let go. Scared you'd leave me. Just like your mom did. I should've known better. You're not like she was. Not at all. You've proven that to me a hundred times over, but I was still afraid to take a chance. To let you have your own life with him." He nods toward me, a softness I've never seen in his eyes.

Tabby doesn't say a word, so I don't either, knowing she needs to hear him out. Needs to know how truly wonderful she is, confirmed by the one person she's been trying to please her entire life.

I know something about that. Morris reminded me of my father since day one.

"I knew it was inevitable. Someday, some good-looking stranger would check in here and you'd fall in love." Morris chuckles slightly. "Just never counted on it being three of them all at once."

She nods and glances at me. "That's true."

"I know it is," Morris says. "Knew it for certain when you stood up to me. Oh, you'd argued with me before, but never with the passion you had when it came to Rex and AC, and I can accept that. I can accept *them*, Tabby, because they've shown they're made of tough stuff. Just like us."

Morris looks at me. "Rex, if you're still interested, I'd be honored to have you marry my Tabby. Honored to call you my grandson." He stands, holding his hand out to me.

I stand, hiding a flinch at how badly my ribs bother me, and take his hand. Shake it hard. "Marrying this woman's all I'll ever want. Thank you, Morris, I'm honored, too. Honored to become part of your family." Although I'm happy to have the man's approval, I'm extremely happy for Cupcake, knowing how much his consent means to her.

"It won't be easy." Morris lets go of my hand after giving it a final firm shake. "She's a handful."

"Oh, I've discovered," I say, my smile growing wider than the sky.

He chuckles, bends down and kisses Tabby's cheek. "I love you, Tabby-kitten."

"I love you, Pops," she says, kissing his cheek right back.

They both laugh, and I feel as if I've been left out of a secret, but I don't mind.

Morris looks at me, "By the way, I have another job for you, soon as you're better. The spa room needs to be remodeled. It's about time. Got ourselves a brand new hot tub ready to go in, courtesy of an estate sale from the Caspians. They're upgrading to an indoor pool, I hear. Those billionaires can buy anything." He nods towards Tabby. "You remember them, don't you?"

She nods.

I know the name. Ryan Caspian's enormous palatial property backs up to the acreage next to the lodge. I've barely seen the house – the *castle* – through the trees. Him and his company are the reason Split Harbor's back on the map in Michigan.

"Caspian wants to talk to you, Rex," Morris says. "His wife, Kara, heard about the work you did in the barn. Wants you to do some for them next, if you're game."

"Sounds good," I say, trying to hide my excitement.

I'm not used to this, my good luck multiplying. Working for this billionaire could open doors to God only knows what. I'm beyond willing to start a new business right here in Split Harbor as soon as possible, maybe resurrect the T-Rex Construction brand and see how many of my old crew are willing to relocate.

My future thoughts are interrupted a second later. Adam and Chase, each carrying a small tray, along with a woman who cleans for the lodge during the week, walk in the room. "Dinner, Daddy!" they both chime at once.

"Easy, boys, let me get them some TV trays," Morris says, scurrying across the room to a stand holding several wooden flip top trays. "I was too busy talking."

"Well, look at you two!" Tabby beams at the boys.

"We're helping so you and Daddy get better faster," Chase says.

"We are," Adam says. "And it's fun. And we're sorry."

"They're doing a great job," the woman, Betty, says. "Even that other little rascal is minding his manners."

"What'll happen to Brandon?" Tabby asks, looking at me.

Before I can form any thoughts, Betty says, "The FBI already contacted his parents. His mom's on her way to get him." She shakes her head. "Poor little boy, stolen away from home like that. We were harboring a kidnapper and didn't even know it. Can you imagine? Right here in Split Harbor."

Neither of us want to think about it. From what I've read about the Caspian's drama, things as dark and crazy as this have happened before in this little town. And I hope this is the last time.

Morris had already stood two trays in front of us. As soon as Betty and the boys fill them with plates of food, utensils, glasses of water and some condiments, she ushers the boys out of the room.

"You two eat up," she says. "We'll be back to see if you need more in a minute."

"I feel sorry for him," Tabby says once we are alone. "Brandon."

"Me, too," I admit, staring at the food before us.

The room takes on a heavy silence while we eat. Earlier, I'd felt the weight lifting off my shoulders, but there's still too much unknown. Too many loose ends. Too many complications that can still crop up like jungle weeds after all that's happened.

Too damn many lives damaged, destroyed, and all thanks to my mistakes.

Me. And I'm imagining how the good folks of Split Harbor will gossip once they learn the full story. The whole truth about Nelia, hit men, my escape, the boys.

Can Adam and Chase have a normal life here?

What about the lodge?

We'll need every lucky break we can get.

I realize I'm picking at my food and lift my fork. "We'd better eat something, or Marcy will spoon feed us."

She nods. "You catch on quick."

There's a tiny smile on Cupcake's face, but it's strained. So is mine.

My ribs hurt like hell every time I twist, and now the weight returns to my shoulders, sending an ache deep through my bones.

We eat what we can and set our forks down after barely making a dent in the hefty portions. I lean back, wrap an arm around her, and pull her against my side.

As her head settles on my shoulder, she lets out a heavy sigh. "It'll all work out. I know it will."

"It has to," I agree. It fucking *has to*. I can't be this close to a perfect life and have it shattered. I've already had that happen once.

I don't want her happiness shattered, either, but can't deny the fact Knox never said anything about me being cleared. Though the FBI said they're on our side many times, they also know I was money laundering. That doesn't just go away. There'll be consequences to pay. Possibly money or even jail.

My thoughts are turning darker when I hear the front door open. Tabby lifts her head off my shoulder as the sheriff walks in the room, followed by one of the FBI agents who'd gone to town earlier, and a third man I don't recognize.

"Ms. Danes, Mr. Osborne," the sheriff says. "This is Dr. Mumford, he's here to examine you both."

I didn't know doctors made house calls, especially not under these circumstances. However, I do know they make jail visits.

My heart starts thudding. "Why, Sheriff? We were already checked out by the paramedics."

"Precautions." One word is all he gives.

"If that rib's broken, you could have a punctured lung and don't know it yet," the doctor adds, taking off his coat. "And I should look at that hand." He's staring at Tabby now.

I glance her way. Her face turns pink as she pinches her lips together and looks the other way. I reach over and gently lift the hand she has lying on her lap under her T.V tray. Remorse washes over me.

"Why didn't you say something?" I ask, examining the hand that's almost twice as big as it should be. How had I missed it? Or the welts on her neck. She'd straightened her sweater, buttoned it to cover herself, but not just because of modesty.

She was trying to hide just how hurt she is. No different than me.

Fucking fool, this is your fault, I tell myself. I should've been honest up front. *No more secrets.*

I remember her words after we got engaged and quietly vow to make them law, from here on out.

"It's fine," she says. "I'm fine. Really."

That fucking bastard, Alan. Call me a fucking-bastard, too, but I'd never been prouder of her than the moment she'd smashed him in the nose. "Let him, Cupcake. Better to be sure. Go ahead, doctor," I say. "Let's get this done. I'll be next in line." If she won't participate unless I do, so be it.

"I'll need an examining room."

"Right this way." Morris is in the doorway, gesturing towards the elevator.

The TV trays are lifted away and every muscle in my body screams as I stand up, but the real pain comes when I see how much agony getting off the sofa causes Tabby. She winces, using her good hand as much as she can for leverage.

"We should get her to a hospital," I say. "Now."

"If I deem it necessary, certainly," the doctor says. "For either one of you. Or both."

We're escorted to room 205. Soon, she's on one bed, me the other, wearing nothing but our underclothes and draped with hotel bathrobes. I *insist* the doctor examine Tabby first.

A mixture of sorrow and anger roils inside me at the sight of the bruises marring her skin. I know that body.

Every inch of it, and there hadn't been a mark on it anywhere this morning.

Marcy is in the room with us, just around the bend so she can't see, listening intently to everything the doctor says. There's an FBI agent right outside the door. Which makes me believe they aren't here in case there's another hit man out there.

They're here to make sure I don't run again. Couldn't be more obvious.

The doctor sits on the edge of the bed beside Tabby and touches the ice pack on her hand. "Ice will help with the swelling. Don't think anything's broken, but if it's not better in a couple of days, we'll need to have it x-rayed to make sure." He waits for her to nod before saying, "You'll be sore for quite a while, especially your throat. He was quite forceful, I'm afraid. If it starts to swell, or you lose your voice, come to the clinic right away, or the hospital if it's after hours."

She nods again and it dawns on me then how little she's spoken since we got home. Alan had strangled her, almost to death.

Fury knots my stomach tight. I'm starting to regret not killing that sick fuck.

"There'll be a prescription waiting for you at the drug store in the morning," the doctor says. "For now, I'm going to have you take these. One's a muscle relaxer, the other a pain pill."

Tabby pulls the robe around her as she sits up and takes the pills. The pain on her face renews the agony in me. This was the last thing I'd wanted. Her to be hurt.

"Your turn," the doctor says, standing next to my bed.

"I'm fine."

"I'll be the judge of that."

If my rib wasn't broken before his examination, it might be by the time he's done prodding, but even that would be nothing compared to Tabby's shins. I swear new bruises are appearing on her sweet skin the longer I stare while she sits on the edge of her bed. She's asking the doctor a multitude of questions about broken ribs.

Her concern is for me. All of it.

I don't dare close my eyes or even blink. When I do, I see Alan dragging her up to the top of the lighthouse, her fighting the entire way. If I'd been too late, if I hadn't saved her...

"You'll have a prescription waiting, too," the doctor says, reaching for the pill bottles he'd set on the table after giving Tabby some.

I sit up and shake my head. "I don't want anything."

"Take them," Tabby says. "Please."

The way my hand goes out to take the pills and glass of water from the doctor tells me something I already knew but hadn't recognized until this moment.

My heart no longer belongs to me. It's hers, forever bound to her happiness.

There's no more me. There's just us, her and I, two souls forever lost in shared passion, pain, fury, and grins.

As soon as the doctor and Marcy – who says not to worry, that the boys will be with her all night –

leave, I climb off the bed. Folding back the covers, I ease the robe off Tabby's shoulders. "Hot bath or bed?" When she doesn't answer right away, I sit down next to her. "You can point if it hurts to talk."

"It doesn't hurt that much to talk."

I softly run a finger along the side of her face. "You haven't said much since we got home."

She shrugs. "I haven't had much to say. I'm just glad you're safe." Sighing she leans her head against me. "I want to believe it's all over, but..."

She pauses. Shaking her head, she continues, "I just don't know, Rex. I want it over, I want it done, but nothing's this easy."

I kiss the top of her head, agreeing completely, but I don't want to admit it.

I'd rather assure her it's over, make her believe. At the same time, I can't lie to her. Can't tell her another fact that eats at me every time I see one of her bruises, either. With a good enough lawyer, Alan could get off free. Maybe not for years, but damn it, someday.

In the best scenario they charge him with kidnapping Brandon – if the boy's mom presses charges –

and with abducting Tabby. Serious crimes, but neither guarantees a life sentence.

Not like murder. Knox never mentioned that. Aiden's dead and I killed him.

Accidentally or not. I can't run from the truth. Have to face it, but Tabby doesn't. She doesn't have anything to do with it, thank God.

She lifts her head and stares at me, her dark eyes bore deep.

Stepping back, out of my arms, she shakes her head. "Stop. Just stop."

"Stop what?"

"Stop thinking."

"Cupcake, I'm not –"

"Yes, you are." She grabs the robe off the bed and

grimaces while shrugging it on. "Don't lie to me, Rex. And don't you dare try running this time. You're completely lost inside your head."

"Darling, I can't. We've got the FBI right outside."

"But that's what you were thinking, isn't it?"

How can she know that? My deepest, fucked up fears? She can't truly read my mind. *Right?*

"I know," she says. "You had the same look in your eyes when you left the cabin that morning. The day you loaded up Adam and Chase and skedaddled. You're afraid. For me."

"Skedaddled?" I say, a sorry ass attempt to ease the anger flashing in her eyes.

"Yep," she snaps. "Skedaddled. And the only reason you came back was because you needed –"

"You," I interrupt. "You, Tabby, are the reason I always come back. Hope you know it. Whatever the fuck happens, there's nothing that'll *ever* tear me away. Not anymore." Now I've got her attention. "No running. No skedaddling. No surrender. Not this time, Cupcake. Even if there's heavy, fearsome shit to work through."

"I know," she whispers. But I'm not convinced yet she believes it.

"Things *I* need to work out."

"You?"

"Yes. Me." I sigh at the pressure inside me. There's no other choice. "If it's too much, Cupcake, we can slow down."

"Slow down?" She nods. "Slow down what?"

"Us. Just till we heal and fix this shit. Wait for things to get worked out, and –" I'm babbling like a madman, but fuck, I just keep seeing her in the lighthouse. Hurt and afraid and under the gun, literally, thanks to me.

"No. You're *not* getting cold feet now."

"No, no cold feet, darling. Everything happened so fast." I shake my head. "Hell, everything you do to me comes fast. You *never* sit down and rest. Never sit still. Never quit, every second you're in my head."

"Rex..." my name sounds like a curse on her lips.

"Darling, I'm not done. I don't want you hurt. Can't stand the thought of anything else ever happening to you because of my past. I –"

"Bullshit!" She moves suddenly, shoving at my chest with both hands. "Bullshit, Rex! You can't run away this time, so you're trying to run from what you can: me. Well, I won't let you. You hear? I won't let you! So take your doubts and second guesses and scary nightmares and shove them –" She pauses while my eyebrows try to bolt off my face. "Rex, you know what I'm trying to say. Whatever happens, whatever we have to do, we'll do it together. There's no more me and you. There's us."

Us.

Fucking-A, she's right.

Right about everything.

So painfully correct I want to kick my own selfish, battered ass.

That's exactly what I was trying to do. Run. Push her away without even realizing it. Still seems like my only choice, but it *is* a choice, isn't it?

"You can't suffer due to me. Not again," I growl.

"And I won't. That's over, Rex. Over and done. Remember?"

Yeah. Maybe, just maybe, she's right about that, too.

"Fight this time, Rex. Fight just like you did with Alan. Stay, join, and fight. Fight for yourself. Fight for the boys. For us." Tears glisten something fierce in her eyes, the truest thing I've ever seen. And she's not done. "Fight for me." She takes a hold of my hand. "And I'll fight for you. Always. You and the boys. We'll work this out, Rex. I know we will. Together."

I pull her forward, wrap my arms around her, and hold on. Give her a grip so tight I finally see the naked truth.

She's right. Again. Always.

Hell yeah, I'll fight this time. Fight to my last breath. Whatever it takes. As long as it takes.

Fighting for us, all of us, is worth it.

It's worth damn near everything.

She sighs and nuzzles my chest with her nose. "You don't have to admit I'm right, but I am. And I'm not too fast. I'm efficient. There's a difference."

She looks up at me, and the smirk on her face does what it always does. Makes me grin, makes me happy. "Efficient?"

"Yes, I'm very efficient."

"Too efficient," I whisper.

That's her, the first time in my life I've heard that word without it being attached to some cold, boring crap. But it works because Tabby Danes really is 'efficient' in everything, including making me see the light in this endless dark. I kiss her, carefully since her lip is still swollen, and watch the darkness go like a bad tide rolling out to sea.

Won't always be as easy as tonight. But with her on my lips, reminding me how real *us* can be, it doesn't stand a chance.

A knock sounds on the door, breaking us apart. My

disappointment must show on my face because she laughs softly.

"Let them in," she says. "Neither of us are in any condition to do more than talk, anyway."

"Soon," I promise, kissing the tip of her nose. I wait for her to tie her robe closed before saying, "Come in"

The door cracks open slightly. "Are you decent?"

"You've seen me in less," I tell Knox.

"I have, sad to say. War and privacy don't exist in the same universe," Knox says, entering the room. He closes the door behind him, a mysterious smirk on his face. "You both doing okay?"

"We'll live," I say.

Knox folds his arms across his chest and leans against the door. "Almost went to the airport without the big news, but it came in at the last second. Listen, I didn't get a chance to say much earlier, and I know you, Osborne. Your mind's coming up with every fucked up scenario. You're busy trying to figure out what you can do about each and every one of them."

He does know me. Almost as well as Cupcake. I wrap an arm around her shoulders. "There's more than just the money laundering?" I ask, knowing there must be. "What did the Feds decide? Do they know the rest?"

"Enough. You know you can trust me when I say, stop worrying." Knox shakes his head. "At least you should. You did everything you could and you did it the right way. Kept your nose clean. The profit and loss records you had your accountant email to your lawyer every month, your tax filings, it's all there. The Syndicate thought they were dealing with a pansy, a dickless, sloppy boy scared out of his mind. Not the man who'd take them down."

"There's got to be consequences. What I did was illegal, Knox. And I knew it." I huff out a breath. "Plus Aiden's dead. That's on me, too."

Knox nods. "He is. Good fucking riddance. What I couldn't tell you downstairs, Osborne, is that Aiden didn't die from a blow to the head. He was shot. Killed along with his bodyguard while his man tried to stuff him in the back seat of his car. The drive-by happened quick, not long after the guard reported you to the *capo.*"

"Drive-by? I didn't shoot him." My mind searches, making sure I'm remembering correctly. "I know I didn't, I had the boys and we had to get the hell away."

I grab my head. This doesn't make sense.

"There was no one else there that night. Just the bodyguard," I say, recalling every dirty detail.

"Wrong. Someone else was there, all right" Knox tells me. "Turns out it wasn't just you and his own mafia Aiden was screwing over, skimming money and drugs. He'd just done a big cross-country shipment to Chicago and stiffed the man in charge of the escort on pay. And right after you left, he showed up. Shot both Aiden and the bodyguard right behind the penthouse." Knox's smirk grows bigger. I remember how much fun he liked to have leaving us in suspense during our Army days.

"Enlighten me?"

"His pissed off security chief and part-time bounty hunter. Alan Schweikert."

XVII: ENOUGH FOREVER (TABBY)

Four months later

IF SOMEONE TOLD me four months ago that I'd be standing here on this gorgeous summer day, about to marry the love of my life, I'd have called them a liar. Today, I'd invite them to my wedding.

Probably did. The entire town is here, people from around the world. Literally.

Rex's mom is here from Italy, and his father from Hawaii. Army buddies from too many places for me to remember, old business friends, and family. Cousins, aunts, uncles from everywhere.

There are even a few FBI agents in attendance. The case is almost wrapped up. These are just the people we got to know *very* well during those first six weeks after Alan was arrested. We'll be working with them again, once he goes on trial, and everything says it should be a slam dunk. The murder charge will put him away for good.

The back lawn of the lodge is manicured to perfection, flowers with more colors than the rainbow popping out of the rich soil. People are already filling up the many rows of white chairs. The caterers began filling the kitchen hours ago in order to feed the masses later on, and the band is set up in their stage area, next to the wooden dance floor.

My favorite spot is the large white gazebo Rex built with his own hands, where we'll tie the knot, officiated by yet another one of his army buddies, a chaplain, very, very soon.

It'll just be the two of us up there, plus Adam and Chase, who are sharing ring bearer duties.

I turn to Gramps, who fusses with the tie that came along with his shiny black tuxedo. "If I'd ever imagined my dream wedding, this would be it," I say. "I don't know how to thank you."

"Then don't." His tone is serious, not grumpy. "I owe you this, Kitten. Best money I ever spent."

His nickname doesn't bother me in the least.

"I started a savings account in your name the day you were born. Backup money, in case you ever needed it." He nods towards the cabin window I'd been gazing out moments ago. "That man you're about to marry will make sure you never want for anything in your life, he's already proven that, so the very least I can do is pay for your wedding. And there'll be plenty left over after this shindig."

He winks one eye. "I'm not even charging the guests for their overnight lodging."

I kiss his cheek. "Thank you for that, too."

Marcy, dressed in ruffled pink from head to toe and wearing a floppy hat, pokes her head through the door. "It's almost time!"

I bite my bottom lip to keep from laughing. Rex believes I'm wearing a dress exactly like the one Marcy is wearing. I've had her dress hanging in my closet for a couple weeks, mostly as a joke because he teased me, saying he knew my wedding dress would be pink. I swear, sometimes I think pink is his favorite color now, not mine.

My dress is white. No ruffles. No lace. Just a long flowing piece of silk that hugs me all the way to the ground, except for my back. There's an open V that goes almost down to my hips, and a slit along the side of the skirt that goes all the way up past my knee. He'll love it.

I'm not wearing a veil, but am carrying a bouquet of pink roses. I *had* to get the pink in somewhere, after all.

"Ready, Tabby-kitten?"

"I am, Gramps. More than ready."

Marcy pushes the door open wide and we step out. He's yards away, clear on the other side of the rows of chairs, but I feel Rex's eyes on me, and it makes me smile.

"I'm happy about this, Tabby," Gramps says as we start walking. "Very happy."

"Me, too, Gramps, and thank you. Knowing you're happy makes me even happier."

He walks me all the way to Rex, who can't help grinning. The mischievous glint in his eyes tells me how much he likes my dress already.

"Tabby, you're pretty" Adam bursts out over the music.

"Princess Tabby," Chase says, smiling.

I kneel down in front of them. "Thank you. You both look so handsome." They really do. Both in black tuxes, just like their father. I kiss each of their cheeks. "I love you both and I'm so happy I get to be your mother."

"We are, too!" they say together.

Adam then looks up at Rex. "You want the ring now, Daddy?"

"Not yet," he says, holding his hand out to me.

I take it, stand, and then step up next to him.

"You do look like a princess," he says next to my ear. "A fucking sexy one."

I laugh and nod toward the chaplain. "Good thing he's the only one with a microphone."

"Who gives this woman into holy matrimony?" the chaplain asks.

"I do," Gramps says.

"And who gives this man into holy matrimony?"

"We do!" Chase and Adam shout.

Gramps moves over and stands beside the boys as Rex and I walk up the steps, into the white gazebo, to stand before the chaplain.

The service is scheduled to be short and sweet and perfect. It is.

It's also flawless. Gramps makes sure the boys hand first Rex, then me, our rings at the precise moment. The kiss Rex initiates and I *fully* melt in, has the entire yard clapping and cheering.

He has me bent backwards, over his arm, and the way he's looking at me, his eyes twinkling...holy hell. If I wasn't already head-over-heels in love with him, I'd have fallen all over again.

Slowly, he pulls me upright, and kisses me again, before we turn to the crowd.

"Ladies and gentlemen," the chaplain says, "allow me to present, for the very first time Mr. and Mrs. Rex Osborne!"

The crowd cheers again.

We walk down the steps. He takes Adam's hand and I take Chase's, and Gramps and Marcy follow us all the way back down the aisle between the chairs. The photographer is a few feet ahead of us. I hear the click of the shutter just as Rex looks down at me, and me up at him. We're both smiling bigger and brighter than the sun. I know, without even seeing it, that'll be my favorite picture.

Hours later, after we've eaten, laughed, danced, and had an amazing time, Rex whispers in my ear. "Time to go."

"Go? Go where?"

"I have something to show you."

Convinced I know what he wants to show me – and do to me – I stretch on my toes and kiss his lips. "Lead the way."

The plan is for the boys to spend the night in the lodge with Gramps, as they've done several times, so Rex and I can have the night alone in my cabin. I'm a little worried about that. The party is still going strong, the band has only played a little over half its songs. It doesn't bother me for people to know what we'll be doing in the cabin, I just don't want to be interrupted.

He takes my hand, and then I notice we're walking the opposite direction.

"Wait, where are we going?"

"I told you."

"You said you want to show me something."

"I do."

"I thought we'd do *that* in the cabin, but if you have another idea..." I'm game. I think.

A wicked heat roars between my thighs, imagining the surprises this man might have in store.

He stops, spins around, and kisses me hard. His tongue chases mine until my knees buckle and I swoon – yes, *swoon* – into his magnificent chest.

"I love you, woman."

I laugh. "Don't I know? Not that I'll ever get tired of hearing it."

He takes my hand and we're walking again. "Will you ever get tired of me telling you how beautiful you are?"

It might sound egotistic, but I say it honestly. "No."

He lets out a low whistle. "You knocked me for a loop when you walked out wearing white. I expected pink. And demure. That dress is sexy as all hell."

"Glad you like it. I picked it out with you in mind."

"Bullshit. You picked it knowing it'd get me harder than a rock."

"Did it?"

"Hell, yes. Mission accomplished, Cupcake."

I smile, melding into another kiss. We walk around the newly built stable and towards the woods. "Where are we going? My white dress won't stay spotless for long if we take care of your hard-on in the woods."

"I won't ruin your dress," he whispers. "Not out here, anyway."

"I'm not worried about ruining it as much as I am

about you getting stuck in the back with sticks, because I guarantee you, I'm taking top out here."

I swear, the closer we've gotten to the wedding, the more we've had sex. Indoors, outdoors, morning, noon, and night. Hard and slow and often. And everything in between.

More than once, the places where we've done it weren't the most comfortable. Not that I cared for very long. The front seat of his truck was probably the most awkward, but also the most fun considering we were in the parking lot at the big box store in town. It was dark, a late night grocery run without the kids, and he decided he'd take me then and there.

I'm glad he did. I always am. I came with my hands on his shoulders, rocking my hips into his, kissing frantically at his shoulder and trying not to let the whole of Split Harbor hear my screams.

I'm wet now at the memory.

Thankfully, he has his head together. He pulls aside a branch and with a mischievous grin, gestures for me to go through a small clearing in the trees.

I take a step and pause. Weird. There's never been a trail here before. But it's there now. It's wide, newly made, and gravel has been paved for easy walking. "What's this?"

"Told you I'm going to show you something, Cupcake."

"I know that much. What I don't know is what your something is."

"Soon, darling. Keep moving."

Having lived my entire life at the lodge, I know the moment we leave Gramps' property. "You do realize we're trespassing, don't you? On Caspian's land, no less."

"No. Not anymore."

"Yes, we are!" I'm insistent, but he doesn't fight back.

His lips just silence me, too swift for me to latch on for what I'd call a kiss. Then, he points to the gravel, where there's a single pink flower petal.

I laugh and pick it up. "You truly are a romantic."

The trail turns around a corner and I gasp. The entire walkway is covered with pink petals.

"Come on," he says, pulling me forward.

As the woods end, there's a newly built garden arch. I stop beneath it to stare at the big house with red wooden clapboard and white trim. I've seen the blueprints for this place in his office.

Inside and out. Even helped pick some of the details.

The flooring, counter tops, paint colors, and more than once wondered if we'd ever live in a house like it. That's highly unlikely. I have a job at the lodge, and always will. Might as well keep living there, yet I'm shocked he's been working so close to home all these weeks. I thought he was splitting his time between the crew at the lodge and the one working on Caspian's place?

"This is the new guest house for the Caspians, isn't it? This is closer than I thought. Figured they'd want it out past the lake."

He merely grins and leads me across newly laid sod until we're standing before the house, before the big front porch. Waving a hand, he says, "This stretch isn't Ryan and Kara's anymore. He sold off a chunk. Traded it, really, as a bonus for a job well done. It was after I finished the real guest house out by the lake."

Real guest house? He *can't* possibly mean...

I'm stunned. Can't even speak.

"I built the pathway so we can walk back and forth to

the lodge. It's less than half a mile. Those trees helped give me cover, they'll be trimmed back now that you're in the know, Cupcake."

"You bu-built us a-a –" I'm still too stunned to speak. To comprehend.

"Yours, Cupcake. Ours. Our house. Our home. Just you and me and the kids." He wraps his arms around me from behind and bites gently at my ear. "Surprise."

Oh. My. God.

"Rex!" I spin around. Hug him. Kiss him. I thought I couldn't get any happier, that my life couldn't get more perfect, and then he does this! Builds us a house next door to the lodge. I spin around. "Can we go inside?"

"Hope so. Cupcake, do the honors."

We run up the steps hand in hand. He opens the door. "It's not furnished yet. Thought I'd leave that up to you. Except for a bed and a couple tables in the master bedroom, that much I took care of."

"Ah, the most important part." I run a hand over his hard stomach as I walk into the big, open space. The wood flooring is the golden oak I'd picked out, the walls painted the soft beige I'd chosen, too, and the trim is a glistening white. Again, the shade I loved. "It's gorgeous. So freaking gorgeous. And perfect. Just like I imaged."

"I listened to every one of your suggestions. Burned them into my brain, Cupcake. Wanted it to be us, exactly."

I spin around and hug him. "*You're* exactly what I want. And always will be." I plant a wet promising kiss on his lips. "I want you, Rex. Here. Now."

"We're getting to that," he says. "But I'm not done with my surprise."

I shouldn't be disappointed. The house is beautiful and

I love it, but I've been thinking about my husband's hard body all day. He looks so good in that tux, shoulders square and broad, his ink civilized and oh-so-ready to break out the second he's naked again.

It wouldn't take much to go over the edge.

He pulls me into the kitchen area.

The cupboards I'd picked out, the marble counter top. I have to take a second look, and then ask, "Is that?"

He nods. "Cupcake for my Cupcake."

I walk towards the counter where a cupcake the size of a five-tiered cake sits. "It's flipping huge!" I swipe a finger in the frosting. "And it's real."

"Of course it's real."

"Where?" I shake my head, not really wanting to know.

I still like baking them a whole lot more than eating them, honestly. But tonight, for him, I'll feast on anything and I'll love it.

He picks up a knife and cuts into the big cupcake. I don't want to be ungrateful, but I hope like hell he doesn't want to stand here and eat that damn thing. I spin away, looking out the window, to a yard where I imagine a swing set for the boys, and a tree house in one of the big tall oaks.

I'm still excited, but am starting to think about reality. "How did you afford all this? *Can* we afford all this?"

"Of course. I made the deal on the land with Caspian, like I said, soon as the insurance company paid out on my house."

"You used that money to start your company here," I point out. The insurance company had gone after the Stone family for burning down his house in Chicago. When he'd received his payment, he'd resurrected his construction company here. Even a couple of the men who'd worked for him in Chicago had moved here and are working for him now. That's how the spa remodel at the lodge and the new stable got done so fast, as well as this place, evidently.

"No, that was the money from my shop. They were two separate properties." He steps over and takes both of my hands, pulling me back towards that cupcake. "I wasn't trying to hide anything, just wanted to surprise you."

"Congratulations, I'm *thoroughly* surprised." Glancing at the cupcake, I say, "And, the cupcake is sweet, but I'm not really hungry."

He laughs. "You don't even like cupcakes."

I'm stunned. "You remember?"

"Darling, I remember everything about you." He grabs my hand and shoves it inside the cake. "Tell me when you feel something."

My fingers have already encountered something hard. "What is it?"

"Pull it out."

My mind goes to something much more fun to pull in and out, but I pull out the small plastic container. "What's this?"

"Open it."

I take off the lid, and pull out a piece of paper. It's a computer print-out. A flight itinerary. With tomorrow's date. And a destination. My heart leaps. "Hawaii?"

He nods.

"We're going to Hawaii? Tomorrow?"

"Honolulu, Tabby. And then whatever island we damn well please."

I scream. Hug him. Kiss him. Then I slump against him. "There are no more surprises, right? Right?! I can't take any more. This was already the best day of my life, and then you did...all this."

He takes the print-out and lays it on the counter. "We don't fly out till tomorrow night, so there's plenty of time to pack. My parents and their spouses are going to stay at the lodge for a week, to help Morris with the boys while we're gone."

His parents are very nice people, so are their spouses, yet I quiver slightly. "A week with Gramps can be a lot."

"So can a week with my folks."

I glance at the cupcake. "How –"

"Don't ask." He shakes his head. "I was trying to come up with a way to surprise you with the tickets, and mentioned it to Shirley."

"At the gas station?"

"Yes, her daughter wants to be a baker, so..."

Laughing, I step up and run my hands up and down his chest. "Talk about a tough act to follow. All your surprises makes mine seem so insignificant."

He runs a fingertip the length of my arm. "There's nothing about you that's insignificant. And I love the shit out of surprises."

I nuzzle his chin, marveling at how wonderful he always smells. "I hope you truly feel that way."

"I do. Always."

Stepping back, I slip one thin dress strap off my shoulder, and then the other. As my dress slowly slides down my body, I say, "Because I went commando all day, just for you."

He lets out a husky growl while stepping forward. "I

knew I didn't feel any panties every time I rubbed your ass." After a long mouth on mouth kiss, he says, "Let's move this surprise to the bed."

He scoops me into his arms. I hug his neck, loving how his muscles ripple against my fingertips.

While walking down the hall, he licks my nipple, adding flames to the fire that's been smoldering inside me all day long. I nip at his earlobe. "What *are* we going to do in our new bedroom?"

"I'm going to put my cock in your pussy over and over again. Then I think I'll swallow every moan, swat your ass red, and make you scream so fucking hard we shake the brand new roof."

"Perfect." I try to whisper into his shoulder, but it's more like a moan. A whimper.

This is my life now with this man. Unscrewed and loving it.

He walks into the bedroom, carrying me over the threshold. I recognize the windows and closet doors I'd picked out. "This room is *huge.*" I laugh. "I can hear my own echo."

He spins me around so I can see the bed. "I bought us a king-sized, so there'll be plenty of room for us both.

"Are you calling me a bed hog?"

Swiftly, he crosses the room and drops me on the bed. "No, Cupcake. I'm saying I want plenty of room to fuck you all seven ways to Sunday."

Oh, God. A hot flush lights up my cheeks.

"Better than being a bed hog." I laugh, scooting up on the bed to lean against the pillows. "We sound like an old married couple."

"We are," he says, shrugging out of his suit coat. "It's been five hours."

"Five hours, and you have yet to fully make me your wife." I stick out my bottom lip. "I'm feeling...neglected."

"Where?" he asks, climbing on to the bed. "Here?" He traces a circle around one of my nipples. "Or here?" He traces around the other one. Then his hand sinks between my legs. He finds my clit with his thumb and presses until I twitch. "Fuck, it's here, isn't it?

"Yes!"

His blue eyes are on fire when he dips his head. Rex takes one nipple in his mouth, teasing it with his tongue. His stubble burns so good against my cleavage, ignites fires across my bare skin.

I sink into the softness of the bed, relishing the pleasure I've been waiting for all day.

He sucks my nipples soft, pulls with his teeth, leaves me wet and begging him for more. Then comes the trail of kisses down my stomach.

"Love this, darling. Love how bad you want your husband's mouth all over your sweet little cunt."

I raise my hips instinctively. So ready. So wanting. "I want, Rex Osborne. Want your dick inside me right now."

"Clothes are still on," he growls, running his tongue through my folds. I shudder. "You'll have to settle for my tongue, Cupcake."

I can't talk. Can't think. Can't even beg.

He knows how to play me so well, how to get every fire roaring. He's licking, sucking, fucking me with his tongue, taking me to the brink and easing off just before I lose it.

I'm gasping, my muscles quaking, my hips pumping, and of course I'm loving it.

My entire body goes rigid a few licks later. Pleasure peaks. My hips arch off the bed, pushing into his face, his hands cup my ass and pull me to him, his tongue owning me the whole time my O breaks loose.

Our sex was amazing before.

Tonight, it's off the scale, off the chain, off the confines of the known universe.

There's nothing like the rough satisfaction his mouth licks through me, again and again. An aftermath of pure bliss has the air rushing from my lungs as I drift home. I slump deeper into the soft new mattress, wet and intrigued.

"*Still* feel neglected?"

I shake my head. "No, but you must." I draw in a deep breath, still basking in that amazing O. "Give me a minute and I'll take care of that."

Rex wastes no time. The rest of his clothes come off, piece by piece, baring his insane, hard, awesome valleys of muscle and black magic inks. I spread my legs, suddenly feeling like a virgin all over again.

How could anything be better than our very first night? I didn't think it could, but now –

"Rex!" My eyes pop open as his cock, hard and hot, slides inside my pussy with one smooth thrust.

His grin quirks up, deviously wicked, as he slides out of me. "Fuck, Cupcake. My wife's pussy feels like heaven tonight."

I answer with a moan. The only sound I'm able to get out. Then he grips my hips with both hands and slides back in. "I want an encore. I want to fuck you like crazy. I want to empty every fucking drop that's burning in my balls deep, *deep* inside you."

There's no question. My legs fold around him and I match him pump for pump. Our tongues clash and our bodies fight, a delicious battle to see who can fuck the hardest and give it up quickest.

Finally, a battle we both love. We hold nothing back.

My tits, my hips, my entire body bounces as we go at it. Thrust for thrust. Our mouths ambush, conquer, then break so we can both drag in a breath of air before going at it again. It's like a lake storm in this bed. It's wild, it's crazy, and we both let out a triumphant cry as ecstasy builds, shoving us upwards, onwards. Together.

"Hurry the fuck up, darling" he rumbles, back arched. "I'm about to come in my wife and I need her to come the fuck with me. I need –"

"Rex, yes!"

Oh, yes.

It hits, welding us together. Perfectly, distinctly one.

We're locked together, arched into one another, thrusting like maniacs as wave after wave of ecstasy encompasses us, and then slowly folds its euphoria across our skin. It's the hardest I've ever come, and the softest I've ever come down.

Rex roots himself in me, still thrusting, emptying himself hard and deep. His heat adds to mine, forcing intensity. I give up a full body shudder as one O blurs into the next.

Then I open my eyes, sane again, my mouth melting on his.

The aftermath lingers forever as we kiss, softly and slow and leisurely.

I let out a happy moan as he rolls off me and flings his legs wide. He crashes back down, pulling me to his chest. His hand sifts through my hair, soft and calming.

I nudge him. "See? I'm no bed hog."

"Never said you hog the bed, Cupcake." He gives me a wink. "The covers, on the other hand, are a different story."

I slap him playfully. We kiss again.

Then I lay my head on his chest, watching his lightning blue eyes, waiting for them to light again with lust. They never dim.

My husband, my stranger, my passion, my sweetest sorrow, my eternity stares up at the new ceiling for the next minute. When he looks back at me, I see the man I've sworn to love. Till death do us part.

It's the same incredible being who came into our lodge, two little miracles in tow, man enough for cupcakes. Tonight, he's man enough for us.

Man enough forever.

XVIII: ONE YEAR LATER (REX EXTENDED EPILOGUE)

"I can't believe they have homework. They're *only* in first grade."

Not letting her see my smile, she's too irritable for that right now, I walk up behind her, wrapping my arms around her sides. I can't resist a quick rub of her round belly. "Cupcake, it's not homework, it's just some worksheets for them to practice what they've already learned."

"No, it's homework. I should've asked for a different teacher. I had Mrs. Thurston when I was in first grade, and she hated my guts. Still does, I think. And now she's taking it out on poor Chase and Adam. My sons deserve better." She tugs my hands off her stomach and marches across the room. "Enough games. I'm calling the principal."

I follow her path and take the phone out of her hand. "It's nine o'clock on a Saturday night. You can't call the principal, darling."

"No? Watch me!" She reaches for the phone, but I hold it over my head away from her. "Rex, come on. He won't be in bed yet," she says, shaking her head. Trying so hard to convince me. "The only people in bed by this time are little boys. Mine would've been in bed an hour ago if they hadn't had homework to do."

I set the phone down and grasp both her shoulders. "Chase and Adam are in bed, and have been for an hour." Looking her straight in the eyes, I continue, "You, on the other hand, have been going crazy over two worksheets for over an hour."

"Because I can't find them!" She throws both hands in the air. "Jesus, we can't let them do all that work for nothing. Help me look. I *know* I put them right here on the counter, and now they're gone. Gone, Rex."

They're in the drawer, where I watched her put them, but I'm not about to point that out. Not yet. I've learned a few things the past few months. Pregnant women are the apex of Jekyll and Hyde. You couldn't love them more one minute, and they scare the living shit out of you the next.

She's at the fridge now, head buried in it. Her cravings are unholy.

Nope. Nothing there.

The pantry.

The cupboard.

The fridge again.

I have no idea where she finds the energy or speed she has some days. I'm exhausted just watching her.

I lean against the counter while I'm doing just that, watching her. She pulls down the edge of the cupcake paper and takes a big bite. I wait for the reaction. When she takes a second bite, cock my head. "Fuck, when did Tabby Osborne start liking cupcakes?"

"I don't like cupcakes. Never have. I only make them

for you and the boys." There's more than a little hurried denial in her voice. If I didn't know better, she's savoring that thing.

I nod as she finishes the cupcake off with her next bite.

"Think I'll make some popcorn," she says, tossing the empty cupcake paper in the trash. "Do you want some?"

"No, I'm good. But I'll make you some if you want me to."

She fills a glass of water and drinks it down. "No, on second thought, forget it. I don't want any popcorn. Never really cared for it. Want to watch a movie?"

I'm trying not to smile.

Finally. Once she sits still for more than five minutes, she gets sleepy. "Sure. Living room or bedroom?"

"Living room."

So, we'll be sleeping on the couch again. Once she's asleep, the slightest touch or noise can wake her, and then she's on the go again.

The doctor says this is all normal, especially since she's due in less than three weeks. I believe him, but I also know Cupcake doesn't believe in wasting time. When I tease her about that, she says she's not fast, she's efficient. That she's always been that way. Always had to be in order to manage so many different roles at the lodge all at the same time.

She isn't wrong. The e-word makes me grin like an idiot, even after the darkness is long behind us.

I'm just glad her workload is less. The lodge is busier than ever, paradoxically, but that also means Morris had to hire more people. Finally.

Once he got rolling, the old man discovered the benefits. He's also got more free time to himself to be the best grandfather my boys could ever ask for, and I know he'll love our new baby just as much.

At times, that scares the shit out of me. A baby. Christ.

I'm already a father, sure, that part excites me. The rest? The whole birth thing?

Getting her to the hospital in time?

I have nightmares about delivering our kid along the side of the road because the baby couldn't wait out the ride. I have a feeling this baby'll be just like it's mother, too. Fast and furious. Efficient, as Tabby says.

And I hope the doctor knows what he's talking about. He says first babies usually take a long time. That we have nothing to worry about. We'll have plenty of time to get to the hospital.

Relax, he says.

Bullshit, I say.

I wrap an arm around Cupcake as we walk into the living room, loving her even more than I did on our wedding day. Didn't think that was possible, but it is. The first year and counting with this woman taught me all kinds of things I never knew.

She's the best wife and mother in the world. Can't imagine my life without her. Can't imagine how the boys and I managed without her before.

"Do you think we'll have a boy or a girl?" she asks as we sit down on the sofa.

I pick up the remote and merely shrug. I've gotten caught answering that question before and won't do it again. She didn't want to know, and continues to say that most of the time, but one night last week, around midnight, she was about to call the doctor. She couldn't stand not knowing any longer.

I wrestled it out of her hand just in time, of course. She'd kill me later on if I didn't. Put up enough of a fuss as it was, telling them to blot out the gender from the ultrasound.

She leans her head on my shoulder. "You know...I'm not sure I want to watch a movie. How about we turn in early? Find our fun elsewhere?" She lifts an eyebrow, pursing her lips.

My dick goes hard as diamond. Too bad I'm supposed to lay off till after the baby.

Damn.

"Cupcake –"

"Rex, we don't *have* to have sex." She walks her fingers down my neck and under the collar of my shirt. She's making this difficult. "We could just play with each other, you know."

I swear, I'll be in my nineties someday, and her simplest touch will still give me an instant hard-on.

I'm mulling it over when she drops down with a pout.

"Fine. Too slow." She lets out a tiny groan and twists, pressing a hand to her back. "How about a back rub? My back has been killing me all day."

I set the remote on the coffee table, having never turned on the TV and take her hand. "Come on, let's go to the bedroom."

"For a back rub?"

"Best massage these hands can deliver." My paws are big and calloused as ever. I'm not breaking my back working like I did in the early days, too busy in management, but I still pick up plenty of tools.

"I love you."

"And I love you."

"Even though I'm batshit crazy?"

"Fuck yes." I help her off the couch, kissing her forehead. "Because you aren't batshit crazy, Cupcake. You're pregnant. With our baby, and I love you even more for it."

"Awww." She lets out a long sigh and leans against me. "You're so sweet."

I hold her close. The joy, the contentment she kicks up inside me still catches me off guard sometimes.

Makes me wonder how the fuck I ever got lucky enough to find her. My construction business flourished faster and bigger here than it did in Chicago, and it all happened over months, not years. Just like our love. I never imagined it could happen so fast or be so fulfilling. She's the reason. Everything about her is fast and wonderful and right. *Efficient.*

She arches slightly. Her tiny moan is pain, not delight.

It's my turn to sit up straight.

"Your back?" I ask.

"Yes." She lets go of me to press both hands against her lower back again. "I didn't lift anything heavy today. Doctor's orders. Don't know why I keep getting these spasms."

I take her hand again and lead her around the coffee table. "Let's go. I've got a backrub that'll take all the pain away."

"That sounds heavenly."

In the bedroom, she kisses my chin. "I'm going to the bathroom first. Be right back."

Good move. She knows her body well. Considering the amount of times she gets up at night I truly don't know how she gets any rest, and feel sorry for her. And am amazed at how she takes it all in stride, the amount of work she still gets done. Here, at the lodge, volunteering at the school with the boys...

Shit. I'm also glad Morris hired more people at the lodge for the upcoming summer months so she can rest once the baby arrives. Or work harder. I remember that part, when Adam and Chase were infants. Whoever uses the phrase, 'sleeping like a baby,' has clearly never had a baby.

I fold back the covers and plump her pillows. She comes out of the bathroom wearing only her bra and underwear, pink of course, and I swallow against the pressure building in my cock.

She smiles. "I know what you're thinking."

I laugh. "It's a back rub, Cupcake. Remember?"

Her pout is adorable.

I pat the bed. "I have it all ready for you. Lie down."

She crawls on the bed and lays on her side. I pick up the hand lotion off the bedside table and squirt a big glob in my palm. Then rub my hands together to warm up the lotion before I start rubbing her back.

The sweet soft moans she lets out have the very effect on me that she's going for. So does rubbing her back, caressing her smooth skin, spreading the lotion over the top of her ass.

"Mmmm, Rex, that feels so good."

"For you, woman." I kiss the side of her ear. "You know what you're doing to me."

She giggles. "Maybe."

I keep rubbing her back, getting damn near as much pleasure out of that as making love to her. Her moans end with a long sigh, and then her breathing turns softer, deeper. Almost instantly, she's out. Sound asleep.

I kiss her cheek, cover her with the sheet, and then head for the shower to take care of my hard-on so I can get some sleep.

Hours later, I jerk awake, missing her warmth snuggled against me. She's gone. I hear her in the bathroom. I should have known. Rolling over, I ask, "Everything okay, darling?"

She appears in the doorway, hands on both sides of the frame. "My water –" She grabs the underside of her belly. "Just broke."

It takes a moment for the words to register. Then I leap out of the bed and chaos strikes.

I insist we need to leave. She says we both need to get dressed first. And call Morris. And get her suitcase.

The red one, of course. No, the *blue* one. But fuck, the boys.

We have to get them up. No, on second thought, don't wake the boys. Morris will come.

My head's spinning just listening to her. Within a few minutes, I've called the lodge, got us both dressed, and handed Morris her suitcase the second he opens the front door.

"Move it!" the old man tells us, mumbling up and down the rest is safely in his hands.

I believe him. Not like I have another choice.

Moments later, we're in the truck, driving for town as the sun is coming up.

"It's a beautiful day to have a baby, isn't it?"

I chuckle at how calm she sounds, how mellow and relaxed. "Yeah. We'll be at the hospital in no time. Nothing to worry about."

"I'm not worried," she says. "Everything will be fine. Just fine."

I release a sigh of relief. Thankful as hell everything's calmed down and going so smoothly.

By the time I pull onto the highway, that's changed. The truck tires squeal as I plant my foot on the gas and head for town.

"Fuck, this hurts! Rex." She has her legs pulled up and is bending forward, clutching her stomach. Between gasps, she shouts, "No one. Said. It would. Hurt this bad!"

My heart is pounding as fast as I'm driving. "Hold on, Cupcake. Hold on. We'll be there soon." I grab her hand.

She squeezes my hand hard, then shoves it aside. "Drive. Faster!"

I can't push any harder on the gas without putting us in serious danger. There's a Punch Corp truck up ahead, a huge rig I have to swerve around. My hand slams the center of the wheel, keeps honking at the cars ahead, wanting them to know I'm passing. I want her better right the hell now, and the only way to do that is gun it.

"Almost there, darling," I try. "It's not much farther."

Then, the cab fills with an eerie silence, like a calm after a storm blows over. "Are you okay?"

"Yes." She leans her head back. "It's over. I'm fine now."

My insides quiver.

"In case I forget, tell them I'll need pain medications. *All* the pain meds. This is more pain than anyone else has ever had."

"I'll tell them."

"Thank you. I love you." She sighs again. "Oh, and if I'm not home yet tomorrow morning, the boys need to take something that starts with the letter q for show and tell."

"All right." I make a mental note to make sure I have some quarters.

"Don't let them both take a quarter. Be more unique than that."

I shake my head, smiling how she reads my mind.

"Oh, no," she groans.

"What?"

She bends forward again, hugging her stomach.

"Another pain?"

The glare she casts my way tells me how stupid that question was.

Her growl starts out low and slow, but quickly builds steam and explodes with her screaming, "Jesus. Christ!" Between gasps, she yells again. "Rex. This. Hurts!"

I can see the hospital, and dash around two other cars heading that way. I start blowing the horn as soon as the truck enters the parking lot. By the time I slam on the brakes near the front door, a nurse is running out.

More people appear and we get Tabby in a wheelchair.

As a nurse pushes the wheelchair through the front door, she says, "You'll need to check her in."

"No, she's preregistered," I say, holding Tabby's hand.

"You'll still need to sign some papers," the nurse says.

Cupcake grins up at me, all calm again. "I'm fine. Go check us in."

Against the better judgment roaring inside me, I kiss the top of her head and step aside as the nurse wheels her into the elevator. Tabby blows me a kiss as the door closes and I jog towards the check-in desk.

The woman there takes my name, and Tabby's, and

punches the keys on her computer, asking about our address and insurance.

"Yes, yes, and yes," I answer. "Nothing's changed since she's preregistered." I glance towards the elevator. "Are we done? Shit. I forgot to tell the nurse my wife needs pain meds."

"They'll determine that," the woman says. "And we're almost done. I just need your signature."

"Meds," I growl, giving her the evil eye. "Keep her happy."

She nods, makes a note. I think she's got the message.

I grab a pen out of a little cup sitting there. "Where? What do I sign?"

She smiles and points one thumb over her shoulder. "It's printing." Then she starts punching the keys on her computer again.

The printer spits out a sheet of paper and I clamp my lips together to keep from screaming for her to go get it. Drawing a deep breath, I say, "I think it's done."

"I'll need you to sign four forms."

Fucking-A. I tap my fingers on the counter, staring at the printer.

"Don't worry, first babies take their time." She spins her chair around and stands up. After walking to the printer, she stands there, waiting for the final copy to slide out.

"Can't this wait?"

"No." She carries the papers back to the desk. "Sign here."

She sets one paper down.

I scribble my name across the bottom. More like a

heap of lines, something Adam or Chase would've sketched a year ago.

"And on this one –"

I reach over, take all three sheets of paper, slop my name on each one, and run for the elevator.

No more bullshit. I'm not missing our first born.

Of course, this place has the slowest fucking elevator in the nation. I regret not taking the stairs.

When the damn thing finally stops, and the door whooshes open, I run down the hall, to the double sets of doors they'd shown us during our preregistration tour. I shove through them and glance around. It's empty. No one at the desk. I shoot forward. "Tabby!"

A nurse appears.

"Where's my wife? Tabby Osborne?"

The nurse holds a package toward me. "You'll need to put these on."

"My wife? Where is she?" I'm growling like a bear.

"Down the hall." She nods at the package. "Sir, you'll have to put a gown on. Sterile work environment."

"Why, I'm not—"

"Sanitary reasons."

I take the bundle, rip it open, and throw on the blue paper gown. I hold my hands out, showing her it's on. "Which room?"

"This way." She walks as slow as the one downstairs. It's maddening. At the door, she points to the hand sanitizer mounted on the wall.

I slather it on and rush into the room the second she pushes the door open. Shoving aside a curtain, I stumble to a stop. Tabby's lying on the bed with a baby on her chest. "What the –"

"She's here, Rex," Cupcake says. "Angie's here. Fast and efficient. Just like mama."

We've mulled baby names for the better part of a year, but now Angie sounds as sweet as the soft lips speaking it.

Angie. Our little girl.

Here. At last. Forever.

"You're free to come closer," a nurse says. "Just in time, too. Your daughter was almost born in the elevator."

"You *need* a new elevator," I say, walking to the bed. Watching my wife with that little angel wipes the rage boiling in my veins.

Tabby's knees are up, and there's a doctor sitting on a stool between her legs, still doing something down there. I give him the side-eye, wishing he'd hurry the fuck up and get away from the only place on my wife I get to lavish that much attention on. I lay a hand on Tabby's head, look her in the eye. "You okay?"

She smiles. "I'm fine, and so's our baby. Say hello."

I kiss her, then look at the infant. A tiny little body and a tiny little head covered with matted dark hair. I lay my hand on the baby's back, feel her breathing. Relief washes over me. "She's okay? You're okay?" I ask for the millionth time.

"Rex, we're *fine*." Cupcake kisses the baby's head. "She's beautiful. I hear that's a good pairing with efficient."

I shake my head and kiss them both as pride and joy fills me. "Efficient, huh?"

"Be happy." She smirks at me. "You'd have gotten bored sitting around, waiting for her."

"Would not." This time, the mind-reading thing makes my brow furrow.

"Yes, you would." She sighs sweetly, then whispers to the baby, "I'm right, and he knows it. You'll get used to it."

I'm smiling again. I take the adorable little girl's hand gently, holding it. "Beautiful and efficient," I echo.

Our daughter squirms slightly, opening her eyes. My heart tumbles as I look at her precious little face. I kiss her cheek and whisper, "Mommy's right, precious Angie. Always."

THANKS!

Want more Nicole Snow? Sign up for my newsletter to hear about new releases, exclusive subscriber giveaways, and more fun stuff!

JOIN THE NICOLE SNOW NEWSLETTER! - http://eepurl.com/HwFW1

Thank you so much for buying this book. I hope my romances sweeten your days with pleasure, drama, and all the feels! I tell the stories you want to hear.

If you liked this book, please consider leaving a review and checking out my other romance tales.

THANKS!

Got a comment on my work? Email me at nicole@nicolesnowbooks.com. I love hearing from fans!

Nicole Snow

More Intense Romance by Nicole Snow

CINDERELLA UNDONE

SURPRISE DADDY

PRINCE WITH BENEFITS: A BILLIONAIRE ROYAL ROMANCE

MARRY ME AGAIN: A BILLIONAIRE SECOND CHANCE ROMANCE

LOVE SCARS: BAD BOY'S BRIDE

MERCILESS LOVE: A DARK ROMANCE

RECKLESSLY HIS: A BAD BOY MAFIA ROMANCE

STEPBROTHER CHARMING: A BILLIONAIRE BAD BOY ROMANCE

STEPBROTHER UNSEALED: A BAD BOY MILITARY ROMANCE

Prairie Devils MC Books

OUTLAW KIND OF LOVE

NOMAD KIND OF LOVE

SAVAGE KIND OF LOVE

WICKED KIND OF LOVE

BITTER KIND OF LOVE

Grizzlies MC Books

OUTLAW'S KISS

OUTLAW'S OBSESSION

OUTLAW'S BRIDE

OUTLAW'S VOW

Deadly Pistols MC Books

NEVER LOVE AN OUTLAW

NEVER KISS AN OUTLAW

NEVER HAVE AN OUTLAW'S BABY

NEVER WED AN OUTLAW

Baby Fever Books

THANKS!

BABY FEVER BRIDE

BABY FEVER PROMISE

BABY FEVER SECRETS

Only Pretend Books

FIANCÉ ON PAPER

ONE NIGHT BRIDE

SEXY SAMPLES: CINDERELLA UNDONE

I: PLEASE JUST STAY (KENDRA)

Once upon a time, he was beautiful.

Not because he was my high school crush.

Not because he survived the world crashing down around him like a toxic storm.

Not even because of his rogue good looks, or his family's money – and he had *plenty* of both to go around.

I mean, how could I ever forget my best friend's strapping older brother the second I laid eyes on him? How could I ignore those shoulders, built wide as the Arizona sky? What about the hard blue eyes that cut through everyone? The chiseled jaw framing the world's warmest, sweetest, most mischievous smirk?

How can I pretend I didn't squeeze my thighs together the first time he walked into the room a man, wearing his crisp new uniform, a proud Marine ready for duty? He turned every woman's cheeks in the neighborhood a subtle red. His special gift, and he knew exactly how to use it to get his way.

He was dangerous, scary, and still divine in his heresy.

He kept his charms close, and his secrets closer.

But even when he was a tease, a frustration, and a damn enigma all at once, he was gorgeous.

As long as I live, I'll never see Knox Carlisle as anything less than a striking, brilliant, beautiful beast.

Not even after the night he left, and came home ugly.

* * *

Four Years Ago

"Knox, you don't have to do this. Don't go. A man can only take so much...listen to me!"

Of course, he doesn't. Not until I beg.

"I can't stand to see you hurt. Stay, Knox. Please."

When he spins around and looks at me, I'm expecting scorn. But what do I know, really?

I'm barely eighteen, a year into college. I haven't lived a fraction of his hell, only imagined it.

"No more, Kendra. You want to help? I asked for good karma and a little help making sure Jamers treats my baby girl right. It's long past time for me to fucking go."

I hear the adorable infant upstairs let out a cry. Then Jamie's voice, soothing her little niece, just six weeks old and already losing both her parents. One to business in one of the world's darkest corners, and another to God only knows what.

No one's seen her mom since the week she left the hospital. We don't know where Sam went, or what happened to her. It's got to be eating him alive, but he never shows his pain. There's nothing in his eyes except a tender love for his daughter, Lizzie, his sweetest creation.

Born to tragedy like a typical Carlisle, through and through.

His face is turned toward her innocent cries. The noise stops him with his hand on the garage door. He looks down for a brief second, before he turns his face up, hitting me with a strained spark in his eyes.

I see my chance.

"You hear that?" I say, walking up to him, reaching for his shoulders. I have to stand on my tip-toes to touch him when he towers over me. "Don't leave her. Lizzie needs you."

So do I. That's the part I don't say, but I know he picks it up subconsciously because his strong face softens. He's listening – I hope.

"Look, I get it. You didn't ask for my advice, but I can't help it. You're not the same man who left the military and came home. This job, the stress, chasing that stupid, reckless woman...it's *killing* you. I've read about that place you're going, the chaos and danger. I'm worried, Knox. Scared you'll make a mistake over there, and maybe you won't come home."

"Let me do the worrying, Sunflower. It's not your place. I'll live. And I'll find her when I get back from this gig. There'll be hell to pay when I do, walking out on me and my little girl like that."

My heart sinks, thinking he's done. Then he grabs my

wrist, shoves me against the wall, and holds us there, locked in a gaze beyond words.

He wants me to understand. He wants me to believe he'll be okay. He wants me to think it's business as usual.

But I don't. I'm doubt incarnate.

Having his hands on me doesn't help. Every fiber in my being wishes he'd do more than a friendly touch, but I have to remember my place, who I am in his eyes.

I'm his annoying little sister's friend. Practically a surrogate sis.

To him, I'm Sunflower. Too young, too precocious, and too clueless to ever be anything more than a stormy night's sick fantasy.

"What if you make a mistake over there?" I whisper, trying not to shudder when I imagine how dangerous his work can be. He's told Jamie before about the friends who never came home. Chasing diamonds is a dirty business, and always has been. It's as brutal, dangerous, and risky as everything he survived in Afghanistan – sometimes more so. "You're a father now, Knox. And that little girl up there doesn't have a mother."

"Sam *is* coming back," he growls, his eyebrows furrowed. "I'll drag her irresponsible ass home and force her to sign over custody when I finally get a fucking break. Can't believe she screwed me over and ran. First chance I get, I'm tracking her down. We both know that can't happen until I've done my business over there. Enough worry, Kendra. Please. I'll be back in Phoenix in a few weeks."

It hurts when he tears himself away from me. I know it's my stupid, careless crush talking, but I also hate seeing my friend in so much pain.

If only I could keep my mouth shut, stop pouring salt in his wounds...but if I'm wishing for impractical things, I'd might as well wish he never knocked up the spoiled brat who left without a trace after their baby was born.

"I'm not asking for me, Knox," I whisper, lying through my teeth. "Just...please...think about Lizzie."

"She's all I think about, Sunflower. She's the reason I'm doing this. You think I'd give a damn about money if it weren't for her? She's the last piece of the world I have left that hasn't gone to shit. She deserves a piece of my company and the family name far more than I do." His voice is hard, but there's no malice. Just raw determination, devotion, plus a warmth I'll never forget.

"Come here," he says, pulling me closer. It's the firmest embrace I've ever had in those arms that used to pick me up, throw me around, and make me laugh to tears. "Wait for me. Focus on school. Find a decent guy. Keep my little sis in line – God only knows she'd get into a lot more trouble without you. You're a good friend, Sunflower. You *will* see me again. Mark my words and cross the fucking T."

Except I'm not a good friend. My mind spins with the painful truths I'm trying to hide. *I'm selfish. I'm young, heart-stung, and stupid. You're everything I shouldn't want...and all I've wanted since at least fifteen.*

"Whatever. Just...come home safe." I try to let the resignation in my voice hide the turmoil, the want, the fear.

"Oh, I will. There are worse places than where I'm going. Comes with the territory when this family's done gems since my great grandpa. We didn't get where we're at being stupid."

"Duh! I know...I'm not an idiot." It slips out in a whine.

His eyes narrow, big and bright full of sympathy. Everything I don't want from him, still looking at me like a child.

Then, before I know what's happening, my face sits on his palm. His warmth cradles it while his thumb traces soft lines up my cheek.

I can't see through the sadness anymore. I'm terrified this is the last time I'll *ever* lay eyes on this walking contradiction caught in my heart like a rusty hook.

"You've been good to me, Sunflower. Sometimes I think you're the only true friend I've got left in this town. My own boys from the service don't say shit anymore, not since I wouldn't – couldn't – join them for another tour. Keep your heart as pure as your pretty little face, woman. You'd better have a good goddamned boyfriend by the time I get home, too. You're in college now. Too grown up to keep pining after what we might've been in another world, one where you're a few years older, and I'm a better man without an axe over my head. I'll send you a postcard. They're everywhere over there when the internet runs like molasses."

Just like that, he tears himself away.

Just like that, I'm flat against the wall and sliding down it while the door slams shut, and I hear his truck's engine become a distant growl as he pulls down the driveway, heading for near-certain death.

Just like that, I'm barely breathing. Too weak in the knees to stand up in time, and run after him, screaming *don't go, don't go, please don't go.*

I do it anyway, and I'm far too late. I run until my knees burn, screaming myself hoarse like a crazy woman, chasing his non-existent truck halfway down the block.

It's hopeless. Defeat sinks through me swifter than the fire in my lungs, knowing I'll never catch him.

Somehow, I get it together, take a few deep breaths, and walk back to his mother's place. I plop down on the sofa with Jamers again. I'm careful to keep my face turned toward the massive TV mounted to the wall so she won't see my red eyes.

"Ugh, did he even say anything about the thirty bucks he still owes me for pizza last week?" Jamie looks up from filing her nails, casting a glance toward the little crib in the corner before she looks my way.

"Nah, his brain was already overseas, I think. Remember how he always got before he went back to active duty?" I turn slowly, and we share a look. Jamie's face is twisted in a sour frown that says she's only concerned with what a big asshole her older brother can be. She'll never understand the bruises spreading in my heart.

"Pig! He's so predictable," she says, shaking her head. "Well, I've got a couple weeks to be a badass aunt, at least, and make sure Lizzie grows up right. Hope he comes home in one piece, and becomes the awesome father he says he'll be."

"He will, Jamers," I say. That, I'm sure.

He has to. Time slows to a crawl.

I keep counting my breaths, watching his baby daughter every few seconds, the closest thing I have to seeing his face. I'm thankful the little girl has so much of him in her. None of the wild, cold bitch who incubated her.

It's a miracle Lizzie's tests were clean after she was born. Amazingly, her mom laid off the drugs while she was pregnant – more than I'd ever give that woman credit for.

Maybe miracles are real.

I still don't understand how Knox had a single hookup with her.

But I don't need to. My brain is too full of fog over the next six weeks.

Life goes on. I pass my mid-terms. Straight As, keeping a flawless 4.0 my first semester at Arizona U.

My design professor keeps inviting me out for drinks, says he wants to talk about scholarships and intro galleries next year. He says he's never seen such grace and ingenuity in my first big project, an elegant evening dress with enough glitter around the cleavage line to make Cleopatra blush from the grave. I try to bask in the praise, but that never comes naturally.

I share fake smiles with my bestie, and real ones when I see Lizzie's little face light up with the cluster of toys her doting grandma fattens weekly.

Six weeks are an eternity. I try not to ask about Knox, and the few times I do, Jamers tells me he's 'surviving over there. Just the usual.'

He's sent their mother a few letters. They're brief, dull, and straight to the point.

Everything I'm sure his reality over there isn't.

When I hear he's finally coming home, safe and sound, I'm stunned. I can't breathe until I see him, overjoyed because normalcy is finally coming back, and all my instincts were wrong.

Except there's nothing normal when he comes through that door, walks right past me without so much as a smile, and scoops Lizzie up in his arms.

He's a changed man.

I watch him kiss his mother on the cheek and take his daughter home without so much as a hello. He barely acknowledges Jamie either. I can't believe my own eyes.

Sure, he has the same good looks, the familiar flame in his blue halo eyes, and a rage against the world. That part stays the same.

The rest has grown colder, somehow. Different. Ugly.

He's as gorgeous as ever, and dead inside.

My instincts were right. My worst fears came true.

Whatever happened over there *killed* him, and sent him home a shell.

* * *

Present Day

Two and a half years is sometimes an eternity.

In the blink of an eye, I'm grown up. Finished with school, working my first post-grad internship, and thinking about a longer one in Paris next year.

But eternity wouldn't sting if certain parts of life weren't eternal and unchanging.

Jamers comes shuffling down the hallway wiping her brow, slick from the summer sweat of a sunny Phoenix day. Her mother's place is elegant, cool, and cozy in Arizona's toughest season.

"Another glass, Kendra?" she asks, standing by the fridge.

"Please. Just don't spike it this time – I'm trying to concentrate."

She pours us iced tea and flops on the huge sectional next to me, adjusting her shorts. I'm nose deep in my laptop, focusing on a new pair of glass heels I need to perfect.

They're the reason *the* Eric Gannon tapped me for his internship. One look at my proposal and he skipped the oral interview. For a couple weeks, I was on cloud nine, but now comes the hard part.

The master designer I'm working under wants these babies on the market this fall. That means my name hitched to his brand, and a lot of money.

But only *if* I can actually finish what I've set out to do. I'm trying to keep the bitchy questions to myself, wondering why my best friend isn't hitting her homework. Again.

Even the quiet doesn't help. She's slumped next to me for a minute before she lets out the world's biggest yawn.

It's infectious. I cover my mouth, and then slap myself on the cheek, shooting her the evil eye. "Do you mind? My day isn't over."

"Sorry. It's brutal out there. Think I'm more toasted and tuckered out than the kiddo," Jamers says, nodding toward the room down the hall. She sips her tea. Toasted is right, it's loaded with so much vodka I can smell it several feet away. "She'll sleep like a charm through the night, guaranteed."

"Sandy will be glad," I say, nodding, never looking up from my screen. "I know she loves being grandma, but everybody deserves a break sometimes."

What do I know about kids? Not much, honestly, but I

don't think Mrs. Carlisle could ask for a better granddaughter than the sleepy little angel in the other room.

Jamers bats her eyes, her lips turned sourly. I don't like it one bit.

"What?"

"Actually, girl...Knox is picking up Lizzie tonight. He's back in town. Just wrapping up business with Mr. Wright before he heads over."

Every muscle in my body stiffens. I keep my eyes glued to the screen, typing gibberish to make myself look busy.

Remember how I said two years can change everything, and nothing whatsoever?

That's Knox. He's the same gorgeous shell with the ugly heart.

The man who decided *just leave me the hell alone* was far too easy when I tried to be his friend.

His ugly heart took a sledgehammer to mine, and didn't stop ramming his message home until he'd demolished my teenage crush.

What happened that night at Danny's party, just a few months after he settled into his life as a single dad...I can't understand it, but it doesn't matter.

I read him loud and clear.

No confusion. No tenderness. No mercy.

It's the past. I can't forgive, forget, or let him get to me a second time.

The asshole rarely speaks to me anymore since that night, except when he decides to acknowledge my presence in the Carlisle mansion with a snide remark or two for appearances. Thankfully, that's rare.

I try to avoid him. Usually, it works. He only sticks his head in to pick up his daughter.

Reality ruined him. It hit after Africa, and wherever the hell he went to look for Sam.

He's realized he'll be a single dad forever, and the wild child mistake responsible for half of Lizzie's genes is never coming home.

Nobody on the planet can find her. I think even he's given up, and it's widened the void in his heart.

"He won't be around long, I'm sure," Jamers says, stuffing a stick of gum in her mouth. "Seriously, don't be afraid of my brother. He doesn't have time these days for more tricks."

Tricks? Not the word I'd use for the poison dart he lodged in my heart. But I haven't told her what he did to me, and I'm not planning to after sitting on it for so long.

"I'm *not* afraid. He's different, is all." I suck in a hurried breath, hoping it'll calm the fire in my blood. "His attitude isn't my problem. I'm just glad he isn't so gruff with Lizzie. It's the only time we see him smile, showing a crack in his armor that says he might still be human."

"He's been through a lot, Kay. Not that it's any excuse."

"Correction: he never *got* through it." I look up, seeing the empathy and sadness lighting up her eyes. She shares a softer version of the same baby blues every Carlisle man, woman, and child seems to inherit.

"What's the latest news? Nothing?" It's been months since I asked.

My friend shakes her head slowly. She sits up straight and sniffs, playing with her long black hair. "I think he hired another detective a few weeks ago. Saw him talking to an older man a few times at his place, when ma and me came by to pick up a few heaps of clothes he didn't need for Lizzie anymore. She outgrows the old stuff so fast. We're all about donations for the tax write off."

I snort. It's impossible to believe a few old outfits make much difference in this family of multi-millionaires. Then again, her mother has always done things differently since losing her husband. Humility and generosity win her a lot of respect, including mine.

"Really, there's nothing new," Jamie says with a sigh. "Just more chasing ghosts. I don't know how he handles it, working with Sam's father everyday. Their relationship isn't the best. Knocking up your boss' daughter will do that. Kind of a miracle Lizzie's turning out as great as she is –"

She stops mid-sentence. "Hey, creep-o, don't you ever knock?"

I do a slow turn, and a double take when I see the tall figure standing near the wall. Knox is immaculate, untouched as ever by today's hundred and fifteen degree weather. His crisp grey suit matches the storm on his face, blue eyes focused on us like pins.

"Not when it's this house. Where's my baby girl?" He casts a demanding glance Jamie's way.

"In her room sleeping. Where else?" My best friend sticks her tongue out. "In case you hadn't noticed, normal people get baked in this sun."

"Baked. I'm sure you know plenty about that, Jamers. I'll let you nap while Sunflower does your homework."

I bristle when he calls me that name. Even after half a dozen encounters where he used it over the years, it hurts. "Hello to you, too, ass."

The delicious chills Sunflower used to bring are gone, replaced by honest, cruel ice.

"I haven't written so much as an outline for her this semester, if you want to know the truth," I say, turning back to my screen. I'm so over him, and yet he somehow makes me blush.

It's a conditioned response. It isn't real. Not anymore.

I've learned to hide the redness when it kisses my cheeks.

It's hard to believe he ever called me a friend, two years and a lifetime ago.

"I don't care. Long as you're letting my sis sink or swim. It's her degree. I'm sure you're busy, putting yours to work on making Dorothy a new pair of ruby slippers." He turns, aiming a quick glance at the heels on my screen.

"Dorothy? You'd have better luck with Cinderella because these shoes are glass," I say smugly. I've heard both names plenty of times. Always one or the other when he wants to insult my career, everything I've poured my heart and soul into.

"I'm too old for fairy tales." It's all he says before I hear his polished shoes hit the tile floor as he walks away, refusing to meet Jamie's sympathetic eyes.

I stare after him even when he's gone, anger burning in my eyes so full it physically hurts.

"Good reminder I'd better get on my crap tonight now that there's an evening without mom and Lizzie," she says, reaching for her backpack on the floor.

I don't say anything, just look at my screen, typing a few more notes. Knox returns a few minutes later, cradling a sleepy little girl in his arms. He stops near the door leading to the garage, the same exit he walked out of years ago as the man I used to worship.

Don't look at him.

It's as bad as eyeing a solar eclipse, and of course, I do it anyway. There's a different man in my screen's reflection, a mirror darkly reflecting someone else.

"Come on, peewee. We're going home," he tells Lizzie, stopping to plant a gentle kiss on her forehead.

I watch their ghostly outlines. It's just enough to tug on my heartstrings, making me wonder for the thousandth time how much of him is left behind his smirking mask. If there's anything, he saves it for his daughter. She's the only one allowed to reach inside the ice chest holding his heart.

He murmurs a few more words to her, soft baby things I can't hear. Alien to my ears, coming from his savage lips.

Then the door creaks open and falls shut with a dull *thud.* Knox never says goodbye.

When I look over, my friend is holding her accounting textbook, probably feigning interest in her classes for my benefit.

"I'm sorry, Kendra. Something's been eating him this last week. More than usual, I mean."

"Really? I couldn't tell. He's just as big a dick as he was three months ago." I'm serious, and more than a little hurt.

I should be numb to it by now. I shouldn't care. I should believe the little words in my head I started telling myself years ago, when I knew he'd never be the same, and I'd damn well better get over it.

But we were good to each other, once. That's what makes this hard.

I remember when we were friends, even if we were never meant to be lovers. I just can't fathom why he's hardened himself to every human being on the planet who isn't his little girl.

Or why he shut me down so coldly when I offered him my warmth.

Why do the worst mysteries always go unsolved?

"More tea?" Jamers stands, grabbing my glass off the end table next to me, forcing a smile. "It's the least I can do. I've talked to him before about his rude fucking temper. I'm sorry nothing's changed. Someday, if we hold out long enough, maybe he'll be normal again."

"Jamers, please. Don't bother. That thing I had for your brother was a *long* time ago. It isn't like he's hurting my feelings." *Yeah, right.* "I've accepted who he is, even if I don't understand why. It's not like we're best friends or anything."

"Yeah, yeah, you're a big girl. You don't need my help. Just sayin'," Jamie says as she trots off toward the kitchen.

It's true. Knox and I aren't friends. Not anymore.

Nothing good lasts forever, or so they say. And if some things are too amazing to be true, or to last, then the ideal I built up was so vivid it killed me when truth threw its first punch.

I have no illusions. The older, massive, otherworldly Adonis I came dangerously close to loving isn't there anymore.

New Knox isn't the man who used to fill my head full of dreams every night, who drove me around town in his first car, or who hugged me so tight it hurt when I threw my arms around him every time he'd lace up his boots and straighten his desert camo fatigues, before he climbed aboard another military plane for the unknown.

I don't know what's eating him, assuming Jamie is even right and it's more than usual.

Frankly, I don't care.

He isn't my problem anymore, and I was never his.

If he ever really cared – truly, deeply, madly – if our friendship wasn't just a fad or a twisted act, then he never would've slammed his soul shut. He never would've become a pillar of lifeless, self-loathing stone before my eyes.

He certainly never would've given me those vicious glances bent on making my heart more like his than I'll ever admit.

GET CINDERELLA UNDONE AT YOUR FAVORITE RETAILER!

Printed in Great Britain
by Amazon